ANGER
Management

BRETTA ELAINE

Edited by Jeanine Harrel, Indie Edits by Jeanine

Proofread by Brooklyn, Brazen Hearts Author Services

Cover art and design by Okay Creations

To the people who put up with my negativity—
and still manage to like me.

CONTENT WARNING

Anger management features strong language,
explicit sexual situations, and mature situations that may be
triggering for some.
Reader discretion is advised.

Chapter One

Clara

I 'm not sure what's worse, having to listen to a group of strangers drone on and on about their problems or the pool of sweat gathering underneath my ass on the metal chair. It truly is a toss-up. I wiggle around on the cool metal, trying to adjust my shorts that are riding up into very indecent territory.

Why is this damn place so hot?

I don't know what I expected. Maybe a nice conference room? Or a plush VIP lounge? Air-conditioning? Nope. None of that. Instead, I am sitting in a rec center gym with no air-conditioning in the middle of May, trying my hardest not to laugh or, hell, bring any attention to myself.

Twelve weeks...

I have to suffer through this for twelve weeks of my life, forfeiting my Friday nights for the rest of the summer.

Goodbye, vacation plans.

Not that I ever had any or intended on taking one. But I enjoyed the option.

All for what? Because a judge told me it was this or jail? Ugh, twelve weeks of court-ordered Anger Management.

To tune out the noise of my classmates, I start on my weekly grocery list:

- eggs

- milk

- toilet paper

- tampons

- fish food

- frozen pizza

- chicken nuggets

"Miss?"

- Cheetos

- guac supplies

- tortilla chips

"Miss?"

Lifting my head, I notice the occupants of the circle of chairs have turned their heads in my direction.

"Sorry, did you say something?" I ask, eyes still darting around in confusion.

"Your name? I asked for your name," the group leader repeats.

He's not what I expected from this jail-type program. His long brown hair is gathered in a large knot at the base of his skull, and his clothes remind me of something a dad in the '90s would have worn. He honestly looks like someone who lives in a van, traveling with his "band" to play the sweet musical styling of the bongos. But apparently, he is a counselor, so there is that.

"Your name, Miss?" he asks again.

"Oh, Clara. My name is Clara, Clara Doyle."

He smiles, leaning forward in his chair. "Pleasure to meet you, Clara. Would you like to tell the group a little about yourself and how you ended up here today?"

"Nope."

He widens his eyes like he's never had someone turn down the opportunity to tell a group of strangers about the worst day of their life. The most humiliating moments, now memorialized as a criminal record.

"No?"

With a shake of my head and my face flat of emotion, I utter, "Nope."

He blinks a few times, leaning back into his chair, plastering a wide, over-the-top smile on his face. With the clapping of his hands together, he moves on to his next victim. An attractive man, maybe in his early thirties, if that. The man looks the epitome of relaxed, with his blond hair perfectly coifed and long legs stretched out in front of him, which in this setting screams sociopathic to me. "How about you, sir? What's your name?"

The man straightens in his chair, clearing his throat. "Kamdyn, sir."

"Well, Kamdyn, would you like to share a little about yourself and what brought you to my support circle, or are you also going to pass?"

Kamdyn's eyes flick across the room to me before returning to our group's leader, whose name I want to say is Steve.

The corner of his lips turn up as he says, "Well, of course. I wouldn't want to be rude..."

I grind my teeth together, taking in his little jab.

"As we have already established, my name is Kamdyn, but please call me Kam. I'm a thirty-year-old high school world history teacher. As for how I got here, let's just say it involved a meter maid on an already bad day."

The rest of the room busts out with a throng of "say no more" and "I feel you, brother," as Kamdyn smiles at them with his stupid, ass-kissing face.

Steve stands, waving his hands around to quiet his students. "Okay, guys, now that we have gotten to know each other a bit, let's go over what we will learn over the next few weeks, along with what I will expect of you to pass this course."

I listen as he passes out a syllabus jam-packed with homework assignments. Each week, we are to complete an extra assignment, along with the workbook, to avoid time behind bars. At the end of the syllabus, it has all the details on how to contact "Mr. S. Buford, anger management extraordinaire." I kid you not, that is how he wrote it.

It's official, my life is the worst. Jail sounds better than this torture. I mean, I bet they have air-conditioning there.

After giving a far too in-depth explanation of the course, Steve asks everyone to look inside themselves and open their hearts and minds to the healing that will accompany us upon this journey...Along with that load of horseshit, he also believes we will all become lifelong best friends. Oh, Steve. Sweet, long-haired Steve.

After my first Anger Management class, I head to downtown Bloomburgh to my favorite dive bar, The Liquor Picker, to decompress. As I walk into the cool, dark room, the feeling of comfort greets me. My shoes stick to the floor as I head over to my favorite spot at the bar. I slide onto the tall, cracked pleather stool and wait for Lexa to notice me.

As she pours a drink for the two old men in front of her, Lexa throws her head back in laughter before glancing in my direction. After a few more minutes, she finishes her conversation with the old men. She turns to me with a bounce in her step. "Is that my favorite hothead Clara over there?"

"The one and only," I say, shaking my head as she brings me my favorite drink, a rum and coke.

"So?"

With a tilt of my head, I flutter my lashes at her, not wanting to talk about the mess that was my evening. My life. Not taking her eyes off me, she pours herself a shot of tequila, shooting it back as her teal hair falls over her shoulders. The carefree attitude surrounding her is something I have always admired about Lexa. Having first met in beauty school years ago, we became quick friends, bonding over our love of skin and hair, dick jokes, and fake accents.

Lex's free spirit has always been something I've admired. I wish I could be as passionate, creative, fun, and full of life as her. Instead of a go-with-the-flow kind of chick, I am a neurotic ball of pent-up stress. So much so that I got myself thrown into an ultimatum of jail or a class for short-tempered fools.

"So, how was your first day of school?" Lex asks, resting her chin on her hands as she blinks at me.

"What do you think?"

"Well, sweetie, did you at least make any new friends?"

With a shake of my head, I take a sip of my drink, choking on the liberal amount of rum Lexa added. My eyes water as I cough uncontrollably. Lex's laugh fills my ears as she passes me water.

"What the hell," I say in between my hacking. I sip down water for a minute or two until I get myself to stop.

"Oh, stop. You love my little surprises. Now answer the question, did you or did you not make any friends?"

"Negative."

She frowns, crossing her arms. "And why not?"

"Well, Mom, correct me if I am wrong, but a bunch of people who had to be there or go to jail really don't seem like the type of people I should be around."

"Ah, little grasshopper, it sounds like the exact type of people you should make friends with because the stories are bound to be amazing."

A laugh escapes me as I relay my day, in extreme detail, to her, in between her mixing and pouring drinks for the constant rotation of customers. I tell her about the insane case of swamp ass I got in the rec center, the counselor I have decided to call "Steve," and the asshole with the golden hair's jab.

"Fuck that guy!" Lexa says.

"Right?"

"No, I mean it. You should fuck that guy. He sounds hot."

I roll my eyes at her. "You are the worst."

"As I said before, you love it. And based on how irritated Mr. Kiss Ass has made you, it seems like you two would have hot, sweaty, animal-like sex."

"Why is everything about sex with you?"

She shrugs. "What can I say? It's a gift. And besides, you don't mind it because you love me, and I am the only thing keeping you from becoming a complete-fucking-loser hermit."

"Well, that's an exaggeration."

She dips her eyebrows into a furrow and tilts her head. "Is it, though? When was the last time you did anything remotely social for fun?"

I wish I could say I had a quick retort. But I don't. I have no idea the last time I did anything outside of work and coming to this bar for a quick drink. Everything in my life has revolved around working toward one goal.

I mumble, "I cannot stand you."

"Whatever you need to tell yourself."

I roll my eyes, taking one last gulp of my drink before sliding off the stool, blowing her a kiss, and heading home.

I wait outside the bar for my Uber to arrive. Rocking back and forth on my feet, I'm reminded how much I hate not having a car and having to depend on others to get around. With my phone out, I debate reaching out to Chloe again. My sister—my twin sister—who has been dodging my calls and me ever since the day she fucked me over. The day she played a part in ruining my life.

My finger hovers over her name. I know she won't answer, but I can't help but hope this time will be different. It's ridiculous that even after everything she has done, she's still the one I want to run to. To talk to about this crazy mess I'm in. But I can't. Temptation ends up winning this round as I draw my phone up to my face, only for her voice mail to be full.

I want to scream. I want to cry. I want to make her pay for everything she has done to me. For betraying my trust. I still don't understand her reasoning. And I doubt I ever will at this point.

I let out a huff just as the ride I ordered pulls up. Climbing into the back seat, I sit in silence, letting the memories of that day wash over me until I find myself back at my apartment.

With my legs propped on the coffee table and my laptop in my lap, I scroll through endless home listings. I was so close. So fucking close to being able to make my pipe dream a reality. But no, I had to screw everything up, using most of my savings to pay for legal fees and a lawyer.

I didn't even want anything fancy. I just wanted something that would be mine.

But instead of owning my home, I am stuck in this small-ass apartment for who knows how many more years.

Chapter Two

Kamdyn

The sun's rays beat down on my shoulders, scorching my bare skin. I wipe the sweat forming over my brows. Summer is in full force, not that I needed the UV rays to tell me that; my over-the-top boredom from being out of work until next school year was enough of a reminder, but still, the heat helped dig that fact into my brain.

"June," I call out, irritation prickling along my skin as I pick up yet another stick from my elderly neighbor's backyard, which is odd because she doesn't have any trees back here and I already cleaned up the yard.

Have I really been so lost in my shit that I didn't even see her throw these in the grass?

"Did you need me, tight ass?" June asks, lounging in a rocking chair on the shaded porch with a glass of iced tea that I am almost positive is spiked.

"June," I say, bringing the sticks to the pile I created on the porch.

"What did I say about calling me that?"

She waves her hand in front of her face. "Oh, pishposh. If you don't like it, then why are you walking around showing off all that skin?"

"Why am I showing off all this skin? Because you conveniently tripped and spilled tanning oil all over my shirt."

"So you would blame an old woman for her failing balance." She tsks. "Shame on you, Kamdyn Cook."

"I won't blame you for that, but I sure as hell am blaming you for all the sticks in the yard."

A grin slivers up from her lips. "I don't know what you are talking about."

"Sure you don't." I shake my head, heading back to the lawnmower. I'm bending over to pull the throttle lever when she lets out a loud whistle.

"June," I groan, turning back to her.

"What? I was just trying to get your moody-ass attention," she says, running her hands through her white hair.

"Well, you have it."

"I made you a sandwich for when you're done. It's in the fridge, along with that casserole from last night you forgot to take with you."

My irritation with her softens as I'm reminded of why I put up with her. She is a pervy stand-in grandmother. She takes care of me, and I take care of her while putting up with her regular blatant sexual harassment.

"Thank you." I smile back at her, pulling the lever. The mower whirs to life, and I continue cutting the last section of her yard, my thoughts diving back into the mess that is my life.

I finish cutting the grass, only for June to direct me to another chore. Black hedge trimmers in hand, I cut my way around the house, shrub by shrub, until my hands to my shoulders shake from exertion.

Note to self: buy an electric hedge trimmer.

My arms feel like lead as I place everything back into the neatly organized tool shed in the far corner of her yard. I march my way up to the house, opening the back door, waiting for whatever torture she feels like inflicting next.

June sits at the kitchen table with a bowl filled to the top with bright-red strawberries. The powerful aroma matches my memory of Steph. The smell of her hair sprawled out on the pillows as we would lie in bed. Strawberries used to be something that made me smile, reminding me of her. Not anymore. No, now they do nothing but dredge up the past that I want to forget.

One month ago

Beep. Beep. Beep.

With my eyes still closed, I rolled over to turn off the alarm on my phone. My fingers swiped over the screen three times before it stopped. Not ready to leave the bed, I wrapped my arms around Steph's warm softness. The strawberry fragrance of her shampoo filled my nose as I buried my face in the crook of her neck.

"Stop it, Kammy. I'm trying to sleep," Steph said, pulling out of my arms.

I smiled at the sleepy slur of her voice, rewrapping myself around her. "I can't help it. You smell so delicious. I need a little taste." My lips moved to the back of her neck, pressing into her skin. I kissed a trail down her shoulder as my hands slid up and down her smooth thighs.

A small sigh escaped her lips as she rolled over to face me. Her mouth found mine as she threw one leg over my hips. I grasped her waist, pressing my growing erection into her. Excitement filled my every cell as she rubbed herself all over me.

Beep. Beep. Beep.

"Fuck," I muttered into her mouth, reaching behind me, trying to grab my phone to silence the alarm again. But instead of stopping the screeching noise, I knocked my phone off the nightstand onto the floor.

Steph grumbled as I broke our kiss to find it and turn it off for real this time.

I sat my now silent phone down, ready to pick up where we left off. I turned back to Steph, only to find her sitting on the edge of the bed. On my hands and knees, I crawled across to her. My hands touched her at the same time as my lips. "Okay, now where were we?"

"Kam."

"Yeah?" My fingers fumbled along the edge of her panties.

Her hand found mine, giving it a light squeeze. "The moment has passed." She stood, leaving me kneeling on the bed with a hard-on that ached to be taken care of.

After taking an extra long cold shower, I headed out at the same time as Steph with a parting kiss and exchange of "I love you." Her to work on a big, high-profile case and me to grade some papers on my "professional day," a random Friday off from my students. It is one of my most dreaded tasks as a teacher.

Once inside my classroom, I picked through the stacks of term papers, hoping it wouldn't be as miserable as I expected. After grading two papers full of sentences like "the war was really bad. Maybe the baddest" and "I think this war was pointless," it became increasingly obvious that my weekend was going to be spent muddling through my high schoolers' half-ass attempts at one thousand words.

I graded what felt like five hundred term papers before calling it quits and packing up the rest to finish at home. With a heavy box under my arm, I headed to my car, only to be stopped by a teary-eyed Linda.

"Linda, what's going on?" I asked, setting the box on the ground.

Her hands shook as she wiped the falling tears away. "The school board is cutting teachers."

My eyes widened. "Did they...did you—?" I felt the panic rise in me. If my hallway neighbor and the best world history teacher this school has ever had got laid off, what hope did I have?

She shook her head. "Not yet. But they told me that one of our classes would be cut."

Shit. There are four of us in the department: Linda, Mr. Boyd, Brittney, and me. Our classes are already overflowing with students. The three teachers who don't get canned will be overrun with students.

"I can't believe this. It's bullshit."

She looked up at me, her face pained with wetness welling in her eyes. She probably assumed it would be her. Linda is pushing seventy-five, and the school board has been hounding her about retirement for the past few years. But this, this would be cruel.

"It won't be you." My head shook back and forth as I gathered her in my arms. "It won't be."

"You are too kind, Kamdyn. You know that, right?" She sniffled, pulling out of my arms. "No matter what happens, kiddo, you will always be one of my surrogate grandbabies."

"Always."

As I drove away, my body tensed, and a heaviness filled my limbs with fear for Linda, for me.

I was almost home when I decided it couldn't wait till tonight. I needed to see Steph. As my girlfriend, I needed her comfort and advice. And as a lawyer. I needed to know what I should do. If there was anything I could do.

I parked on the side of the road, texting Steph to let her know I was going to pop by to talk as I slipped a quarter into the meter before heading across the street to her office. Inside the building, I gave a quick wave to the friendly receptionist, who gave me her usual bright smile.

Once at Steph's office, my hand stilled on the latch, remembering she could have been with a client. As I raised my fist to knock, the sound of a low moan flowed through the door. My hand froze, and I put my ear to the wood. I waited until I heard the noise again.

My heart pounded as I opened the door. I didn't even register that my body had moved until I saw her.

Steph.

My girlfriend of two years.

The woman I woke up to that morning, on her knees for another man.

His eyes were closed as he leaned back on the small couch under the large window. His hands gripped the back of her head, helping her bob up and down. The sound of his moans mixed with sloppy slurping coming from Steph as she sucked his dick had my stomach churning.

Frozen in place, I watched. My mouth filled with saliva. I waited at the door for them to finish, unsure of what I was supposed to do in this situation. My teeth ground together, and I forced myself to swallow down the nausea.

I stared at her, at them, for what felt like hours. Hate filled my body with heat as he continued to thrust into her mouth. With a pop of suction, she darted her tongue over the head of his cock one more time before climbing up onto him. But her pulling her dress up to slide him inside her made me lose it.

"Are you fucking kidding me?"

The two jumped, heads swiveling in my direction. Her face blanched as she widened her eyes. She stumbled up, pulling her dress down while rushing over to me.

Her eyes were already watering, maybe from being caught. But it's more likely from the deep throating she had just been doing. "Kammy." Her hand shook as she reached for me. "Please, let me explain. It's not what you think."

An abrupt laugh came from me. "You must think I am a goddamn idiot if you think I would believe that."

"Please, just listen. Nothing happened. It almost did, but it didn't. I'm so sorry." She flung herself at me, clinging her arms around my body, and every muscle in my body tensed.

I draped my arms around her and leaned down, planting my mouth against her ear. "Steph?"

"Yeah?"

"Nothing happened?"

She tightened her grip on me, shaking her head into my chest before leaning back to look up at me.

With a small smile, I asked, "What do you call swallowing his dick a minute ago?"

She lurched out of my grip. "I…I." That was all she could get out before the tool with his dick still out stepped in front of her.

"You need to leave," he said, his face hard as he glared at me. It might have been intimidating if he weren't tucking his semi-erect dick back into his slacks at that moment.

"You know what, guy-who-just-fucked-my-girlfriend's-face? You're correct. It is time for me to go." I turned, walking out of her office, only to turn right back around, popping my head back in. "Oh, and Steph, I want your shit out of my house by tomorrow."

I didn't give either of them another chance to say a word as I left. My body pulsed. The rage tingled like electricity in my fingertips. It took everything in me not to show my emotions. I needed to get home, to throw her crap in trash bags. Then and only then could I let myself process and feel what had happened.

Once I was out of the building, I spotted my car with someone standing close to it. I jogged across the street. "Hey, what are you doing to my car?" I asked as the woman leaned forward and wrote down my license plate number.

With her back to me, she said, "Sir, is this your vehicle?"

"Yes, and like I said, what are you doing?"

She ripped a piece of paper from her notepad and thrust it at me.

"What is that?" I asked, refusing to take it.

"A ticket, sir."

This cannot be happening.

"A ticket? For what? I put money in the damn machine before I went in not even thirty minutes ago."

She tilted her head to the side, pointing with her pen to the sign a little farther up that stated, "NO PARKING BETWEEN THE HOURS OF 5:00 p.m.-5:00 a.m."

"Are you fucking with me? It's less than five minutes past 5:00 p.m."

"I don't make the rules, sir. I just enforce them," she said, turning on her heels to place the ticket under my windshield wipers.

"Oh, no, you don't." I grabbed the ticket from the windshield and balled it up. I threw it toward her just as she turned back to face me. The ticket ended up hitting her right in the face. More specifically, the eye.

She clutched her hand to her eye. "You just assaulted an officer of the law, right?" she asked while walking back to her car to grab her radio.

"It was an accident." Panic spread up my chest.

Talking into her radio, she requested a squad car, reporting her "attack."

"You know it was an accident," I pleaded with her.

"Accident or not, you are still accountable, sir."

Once again, the anger surged through me. Just when I thought it couldn't get any worse, a squad car pulled up. I threw my hands up with a growl, kicking over the trash can beside the meter. I watched it roll across the ground, trash falling out everywhere before it stopped with a loud clank as it hit the meter reader's car.

It didn't take more than five minutes for me to be escorted into the back of the police cruiser in handcuffs.

It turned out that my little ball of paper scratched the meter maid's cornea, and I was going to be charged with assault and battery of a police officer unless I agreed to take a futile anger management class.

Today starts another week in my short-term stint in hell. I've gone over my story a million times, practicing my lines with my slight twist on what happened last month that led me to this hot shithole of a rec center.

I would laugh and put everyone at ease with my anecdotal story of a mishap with a meter maid. But in reality, it was anything but funny.

I arrive a few minutes early at the rec center, my stomach rolling at the knowledge that I have to go inside. In my car, I soak up every ounce of air-conditioning I can before I get sweat stains all over my clothes. My classmates file into the gym as I rein in my irritation.

When you hear the words court-ordered Anger Management, you expect big, brawny men who could crush you like a bug. But instead, it's men and women who look like they're from all different backgrounds. Some are old, and some are young. Some attractive, and some not. But most of all, they're nice.

Well, except for the girl who sat across the room with her jaw clenched and a glassy, blank stare through the entire session.

Once in the sweltering room, I sit in the large circle of chairs, ready to complete week two. Beside me, a man with a neck tattoo reading "Misti" is showing everyone pictures of his brand-new baby girl named Misti.

"Your tattoo looks healed for being so fresh," I say to him, pointing at my neck.

He pulls his brows together as he looks at me. "Huh? This tattoo isn't new."

"Oh, I'm sorry, I just assumed. Did you name her after that Misti?"

"Nah, that Misti"—he stops to trail his finger over his neck—"was an ex-lady of mine, and a crazy bitch at that."

I open my mouth to respond, but nothing happens. Over his shoulder, my eye catches on her, the girl with the long dark hair whose hand is blocking a laugh at neck tattoo's words.

The corner of my lips turns up at her as I admire the smile on her face. From afar, she reminds me of Snow White. Beautiful with her pale skin and dark contrasting hair. But it doesn't outshine her shitty attitude from last week.

Her face falls, and she straightens in her chair, crossing her legs as our counselor joins us in the circle. My eyes refuse to leave her body. They trail up and down as I take in her toned legs in the cutoff shorts, which leave very little to my imagination.

His talking cuts my line of thought off. I pull my gaze away from her to find him sitting in the same seat as last week, in the same clothes as last week. All I have to do is charm the pants off my new group counselor, Sean, or at least I'm almost certain that's his name. In all honesty, I zoned out on pretty much every introduction. Well, every introduction but Crabby Clara's.

Normally, I excel with names, memorizing faces and names on the spot. It comes with the teaching profession. But lately, I am far too caught up in my own shit to pay attention.

"Okay, group, this week in AM"—he pauses before continuing—"that's short for Anger Management. We are going to learn about three things. One: the cycles of anger. Two: myths about anger. And three: fight-or-flight.”

I can't help but rub my fingers across my forehead as I listen to him.

“Anger begins with a trigger that leads to a negative thought or response. Soon, manifestations begin, such as emotions, like shame or hurt, and physiological signs, like your heart racing and your body shaking, eventually leading to an action. A behavioral response to the trigger. To your anger. It could be yelling. It could be punching.” He looks around the room as he speaks, stopping to look us each in the eye for a moment before continuing. “Once we understand what anger is and what it looks like, we can learn to manage it. To stop it before it gets out of hand.”

He stands, passing out a stack of papers to everyone. “Here is a list of fight-or-flight responses to anger. Anger is a ‘fight’ response in fight-or-flight. We need to learn to recognize that in ourselves so we can move on to the flight. I will separate everyone into small groups to work on the worksheet. Try to identify your responses to rage, as well as what others may experience.”

Much to my amusement, I end up in a group with “Misti,” snarky legs, and somehow Sean himself.

With a clap of his hands, Sean looks at the three of us with excitement. “Who wants to go first? Kamdyn? Or how about you?” He gestures to the neck tat.

I glance over at snarky Snow White on my right to see if she also noticed how he skipped her. With her hand in front of her, she picks at her nails in a way that looks like she's admiring and despising them all at once.

“Well, since no one wants to volunteer, I guess I will go,” Sean says, his face falling slightly. “When I get upset, I clench my fist, so I am going to circle that one on my paper. Kam, how about you?"

My eyes fall to the paper before me. "Ugh, I don't know. None of these fit me. I'm not an angry guy."

A mumble comes out of Clara's mouth, and we all turn to look at her.

"Clara, is there something you want to add?" Sean asks.

"Yeah, Clara, tell us what you're thinking," I say, tilting my head. I want—no, need—to take her down a notch.

A smirk graces her face as she stares me down. Her blue eyes pierce mine. They look like a storm waiting, blowing in. "Oh, just that you're full of shit, Kam," she says, adding emphasis to my nickname, sounding like an insult.

I grind my jaw together as I lean forward in my chair. "Is that right?"

Her body mimics mine as she scoots to the edge of her seat, leaning in closer. "Yep."

Chapter Three

Clara

"Okay, okay, guys," Steve says, putting his hands up to tamp down some of the tension building between Kam and me. "Good job, you two, showing examples of some emotional and physical responses to anger."

With Mr. Perfect's eyes still on me, I wink as I shift back into my seat. I swear I see a little twinkle in those enchanting hazel eyes of his as my smirk grows bigger, watching him retreat to his put-together facade.

I continue to appraise him—his attitude, his body language—for the next hour. From the way he tightens his jaw every time he finds me staring, to the way he gestures while he talks with a sort of fluid grace that screams control.

As the class wraps up, I don't linger around like others. I dart out of my chair, picking up this week's homework assignment. I make a beeline for the door, only to be cut off by none other than Mr. Perfect.

Not bothering to give him a second glance, I step to the side to move around him, only to find him stepping into my path again.

"Do you want something?" I ask.

Instead of answering, he looks me up and down, sending an agonizing wave of heat through my already feverish body.

"Okay then, Asshat, if you have nothing to say, I'm gonna go." I point over his shoulder at the doors.

"Asshat?" he says, snickering to himself. "Did you just call me an asshat?"

"Well, if the ass fits," I deadpan, sobering him up. He moves out of my way, giving me room to walk out into the sun's sweltering heat.

It doesn't take more than a minute of me being out here for my skin to start burning. Needing a shady spot to hang out in until my ride gets here, I have two options.

Go back into the rec center and force myself to mingle.

Or sit under a shaded tree that might be surrounded by ants.

Ants. I will always choose ant bites over people and small talk. It's something a lot of people don't understand about me.

How can a beautician be so antisocial? is a question I am constantly asked. Well, for starters, I am an aesthetician. I work on skin, more specifically, the face. Most of the services I provide at The Spa require my clientele to be still and quiet. They wouldn't want to fuck up what they paid for. And trust me, they pay out the ass.

So yeah, I am a beautician who hates small talk.

I scour the ground for signs of ant life, finding nothing. With the tree behind me, I sit, leaning into it as I request my ride.

Twenty minutes. Ugh, I have twenty more minutes to kill until my Uber is here.

This is what I get for choosing a Friday night group, hoping to make my life a little easier by not having to take off work for a class they're already pissed about. Well, not necessarily pissed about the class, as much as mad at me and the whole situation.

I lean my head back against the tree, closing my eyes as a small breeze brushes against my hair. Strands fly across my face, sticking to the sweat dripping down my cheeks.

In my attempt to clear my hair from my face, I note the dirt now clinging to my palms.

Red and brown smear on my damp skin.

"Ugh," I say, letting out a heavy sigh while still fidgeting.

"I feel like Mother Nature wins this round," a man says from beside me. I jerk back, scraping my elbow on the tree.

"Fucker," I hiss through clamped teeth. I snap my eyes shut as I let out a deep breath through my nose.

"Another point for the environment."

I snap my eyes open, darting to where the man stands. I was so busy focusing on the pain in my arm that I had completely forgotten about the asshole who startled me.

Kamdyn, aka Mr. Perfect.

"Of course, it's that asshole," I whisper, not caring that I said it out loud for him to hear.

He lets out a whistle. With his hands in his pockets, he stares at me, waiting for me to respond. When I don't reply, he doesn't resist speaking again.

"So it isn't just the class?" he asks.

"Huh?"

"The hostile thing. It's not just for class, I guess."

His words sting. I lean back to look at him through my widening eyes. My chest tightens as I try to conceal my expression.

I fight to hide my emotions, repeating the words of my favorite cartoon ice queen in my head. Yes, Elsa's words have resonated with me over the years. I'm not afraid to admit it's my mantra.

I won't let anyone, let alone him, know they have gotten under my skin again. Not after the last time landed me in this shithole that I can't seem to dig myself out of.

"Wow, a woman doesn't respond to you and that automatically makes her a bitch? Way to be the average white man." I push my hands into the ground to stand up. I am being a bitch, though, and I know it. I just can't help it. This whole situation has me on edge.

His jaw ticks as he crosses his arms, his eyes sharpening as he looks me over. The stare is intense and suffocating. I can't help the shiver that runs through me when his eyes meet mine.

"You know what, never mind. I wanted to apologize for last week, but I can see this was a mistake." A pleased look washes over his face when he catches my involuntary squirm.

Just as I open my mouth to spout another insult, my phone "pings," alerting me that my Uber has arrived.

Thank you, Universe.

I walk past him, bumping my shoulder into his for a dramatic, spiteful effect. Only to hit an unfaltering, hard stone wall.

"Fuck," I mouth, wincing as the pain from my childish dick move sets in.

Not wanting to see him or hear another egotistical word, I hurry into the car. Without looking back, I head home for the night to get a jump start on this week's homework.

The moment I walk through my apartment door, I go straight to my small gray couch. I flop down onto a pile of throw pillows covering it and groan inwardly at the sheer ridiculousness that is now my fucking life.

"I can feel you judging me," I say, face down into a pillow. "Stop." I lift my head just enough to give my small, disapproving goldfish, Sir Swims-A-Lot, a glare. He returns the stare in his normal fashion before leisurely swimming away into the back of the tank.

Resolved to bask in my misery, I lie like that for a good chunk of an hour before turning on the TV to find my next assignment.

An hour into the movie, I am as restless as ever. How on earth is a movie about sisters supposed to help me let go of this anger and resentment that has been building for longer than I want to admit to myself? Hell, it's doing the opposite. It's reminding me why I'm so pissed at Chloe—and myself.

Instead of doing the smart thing, like turning in for the night, I do the very unhelpful thing of text bombing Chloe.

Me: Where the hell are you?

Me: Why are you such a selfish hag?

Me: In tenth grade, your boyfriend Nathan told me I was the pretty twin.

It's a lie. But it's something that will get under her skin since he cheated on her. I'm being a dick, but I will try anything to get a response from her. Even goading her with mean comments.

But she doesn't take the bait. My phone sits in my hands, waiting for a reply.

After a while, I give up on waiting for her to respond. I'm halfway to my bed when I hear my phone ring.

I leap onto the couch to grab it, only to see my mother's picture lighting up the screen. My thumb hovers over the answer button before moving to ignore her call.

She's been hounding me for weeks to set up a lunch date, to which my response is always "*maybe next week.*"

I love my mother with all my heart, but I don't have the patience or stomach to dodge all the Chloe questions that will undoubtedly come up.

Chapter Four

Kamdyn

As the overachiever I am, I complete week two's homework on Friday night. Well, I could also attribute it to the fact that I'm single and have nothing to do. But I'm going to stick with the overachiever reasoning. It makes me feel better about my newfound patheticness.

With summer in full swing, I don't have the most normal routine. I spend most of my days either running errands for my elderly neighbor, June, volunteering at the animal shelter a few blocks away from my house, or working out.

Most teachers live for summer break. The relaxing time of zero work. Zero responsibilities.

In the past, during summer break, I would visit my mom and her wife, Amanda, wherever the hell they ended up in the world. Last year, I spent four weeks with them in Brazil. We hiked, went sightseeing, and ate everything in sight. It was perfect. But this year, I'm stuck, both physically and emotionally.

Bound in place by the consequences of my actions. Of my reaction to Steph's cheating. And the fact that I've received at least one text a day from her since. Apology after apology. Lie after lie.

The worst part is that I had to lie to my mom about it. I gave her some vague excuse about why I couldn't go on our annual trip this year. She was crushed, but if she learned the real reason, she would be heartbroken over how dumb the man she raised had been.

I can't fuck this up. Too much at risk. If I mess this up, it's my career on the line.

This week's homework was easier said than done. Watch a Hallmark movie and write a report on the characters' actions. Yeah, first, I don't have that channel. So subscribing to it was ridiculous. But the actual movie is the most irritating thing I have ever experienced.

The movie is sappy and predictable.

But I do it. I write my report on the ridiculous and wholesome actions of the characters. I'm not sure how watching a movie about a woman falling in love with a rival business owner is supposed to help with anger and aggression management.

But nevertheless, I did it. I kept up with little attention to the actual movie. I can only hope this next week's assignments and class will be less painful for my brain.

Days pass by of me doing the same thing over and over again.

Help June with the lawn and groceries, walk the dogs, and work out. And repeat.

I need human interaction, more than just strangers and elderly women. Lucky for me, on Wednesday, my best friend needed the same thing, only for different reasons.

"You know I've missed you, brother," Marcus pants with his hands braced on his knees. "But this is not what I had in mind when I said I need to stretch my legs."

We just finished running three miles through the city. I had planned on doing my usual four, but from his heavy breathing, it's time to call it for the day.

I slap his back, and he goes flying forward an inch, giving me a glare that would scare anyone else.

The two of us from the outside might appear to be opposites—him with his dark skin full of cool undertones that always make him look flushed, and me with my summer-tanned beige skin.

But that's where the differences end. Marcus, like me, is a teacher a few towns over, only instead of history, he teaches geometry, which he still tries to get me to understand without success. We both could eat our body weight in cheese. In fact, we once tried and failed miserably in high school to do so. It wasn't pretty. Both of us ended up having to be plied with laxatives. We vowed never to speak of it again. Along with that, we have matching tattoos symbolizing our friendship. The Latin words *caseus fratribus* are hidden among all the other tattoos on our arms. The words meaning "cheese brothers."

"It's not my fault you've let yourself go," I say, still jogging in place.

"Oh yeah, asshole, because juggling a wife and a baby along with tutoring this summer leaves a shit ton of time for running ten miles every day."

"Hey." I hold my hands up. "I'm not the one who told you to marry the lady and procreate."

He stands up straight, his breathing almost to a normal rhythm. "Yes. Yes, you fucking are."

I shake my head. "I don't remember that."

"And I quote, 'if you don't marry her and put a baby in that uterus, I will.' Or was that my other best man whispering in my ear as Tay walked down the aisle?"

Grinning from ear to ear, I slap his arm. "Want to get something to eat?"

"God, yes!" he says, following me to my car. "Mexican?"

"You want queso, don't you?" I ask.

"Fuck, yeah, I do." He climbs into the passenger seat.

It's a ten-minute drive to the restaurant, but the way we talk with each other makes it feel like thirty seconds.

Once seated inside, we pick right up where we left off. "Anyway, these kids I was tutoring didn't have the first clue about geometry," he says in between a bite of chips and queso.

"So? Neither do I."

"Kam, when I say they had zero knowledge of the subject, I mean it. Like right angles were lost on them."

"So what I'm hearing is you needed this get-together more than me."

"Fuck, yeah, I did. Wait, why would you need it? Aren't you and Steph supposed to be meeting your mom, like, in a week for some awesome worldly adventure that my ass can't afford with a child at home?"

I shrug, avoiding his eyes. "Canceled."

"Why? You go every year," he says, looking baffled. "Wait, let me guess, Steph. She's the reason, isn't she?"

I give him a pointed look that he takes as a yes.

"Look, you know I love you and only want what's best for you, right?"

"Yea—" I say before he cuts me off.

"You need to stop letting her control your life."

I don't disagree with him. Instead, I just don't respond. I hate lying to him about this. He wouldn't judge me, but the shame burning through me makes it impossible to let him know about this.

When Friday rolls back around, I walk into the sweltering-as-usual rec center, only to be met with the sight of my chosen seat for the past two weeks being taken. Even without seeing their face, I know who it is. I would recognize that long, dark hair and pale skin anywhere. Clara. I move around the chair to find her looking up at me with a smirk on her face.

"Oh, hey, Asshat," she says, quirking an eyebrow at me, waiting for me to respond to her seat stealing and use of the nickname she has now graced me with. The woman is trying to piss me off.

"Clara." I stare down into her steel-blue eyes beaming up at me.

"Yes?" She crosses her legs, placing her hands on her bare knee. There is no doubt she's enjoying this.

"You're in my seat."

"Oh dear, am I?" Her hand flies up across her chest, landing right over her heart. "Well, look at that, I am. What are you going to do about it?"

I lean toward her as she leans away, pressing her back flush against the metal chair. Bracing one of my hands on the chair behind her and the other beside her thigh, I brush my thumb across her skin. I watch as her skin goose bumps under my touch.

Warmth flows through me, knowing I caused that kind of reaction from her. Why do I care, though? She's standoffish and rude.

But the better question is, why is it causing her to react like that? She has told me time and time again how much she dislikes me. Yet, her body is saying the opposite.

My lips brush her ear, and the sweet rosy aroma of her hair fills my nose as I whisper, "Oh, I don't think you could handle it." Her breath catches in her throat as I push off the chair, watching her skin flush crimson.

She's speechless as I take the seat right next to her, pulling my chair only inches away from hers.

Legs pivoting in my direction, she opens her mouth to say something, only to have our attention stolen by Sean entering the circle.

"Okay, my amigos, how was everyone's week?" Sean asks, waiting for the circle to reply. Everyone is silent, staring at our fashion-challenged leader. The big, bright smile on his face falls. "Come on, guys. Where is your energy and enthusiasm?"

Beside me, Clara mutters, "We left it in the '90s, along with your sense of style."

I catch a laugh in the back of my throat and end up choking on my saliva. My eyes water as I cough repeatedly.

With all eyes on me, I hold up my hand, signaling that I'm okay. Sean's raised eyebrows aren't helping the situation either. He hands me a small cup of water to sip on. It helps.

With a darting glance at Clara, I can see the smirk she's trying to hide. Her lips curve in as she bites back her laughter.

Sean brings the attention back to himself and off me, announcing that today in class, we will team up to role-play situations, showing how and how not to react to anger. The entire room releases a groan as we wait to be split up.

He has us all draw slips of paper from a hat with a scene written on one side and "aggressor" or "triggered person" on the other. Once everyone has drawn from the hat, we have to find our partner who has the other role.

As everyone pairs up, it becomes increasingly obvious who my partner is.

None other than the grouch, Clara.

Still sitting in her chair with her legs and arms crossed, she turns her body away from me.

"Are you going to refuse to do the assignment?" I ask her.

She lifts her hand and examines her black fingernail polish, fanning and extending her fingers out, then pulling them into her palm. Yep, she plans to ignore me.

"Listen," I say, scooting my chair in front of hers. "I don't want to do this either, especially with someone like you." She snaps her head in my direction and widens her eyes at me. "But we have no choice. I don't know about you, but I would prefer not to go to jail."

"Fine," she says, turning to face me. "Let's get this over with."

We brush over our plan for acting out our scene. After ignoring each other for most of the time we were given to prepare, we're unprepared when called to perform our stolen-lunch scene in front of the class.

I walk over to an imaginary fridge, opening the door to find my lunch is missing. Using my classmates to my advantage, I turn to ask a few if they know where my lunch is or if they ate it. All shake their heads, denying their involvement. That is until I walk over to Clara.

Standing in the middle of the circle, she looks at her nails again. She looks unimpressed, almost bored.

"Did you eat my lunch?" I ask her with an over-the-top scowl on my face.

Her eyes travel up and down my body before returning to my face. "Um, was this yours?" she asks expressionless, motioning with her hands to another imaginary item.

"Yeah. That's why my name is on it."

"I didn't see your name. Maybe next time, do a better job of making sure you label your stuff." She quirks her eyebrows up, and I realize she's throwing a barb about the chair.

I stalk close to her, stopping a few inches in front of her. "Maybe next time you shouldn't be so selfish."

She stares up at me, eyes twinkling, daring me to say more. To overreact. The blue iciness of her attention has me frozen in place, but inside I'm set ablaze with irritation. She's trying to gaslight me, wanting, tempting me to lose my cool.

"Don't you think you're overreacting?" She curls her lips into a wicked grin. "It's not a big deal, just a piece of food."

I close my fists, cracking my knuckles as I step even closer to her. Our bodies almost touching. We're so close the warmth of her breath skims over my skin. The sweet and spicy aroma of her cinnamon gum fills my nose as my eyes snap closed.

With a slight lean forward, I open them to look at her. The rapid rising of her chest makes it impossible for me to do anything but admire her breasts as they move with her every breath.

Clara lets out a snort, bringing my eyes away from her chest and back to her face. I feel like an obtuse jerk. She must have just observed my unintentional ogling.

"Ahem."

Clara jumps slightly as Sean brings our focus back to him. Back to the scene. Back to Anger Management class.

"Good job, you two." He waves us back to our seats. "Excellent job showing a situation where both parties handled the situation wrong."

I do my best to ignore her for the rest of the class, biting my lips and cheeks to keep a straight face when I hear her mutter insults and jokes under her breath. If she weren't such a trying woman, I would admit she was actually pretty funny. But she is catty, and I refuse to acknowledge her or her actions anymore.

Chapter Five

Clara

The past few weeks have been a blur. Between the extra clients I'm taking on to help with the mess Chloe landed me in and the Anger Management course, I am a ball of stress and sleeplessness.

So this week, when Steve announced that lesson four's homework was to blow off steam, I relished the excuse to take some me time.

I sit in my usual metal seat beside Asshat, who continues to be a charming kiss ass to Steve, which is grating on my every nerve.

Kamdyn laughs as Steve tells joke after joke.

"Okay, okay. What about this one, guys? Why did the vegan get sent to Anger Management?" Steve's face is bright red as he tries to contain his laughter. "Anyone?"

No one responds.

Cackling to himself, Steve says, "Because he had a bad tempeh." The room breaks out into laughter while I fight the urge to roll my eyes.

Apparently, Steve's way of letting off steam is telling lame jokes.

Beside me, Kamdyn elbows me, whispering, "Just throw the guy a damn bone."

If looks could kill, Kamdyn would be dead right now from the daggers shooting out of my eyes. "No."

He huffs. "You know you don't have to be this sad, snarky bitch all the time?"

My head cocks to the side as I stare him up and down. Did this man just call me a sad bitch? Oh, fuck no. I am a bad bitch, now borderline mad bitch.

"Tell me, Asshat, do you enjoy the taste, or is it something else?" I ask.

He raises an eyebrow. "What are you talking about?"

"Ass? Do you enjoy the flavor, or is there another reason you kiss everyone's ass?"

His left lip twitches like he's fighting the urge to smile. I wait, staring at him, wanting to see him break.

"Time's up, guys!" Steve says, waving goodbye to us all.

I grab my chair, put it away, and rush the hell out of there.

Saturday morning, after chugging a huge energy drink, I go downtown to the cute one-room yoga studio, Pose. It's been a while since my last class because of everything that's been going on. That's a lie. I've been neglecting practicing yoga for a while now. It used to be something that I loved. Something I was passionate about.

I loved the sensation of my body being pushed and stretched

to new limits. The strength you gain both physically and mentally from it. Hell, at one point, I was looking into getting my instructor certification. I'm not sure when I stopped coming to classes or even practicing at home. Or why I stopped, but today feels like a step in the right direction.

With my mat over one shoulder, I find a spot near the back with room on both sides. As I settle in, placing my mat and water on the floor, I wait silently for the class to begin. Not recognizing a soul in the room.

With a loud thwack, a black mat rolls out beside mine. A hum of heat runs through me as I close my eyes and try to get my head in the zone. My attention shifts to the creator of the noise. I crack one eye open, catching the sight of blond hair and stubble.

I try to bring my mind back to preparing my body, but I can't. My focus is stuck on that hair. Tousled in just the right way, the honey strands shine in the light coming through the large window making up one wall.

I rear my head back as the realization of who is next to me sets in. Kamdyn.

Kamdyn is here.

In the yoga class.

My yoga class.

Stretched out next to me on the solid black mat, he meets my gaze with a wicked smile, causing my heart to race. With a little wave, he leans closer to me, taking his time to examine my chosen yoga apparel. My body stills under his scrutiny.

My teeth grind together as I ask, "What are you doing here?"

He furrows his brow at my question, looking around the room before turning back to me. "Isn't it obvious? I'm here for yoga."

He pauses for a minute, tilting his head. "What are you doing here, Clara?"

"Don't be a dick, Perfect. Why are you here, at the same studio as me?"

"For yo-ga." He says the words slowly while overaccentuating his mouth.

"You know that yoga isn't easy, right? It's not something any asshat off the street can magically do."

He says nothing, just gives me the same shit-eating grin he always has plastered on his ridiculously perfect face.

I turn away as the instructor walks in, settling myself into the easy pose, letting the instructor guide me through my breaths. I try to ignore that Kamdyn, the ass kisser, Mr. Perfect, is sitting on the mat next to me. And will be for the next forty-five minutes.

A bubble of laughter escapes from me. This is hot yoga. His ass has zero idea how hard of a workout he is about to get. He will shake and fall in the first ten minutes. But what really makes me want to crumble over in laughter is the fact that no one comes out of hot yoga looking good. Or hell, even decent. Everyone walking out of the studio in forty-five minutes will look disgusting, including Mr. Perfect.

I slam my mouth shut, hoping no one heard me. By the looks of it, no one did—well, no one that counts.

Kamdyn looks at me from his mat with his lips slightly parted and his eyebrows raised in question.

Facing the front of the class, I whisper to him, "Are you following me?"

There's a pause in his breaths as we both move into the next pose. "Are you kidding?"

"No." It's barely a sound, but from the way his jaw just ticked, I know he heard me.

For the rest of the class, Kamdyn ignores me. Never giving me a response or even a glance in my direction. He's mad at me. More mad than normal. Something about what I said must have hit a nerve with him.

I watch as Kamdyn moves through the poses with grace and ease. His muscular legs drip with sweat as his black shorts ride higher up his thighs. A rush of warmth fills my face down to my core.

And just when I didn't think Mr. Perfect could get any more, well, perfect, he unzips the light jacket he was wearing to reveal his entire left arm covered in tattoos.

My breath hitches at the sight.

He has a sleeve.

Has he always had those? Every time I've seen him in the past few weeks, never once has his arm been bare. He always has them covered in long sleeves or a jacket. Which was ridiculous and weird considering how hot the rec center gym is, but now I realize it was to conceal what lies underneath.

That Kamdyn, Mr. Perfect, has my goddamn kryptonite.

I've always found arms covered in tats so attractive. It's been this way since I was a teenager. I always wanted or dated the guy with them running up his arms.

But why does he have to have them? Ugh, why can't he be unattractive? Damn him and his perfect balance. My skin hums as I can't take my eyes off him.

I've never been so grateful for the heat of the studio until now. I would've had to explain the extreme flush to my skin in any other situation.

Once I force myself to stop my creepy staring, I focus on my breathing and body movements for the rest of the class. After finishing up our savasana, my body is like Jell-O. Every part of me is warm and loose—it's like I'm weightless. There's no other way to describe it.

Kamdyn hangs back, chatting with the instructor and a few of the other women in class as I gather my things.

Predictable as ever, Mr. Perfect has to go and charm everyone he meets. I don't bother stopping to say bye to anyone there. He's the only person I recognize, and the last thing I want is another shit show conversation with that asshat.

Later, once the calming effects of yoga have worn off, I need something, anything. Maybe some human interaction. The only problem is I have no one to do said interacting with.

Well, that isn't exactly true. I have Lexa, but she's always working when I'm feeling friendly or talkative, so that doesn't exactly work out very well.

It's times like these I wish I were more of a social butterfly. That I could click easily with others. Or maybe I just wish my best friend wasn't also the sister who stabbed me in the back.

I should've known better than to put all my stock into one person. If you lose them, it wastes everything. Every memory is tainted. You have no one to cry to about them. No sister to go running to when your best friend hurts you. No best friend to talk to about all the shitty things your sister said to you during the holidays.

At least I learned the lesson to never again invest that much of myself or my time in one person.

I try my hardest to get out of my funk. I paint my nails a shiny pale pink instead of the normal black I like to sport while watching my favorite trash reality TV shows. But no, not even the dating show with a sleazy make-out session with one person ending up getting mono could hit the spot.

After what seems like hours of staring at a TV screen, I give up and throw my hair into a high ponytail before slipping on some skinny jeans and an old baseball tee. I head out for a drink at The Liquor Picker.

Once there, I find my usual spot at the bar taken, with a jacket and a drink in front of it. I can't help but be a little pissed off, even though I have zero right to be. So I shake off my rigidness and sit two stools over.

Lex's eyes light up as she notices me. She moves to make my favorite drink without bothering to ask me what I want. She calls it her bartender intuition but also chalks it up to the fact that my drink order hasn't changed in all the years she's been my friend.

While giving me a waggle of her eyebrows, she sets the drink in front of me. It's Lexa code for "hottie in the house." She has never been very subtle. It's the thing I like the most about her. She is unapologetically herself.

Unable to resist looking at the man or woman who has her drooling, I glance as discreetly as I can muster, only to see him.

"Fuck."

Chapter Six

Kamdyn

It's a Saturday night, and I am sitting alone in a dive bar, drinking my sorrows away. Yeah, totally healthy.

Today was supposed to be a day to blow off some steam in a productive, non-future-alcoholic way. But fate or karma had other plans for me.

When I walked into yoga today, the last person I ever expected to see was the snarky girl from AM. But there she was, looking like every man's sad, wet dream. Her hair, braided into an intricate crown on her head, made her look like the Disney Princess she reminds me of. But the thing that had my heart thundering in my chest was her outfit.

Dressed in tight white marbled leggings and a black sports bra, it took everything I had not to let my gaze linger on her body. I couldn't help myself when I laid my mat out beside hers, creating as much noise as I could to get her to glance over, to notice me.

I don't know why I wanted to be by her or even have her know

I was there. Every time we're in the same vicinity, it's nothing but torture for me. From the way she always looks and speaks to me, I could guess it's the same for her, too.

She squirmed, realizing I was in the same yoga class as her. Her gaze wandered around the room as if she couldn't believe I was there. I soaked up her shock and irritation, basking because she was flustered, yet again, by me. My entire body filled with light vibration as the class began. It was like a new type of high. The type your body gets after doing something that demands an extreme amount of endurance. That lasted a few blissful moments until she leaned over and accused me of stalking her.

I didn't bother to peek at her for the rest of the class. I didn't say goodbye when she left. Instead, I chatted it up with a few people I recognized from the last time I had come to the class. Once she was gone, I let her words sink their claws deeper into me.

She thinks I'm following her...

I filled the rest of my day with things to take my mind off her comment. Why is it pissing me off? Scratch that. I know why. Steph.

If Clara had made a comment like that toward me a week ago, or hell, a few days ago, I would have brushed it off as her being her normal snide self. But today, it stung, all because of Steph.

I took a few of the energetic dogs from the rescue on a walk around the lake. I say walk, but what I really mean is a half run, half stop to pee on everything in sight. During our many pee breaks, I was lucky enough to be approached by a multitude of people, thanks to the three dogs whose tails hadn't stopped wagging since we left the rescue. Wearing bandannas around their necks with the rescue center's logo and the words "Adopt Me" was like running a moving adoption fair the whole time.

After taking another group of dogs for exercise and socialization, I dropped them back off at the rescue. I have a sense of fulfillment knowing that I helped them. If not to get adopted, at least I'm part of bringing some fun to those rambunctious hounds. But the moment I left them behind, the words uttered to me in the studio today crept back in.

Unable to take the itching anger stewing in my gut, I sit on my porch steps and call up my oldest and closest friend, Marcus.

He answers on the third ring. "What's up, brother?" Marcus sounds like he's shouting into the phone. Anyone who didn't know him might think he was. But he's been my friend since middle school, and the guy has no volume level. A normal person's inside voice is a whisper to him. He's a loud guy through and through.

"Not much. Can you sneak away from the wife and kid to grab a beer?" I ask, closing my eyes to send a silent prayer into the universe that he'll say yes. I need my friend today.

There's a pause from him before he responds in a low, quiet voice. "What's going on, Kam?" His voice only lowers like this when he sounds concerned.

"Nothing. Nothing's going on. Can't a man just want to hang out with his best friend?"

"Kam. I've known you for how many years now?"

"Eighteen."

"Yeah, that's right. I've known you for eighteen years. That means I know you. And I know whenever something is bothering you."

"Ugh," I grumble into the phone. "How? How did you get that from me asking to hang out?"

"You asked to get a beer." He laughs into the phone.

"Yeah, so?"

"You only drink beer whenever some serious shit is going down in your life or in your head. So which is it?"

He's right. I do only drink beer whenever I feel like shit. I hate the taste of it and try to avoid it under normal circumstances.

"How about you come and grab a beer with me, and I'll fill you in on everything," I say, hoping he will agree.

He does. But he can't meet until a few hours from now. We agree on this dive bar downtown that's a middle-ground meeting point for us.

I arrive an hour or two early, needing to get my nerves in check to fill Marcus in on the past two months of my life. I'm not sure why I haven't told him about the possibility of losing my job, Steph, the arrest, or even the Anger Management classes.

With an empty beer bottle in front of me and a half-full bottle in my hand, I don't even notice when Marcus slides in beside me. It's not until he tells the bartender his drink order that I'm even aware he is there.

"Brother," we say in unison as we embrace each other in a big hug.

To his credit, Marcus waits a few minutes, making small talk with me and the cute bartender before demanding I tell him what's going on.

Aside from the occasional "that cheating bitch" or "what the fuck," Marcus stays quiet as I recall all the insane recent events in my life. Once I finish, he tips his beer back, draining every bit from the bottle. "Kam, why didn't you tell me all this was going on?" he asks, eyes still wide from the shock of my story.

I shrug my shoulders, unsure what to say or how to answer. Marcus gives me a pointed look, then orders us another round of drinks.

Somewhere between beer number four and six, I find myself

drunk. Not just slightly either. I mean swaying-in-your-seat drunk. The type of intoxicated that can only lead to poor decision-making. Marcus, though, was the picture of tolerance with zero signs of inebriation. Sure, he only had four beers compared to my six. But he also drinks beer more than I do.

Before heading to the bathroom to take a piss, he flags over the eccentric bartender to close our tab. As I wait for him to get back, I stay seated in my chair, avoiding the glass of water he ordered me to drink.

"Fuck."

The profanity and shock in the speaker's voice has me turning to find who it belongs to.

My eyes lock on the last person I would have guessed would be here—Clara. "Fuck," I mutter before turning my head back to my half-finished beer. Tipping the bottle to my lips, I finish the last bits of liquid left, knowing I shouldn't be drinking any more.

Once I polish off my beer, I turn my gaze back to her. With one knee bouncing up and down, she pushes her palm up and down her thigh. "Uh-oh. Looks like your friendly neighborhood stalker found you again," I say as I look around the room. "It also looks like I must be psychic because somehow I showed up before my prey." I watch the knee that was previously bouncing stop when she registers my words.

As her body stills, I can see the insides of her cheeks hollowing out as if she's biting the inside of her mouth to stop herself from responding.

I take that as my cue to talk some more. "If anything, I would say you are the stalker, and I am the stalkee."

"Yeah, no," she says before bouncing her leg again.

Neither of us looks away. Locked in a standoff, a weird staring contest that no one declared. But somehow, I know we both know what it is.

"So," the bartender says. "I assume you two know each other." Her eyes flicker back and forth between us.

Clara responds, "Lex, this is the asshat I was telling you about, Mr. Perfect."

Lex's face beams as she takes me in. "This is Mr. Perfect," she says, pointing her finger at me as she jumps up and down.

Clara gives her a curt nod.

"From your anger class?"

"Yep."

"Oh my God, Clara. He is perfect. Like I said before, you should..." Lex gestures with her hands, a finger going into a hole, and I fight and fail to conceal the smile that pulls at the corner of my lips.

"I get it now," I say.

"Get what?" Clara asks, crossing her arms.

I cock my head to the side. "You want me."

Her mouth falls open as her eyebrows rise up her face before she breaks into laughter. A body-shaking, tears-falling type of laughter. All at the idea of being attracted to me.

"It explains everything."

As she finishes wiping the last of her tears away from beneath her eyes, she says, "What on earth makes you think that?"

"Well, for starters, you talked about me to your friend over there." I attempt to point at the girl behind the bar, only to find two of her. Squinting, I try to focus on which one is the real one. Unable to pin her down because of my alcohol-induced double vision, I give up.

Refocusing my attention on Clara, I say, "Also, you always get all flustered and turn red when talking to me."

"I can assure you, Asshat, that one, I'm not into you. Actually, I think you're an enormous dick—"

I mutter under my breath, "You want my enormous dick." Or at least I thought I was being quiet. The glare she gives me makes it difficult to tell.

"And two, the reason I get red is 'cause I'm angry. It's called fair skin. Google it sometime."

"You know, it's okay to be attracted to me. I happen to be a catch." Just as I stand, my chair moves, causing me to lose my footing. I catch myself mid-stumble on the bar's ledge, letting out a chuckle.

"You are shit-faced." Clara's hand is under my elbow, helping me stand up straight. "How are you getting home?"

A familiar floral aroma surrounds me. The feminine scent of roses invades my senses, filling me with an undeniable heat. Her gaze meets mine, and her expression fades from tight and prickly to a soft one of concern.

"I'm taking him," Marcus says, walking back from the bathroom, breaking whatever strange spell Clara and I were under. "I leave you alone for five minutes and you find a new friend to take care of you."

"I'm not his friend." Her hand jerks away from my arm as Marcus approaches.

My stomach drops the moment her hand is gone, and saliva builds up in my mouth.

With his sixth sense for everything me, Marcus is more than aware that I'm a few minutes away from vomiting. He hurries, paying our tab and getting me out of the bar before I get sick.

I lie in the back seat of his truck, slipping in and out of consciousness, telling him all about how much I hate the mess I've made of my life.

He drops me off at my house, tucking me into my bed with a glass of water and Tylenol like the dad he is before leaving me to sleep off the alcohol.

Chapter Seven

Clara

Last night at the bar was a disaster. From the moment I arrived, seeing Kamdyn sitting there, drunk, everything was destined to go downhill. Mr. Perfect knocked off his high horse. His usual composure gone, traded in for a sloppy, slurring mess of a man. I wanted to laugh, poke fun at him. To get him riled up. To push him until he exploded with anger. But something about the way he looked at me stopped me from pushing him too far. His deep hazel eyes had this glassy dullness to them I couldn't help but stare at. Something inside me wanted to find out what caused him to drink so much, wanted to hold him close to shield him from whatever haunts him.

I can't lie; I kind of liked drunk Mr. Perfect with his hair falling out of place on his forehead. He was still an asshat but less arrogant. If only he would be drunk during class. Not only would he be more tolerable, but the class wouldn't be as painful.

Tucked into the blankets of my bed, I think of how the day played out. How had the day gone from chill to lighting every nerve in my body on fire?

I blink myself awake, rubbing the gunk out of my lids and stretching my arms and legs out like a starfish. A yawn-like groan escapes my lips. With a glance at my bedside table, I see the clock is reading noon.

Shit, I'm going to be late.

Rushing around, I throw on clothes at a record rate, forgoing a shower even though rum radiates from my pores. With my hair in a high pony and last night's mascara smudged, creating dark circles, I grab my phone and keys, locking the door to my apartment.

With my legs moving as fast as I can without actually running, I'm stunned when I arrive at The Spa with five minutes to spare till my client, or I should say, clients, are due. Today I get the unfortunate task of pampering a whole bridal party. From facials to asshole bleaching, they will subject me to whatever they want. The life of an aesthetician on the brink of being fired is never dull.

My boss, Angelica, stares at me as I stroll through the doors, back to my room. She gives me a once-over, and her face turns up at me, her perfectly straight nose scrunching as I pass her. Angelica is exactly what people expect someone who works in a salon or spa to look like. Her tall, skinny, borderline underweight frame is what the world expects of women in the beauty industry. It can be intimidating. *She* is intimidating.

"What?" I raise my eyebrows.

"Is it too much to ask that you actually put effort into your appearance?" She pauses, giving me another once-over. "I mean, you work at a place that sells beauty treatments, for God's sake."

The inside of my cheeks burn with the pain of my bite as I try to keep myself in check. "I overslept. So it was this or nothing." My hand flies down my body.

She gives me a curt nod before turning her back to me. I take it as my cue that she's done with me and this conversation. But just as my body pivots to continue to my room, she says, "You know, you could be quite pretty if you actually tried."

My body freezes in place, and a tinge of metallic touches my tongue as I reopen the cut inside my mouth. My go-to way of fighting off my impulsive, big mouth. I've been doing it since I was a child, but ever since the arrest, I've been in hot water with my job and Angelica, and I have to tread lightly, which has unfortunately caused the inside of my mouth to become a raw mess.

The first of the ten in the bridal party arrives to have their very expensive, all-paid pampering experience with me. I am their servant, or at least that must be what they think because this hoity-toity woman is ordering me around like one. She demanded everything from a HydraFacial to a full-body wax.

At one point, she snapped her fingers at me.

The bitch *snapped. Her. Fingers.*

It took everything in me not to react. Well, and Angelica threatened to fire me in an instant if I embarrass her or The Spa. Apparently, this group is from a prominent family. Probably some wealthy senator's daughter spending her daddy's money. God, what I wouldn't do to have a rich daddy. But no, I got the type of dad who kills himself by eating one too many cheeseburgers and ignoring his cardiologist's warnings.

"So that's when I told him I would not accept his proposal unless he could prove that he could provide me with the means to maintain my current lifestyle," the woman whose name I learned was Michelle says as I apply the tint to her newly shaped brows. "I'll never understand why he expected me to say yes. Insane, right?"

"Completely," I mutter, nodding in fake agreement as I attempt to concentrate on applying the color to her.

"Anyway, you should have seen the ring he tried to propose with. It was laughable. So fucking small and used."

"Used?" That piqued my interest.

"Yes! Can you believe he tried to use his great-grandmother's ring?" She distorts her face, pretending to gag.

"Wow" is all I could manage. This woman is horrible. Thank God that poor man got away when he did. He probably didn't realize it at the time, but that was a blessing in disguise.

She continues on and on for the rest of our time together. Story after story. I listened, learning all about her. I learned she is twenty-four, was vice president of her sorority, and she dumped her college boyfriend when his family lost all their money because of an embezzlement scandal, to no fault of his own. But the most important thing I learned about Michelle was that she was shallow.

After three hours with that vile girl, I was dreading my next and final client. Some in the group are regulars and don't require or want as much work.

With five minutes to spare for a bathroom break, I take care of my business and grab two glasses of water, one for me and one for the next appointment. She ends up beating me to the room. Blond hair drapes over her shoulders as I take in the light, flowing dress that is simple and chic at the same time. She greets me with a bright smile that goes to her eyes. Such a change from Bitchelle's scowling.

After introductions, the heaviness in the pit of my stomach turns to an at-ease calmness. Stevie turned out to be one of the nicest and most down-to-earth clients I have had in a long time. Only asking for a simple facial with extraction, even though her pores are the most flawless things I have seen in years.

We talk as I go through the motions of the face massage, wiping my hands over her face in a light pattern. She tells me all about her full-body massage, where the woman next to her farted while the masseuse was working on her back.

Soon enough, we're both in tears, gasping for air as we laugh about how the woman tried to pretend it wasn't a fart but the cracking of her back. Which would have been fine until the smell took over the room.

"Okay, Stevie," I say, wiping away the last of my tears. "I have to ask, what are you doing here with these women? You're so nice, and they are so...not."

With a hum of amusement in her voice, she says, "Old sorority sisters. And before you say anything, I know. Sorority? Yep, it's true, I was once what they call a 'bow bitch.'"

"Are you all still close?"

Tilting her hand back and forth, she says, "Only with Daisy, the bride. She's still so sweet and hasn't been ruined by her parents and friends yet. The others are a different story. Let's just say they don't like that I work for a living instead of marrying myself off for money."

"Fuck them," I blurt out, forgetting I'm working with a client and not talking to a friend. Wincing, I quickly say, "Shit, sorry."

"My sentiments exactly! I can't help but keep my fingers crossed that Daisy will never become corrupted by society's evil."

"Let's hope so! And how about we circle back to that bow bitch thing? I need to know everything that qualifies one as a bow bitch."

For the rest of her facial, we talk about the difference in our college experiences. Hers was a traditional and high-society experience, while I skipped college for trade school. At the end of the appointment, I am 100 percent certain I want Stevie not only as my client but as my new friend. My stomach flips as I work up the nerve to ask her for her number.

"Hey, Stevie?"

"Yeah?" she says while gathering up her belongings.

"Is there any chance I can have your number?" Her head tilts to the side as she listens to my question. "Sorry to be weird or inappropriate. I just really like you."

Her eyes light up, widening as she opens her mouth to respond.

Realizing it sounds like I am hitting on her, I cut her off before she can reply. "Oh my God, I didn't mean it like that. I mean, I'm sure you would be my type if I were into the ladies, but alas, I am not. I did try it once, but it didn't work for me. It was all fun and games until I was the giver. Then I was like, yeah, I appreciate the vagina and all its wonders, but I can't lick it because of the knowledge of those wonders."

With her eyebrows now reaching her hairline, she tips her head back while snorting.

"God, why am I so fucking weird?" I mutter to myself as I slump back into my chair. "Please ignore me while I die under this table."

"Give me your phone."

"Huh?"

Hand stretched out, she says, "Your phone. I'm going to put my number in."

I hand over my phone, and she types in her number as she smiles at me. "There, done. Now we can become the best of friends."

"What made you agree to be friends with this? Was it the rambling explanation of my one-time sexual encounter with a woman, or did you just feel sorry for me?"

"Can I say both?" she says, handing me back my phone as she leaves. "Bye, Clara. Text me soon, and we can have brunch or something else pretentious."

Did I just make an actual friend?

I filled the rest of my week with the monotonous flow of work. Wax after wax, facial after facial. My mind is bored with the routine. The only little bits of happiness I found in my days were from the overpriced coffee I picked up every morning from the new trendy place on the walk to work, as well as the vastly different texts I was getting from Lex and Stevie.

My new friend is hilarious. Our daily texts are all about her offices, hijinks, and insane coworkers. It was a breath of fresh air not to talk about my shitty life and how I got here.

Then there were Lexa's texts...Meme after meme. GIF after GIF. All inappropriate, all sexual, and all referencing a certain asshat. No matter how many times I tell her things between Kamdyn and me are not and will never be like that, she continues teasing me.

If only I had never reacted to him on Saturday night. She might have let it go, but no, I couldn't help myself. And now I live in a constant state of annoyance.

Outside the rec center gym, sweat pools in my cleavage as I wait for my class to begin. I watch as the others arrive. Their faces are a mixture of scowls and smiles as they walk into the building one by one. How many of those smiles are real? As nice as Steve is, I think any of us would jump at the chance to never come here or see him again.

As I trudge my way inside, the first thing I notice is that Kamdyn is here, and he has taken his chair back. Not only has he claimed that chair as his, but he also placed reserved signs on the two other chairs on either side of him. I grab the sign off the chair to his right and sit down next to him.

"Awe, thanks for saving me a seat, Kammy," I say, my voice high and over the top.

"Kamdyn and Clara, I am so pleased to see you two getting along so well," Steve beams, clasping his hands together. "Now, class, this is a perfect example of the positive relationships and bonds you can form in this class. Good job, Clara and Kamdyn. Good job!"

The jerk glares at me, only making my smile grow until it can't get any larger.

We listen as Steve, who is in the same clothes he has worn almost every Friday so far, tells us this week's lesson. Week five consists of "I messages," identifying problems, and the difference between subjective and objective information. Once again, I do my best to listen as he hands out worksheets, failing as my mind drifts back to what landed me here.

Chloe.

She was the person I could always count on. The person I could tell anything to. I'm not sure when our relationship changed. When we were growing up, Chloe and I were a force to be reckoned with. We took care of each other.

But that was before. Before she became this person I don't recognize, that I don't know. Someone I don't like.

"Clara?"

The sound of someone calling my name snaps me back into reality.

"Sound good?" Steve asks.

With no idea of what he is talking about, I say, "Um, yeah. Great."

"Perfection. Now that everyone has their partner, time to break off and practice some I messages."

Still unsure of what is going on, I stay glued to my chair, waiting for something or someone to clue me in on what to do. As everyone separates, I notice there's only one other person still sitting, Mr. Perfect himself.

"What the literal fuck?" I mumble to myself.

He snaps his head in my direction. "Are you joking?"

Confusion continues to rack my brain. "Huh?"

"You were the one who told Sean that pairing us up sounded like a great idea." His nostrils flare as he looks away from me.

"Geesh!" I throw my hands up to my sides. "I wasn't paying attention, my bad."

With his arms crossed over his chest, he doesn't look back at me but shakes his head in silent disapproval of my daydreaming.

"Look," I say, grabbing hold of his forearm to get his attention. "I'm sorry. I have a twinge of ADD and sometimes have a hard time concentrating on things like this."

Just then, a slew of grumbled curse words escape his mouth, "Motherfucking dick of all things holy."

I clamp my lips together, trying to force the laughter back down my throat. With my face turned away from him, I let the grin flash over me before reining it back in.

"Okay, let's get it over with." I pull my chair to sit directly in front of him. My gaze travels up and down him, taking in his appearance. He's back to the long-sleeved, buttoned-up teacher attire I am used to. But God, do I wish he would roll up those sleeves to show me the artwork covering him.

Sensing my wandering mind, Kamdyn pulls my attention back to the task at hand. "I feel as if you still aren't paying attention," he says in a low tone.

With a shrug of my shoulders, I acknowledge he isn't wrong.

Not missing a beat, Kamdyn continues, "I feel you aren't taking this seriously."

Just like that, I realize what the assignment is—"I messages." That makes sense. Steve gave us a handout on how to express ourselves through "I messages" to improve communication skills and relationships all around.

I follow Kamdyn's lead by saying, "I feel you're judging me unfairly."

"Well, I feel you're being selfish."

Selfish. Did he just call me selfish? Gritting my teeth, I say, "I feel as if you have a large stick stuck up your ass."

His eyes flare as his gaze turns icy. The golden flakes of his irises darken. "And I feel you're a bitch who belongs here."

His words hit me again, right in the middle of my chest. My face falls as I take in his insults, processing the words. My limbs tremble at being called selfish and a bitch. It's the story of my life. People mistake my inability to pay attention as lazy or rude when in reality, I have ADD. Then there's the whole thing with people assuming I'm selfish or a bitch—or both. It's been my label for as long as I can remember.

Both assumptions come from the fact that I'm quiet and reserved. I am not a people person; I never have been. I'm not sure how that correlates to me being selfish or a bitch, but what can I say? I'm an introvert.

My emotions slip through for about twenty seconds before I put my mask back on, wiping away all signs of hurt and sadness. But it's too late. He saw.

His entire demeanor changes. He hangs his head low as he looks at the floor instead of me. The slight slouch of his shoulders gives me hope he's suffering with guilt.

He opens his mouth. "I feel—"

"I feel like this conversation is over," I say, stopping him before he can continue. I study the light strain in his jaw.

With a nod of his head, he agrees to drop it, and I'm thankful. Not sure what to say or do now, we sit silently, waiting to be released for the evening.

Twenty-five minutes. We still have to get through twenty-five long-ass minutes together. Everyone else is still talking and laughing as they work on the assignment. My foot shakes as I stare at the clock. Time is being a little asshole, moving at a snail's pace. It seems like it's been at least fifteen minutes, but the clock tells me differently. It's been all of five.

In any other situation, hell, even in this situation, I am calm and cool in uncomfortable silences. They are my bread and butter. When I was younger, I even went through a phase of putting myself in awkward situations for reasons I can't remember. Once, I even found myself at the church where the pastor was the grandfather of the guy I had been seeing. Said guy had been sleeping around behind my back. And I enjoyed every moment, knowing it made others squirm with unease.

So this should have been nothing to me. But it isn't, and I can't take it any longer. I cave. Turning in my seat to face him, I ask the burning question that has been on my mind since the beginning of our "conversation" earlier. "Who is Sean?"

Chapter Eight

Kamdyn

I can't help the dumbfounded look that graces my face at this current moment. She cannot be that self-absorbed, can she? We've spent the last *five* Friday nights with the man, listening to how AM will change our lives and outlooks completely. The man who looks like the child of Danny Tanner and Goldie Hawn. How could she not know Sean?

I snap my eyes to her face. Serious as she waits for my reply. "You're not joking?"

"No. Who is he?" she says, looking innocent and full of curiosity with her growing eyes and full lips parted. She is clueless.

"Sean"—I point across the room to where he is with his hands full of hair as he fumbles to tie it all up in a bun with a leather cord—"the man who has been leading us through our journey of emotional enlightenment."

She whips her head around as she follows the direction of my finger, dark locks of hair flying around her. I can't help being captivated by her ever-changing facial expressions and how her confusion shows all over her. From a blank expression to the way she pulls her brows together.

With a spin, she turns back around, angling herself in my direction. "Sean?" Her hand gestures back to him over her shoulder. "Are you sure?"

"Yeah." What is so hard for her to understand? Maybe I misjudged her. Maybe she isn't spacey and vapid, but a little slow instead.

Then she giggles. Hand over mouth, reddening cheeks laughter. "Oh my God," she says between gasps for air. "I thought his name was Steve."

A smile threatens to form on my face as I tuck my chin into my chest, shaking my head. "You're unbelievable."

"Me?"

"Yes, you. Who else would I be talking about, Steve-Sean?"

"Maybe. I don't know." She lifts her shoulders, bringing her chest up too. My gaze fixes on her breasts in her flowing green tank top. No bra. She has no bra on. I blink away the shock of her bralessness and the fact that I can see the slight outline of a barbell gracing her nipples.

I'm pulled back into the conversation by her voice.

A bright glow dances across her face. "We should call him Stean. Or ooh, Seave."

"You want to combine the two names? Why?" I ask.

She leans forward, getting closer to me. "Because it will be fun."

Chuckling, I say, "I'm pretty sure we have different ideas of what fun is."

Her lips form a tight line of a smile as she shakes her head, eyes drifting up and down my body with the quirk of an eyebrow, her voice smooth as silk. "Nah, I don't think we do."

Something stirs inside me. I have to blow out a slow, steady hiss of air to rid myself of this feeling. With a smirk on her face, she sits back in her chair.

Stean fills the next few minutes with his voice. This week's homework is art therapy. The assignment is to create a self-portrait of our inner angry monster. Somehow, this is supposed to help us "vanquish" our inner monster to create room for the enlightened version of ourselves.

He hands out a list of businesses where we can create DIY art. Great, it isn't even an assignment I can do at home with some cheap paint from Hobby Lobby.

After a few hours of mindless TV, I look up some businesses on the list Stean gave us in class earlier. Only some offer freestyle painting on the weekend instead of guided paint classes. And lucky for me, the one closest to my house has a time slot on Sunday that will work.

My eyes are heavy as I climb into the bed I used to share with Steph. I hate that I shared a life with her. She still haunts me even as I fight the heaviness pushing down on my lids. It's times like these that I am so goddamn happy I threw out the sheets and bedding that smelled like her when I was still fuming. I can't imagine what it would have been like if they were still there when I went through the heartache and self-pitying that soon followed it all.

Images of today and the past few weeks of Anger Management fill my head as I drift to sleep.

When I wake up in the morning, I'm groggy. Hands scrubbing down my face, I groan, replaying the dream over and over again in my mind. My heart pounds in my chest while my body fights my conscious brain.

I just had a sex dream about Clara. And it was…amazing. So vivid, like a memory, not something my sleeping mind concocted.

Once I climb out of bed, I hit the shower to wash away last night, to wash away the memory of Clara and the itching hunger under my skin.

Under the stream of hot water, I try to fight the urge to overthink what this could mean. So instead, I plan where I'm going to take the dogs for our jog later this morning. Maybe a park this time. The one off Harrison Street has a beautiful garden that would be a nice place to scout for people interested in the dogs.

I groan. Just the idea of the garden has me back to Clara and that dream. Her sweet floral scent. My lids flutter closed as I press my forehead against the shower's cool tile wall. Shallow breaths escape my mouth as vision after vision of Clara on her knees before me takes hold of my body and mind.

With no hesitation, I stroke my shaft with a firm hand, giving into the ache that has continued to grow ever since I woke up this morning. I continue to harden as my grip becomes tighter and more rapid. My muscles tense as I imagine her lips around my cock. Her pink tongue swirling on the head before taking every inch to the back of her throat, engulfing me inside her.

I shudder, gritting my teeth as my orgasm hits me at a record speed. I pant, my hands trembling as I grasp my cock until my breathing returns to a normal, even rhythm.

Shit.

Shit

I just jerked off thinking of Clara. The same woman who called me a stalker and stole my seat. The same woman who doesn't know 100 percent what our counselor's name is.

How am I going to manage to look at her without picturing her sucking me off? Just the thought has my dick twitching with arousal again.

I need to snap out of this. I'm sure I will soon. The moment I see her, I'm sure it will happen. She'll utter a rude comment, and the spell her beauty has cast on me will be reversed. Any ounce of lust will vanish from my brain. It will be fine. I have nothing to worry about.

I, of course, had everything to worry about. As I walk into the DIY art business, Clara's familiar face greets me.

Almost instantly, my face heats. I turn around, ready to leave and go to another studio.

"Stalker boy, is that you?" she asks melodically.

With a deep inhale, I spin to face her as she gives me a wave with her fingers. "In the flesh," I say. She pats the seat next to her, beckoning me to sit by her.

I furrow my eyebrows as I wonder what she's up to. Adrenaline and curiosity propel me closer as I take her up on the offer. "Fancy meeting you here." My voice is tight, lacking any emotion because right now, my mind is racing with dirty images of her and me.

"Ah yes, have you also come to bring your inner mad guy to life?"

She angles her body to mine, quirking her full lips, not knowing the things I picture them doing and what I desperately want to do to them. My fingers itch to touch them, to feel their softness. I wrap my hands around the edge of my chair to stop myself from reaching out.

With a swallow, I bury the need for her body down. "Yep," I say. Her gaze narrows, scrutinizing me for a split second before she turns to face her blank canvas.

"So," she says, picking up a bottle of paint and examining the color before setting it down to pick up another. "Want to make this more interesting?"

My gaze flickers from where she's evaluating colors, bringing them to her face. She doesn't look my way. "What did you have in mind?"

"A bet."

"A bet?" I ask once my hands release the chair, sweat coating my palms. As I run them down my shorts, she smiles at the paint.

"Yeah, to see who the superior artist is."

"No, thanks."

Her hands freeze. "Why not? Afraid I'm going to be better than you?"

"Impossible," I assure her, taking the deep-purple paint bottle from her hand, and her lips form into a pale-pink pout.

"So we're on." She doesn't ask. From the moment she said the word bet, I was on board. A little goading, and I was ensnared in her trap.

"Stakes?" I move my supplies to the opposite end of the table to sit directly across from her.

My question acts as a flint, sending sparks of fire into her eyes that radiate intrigue. She leans forward, bracing her arms on the table. Her tank top gapes around her chest, offering me an unrestricted view of her black bra. A stark contrast against her ivory tone.

I have to fight my instinct to stare. Forcing myself, I bring my eyes to hers.

"Loser buys the victor drinks after and…has to drink the same thing."

I'm on the edge of my seat as she speaks. I move farther back in my seat, considering her offer. "You just want to see me drunk again."

Her head falls back in laughter, dark locks shaking down her body. "You're that confident I'm going to win? That's a little sad, Kammy."

"Kammy?" My nose crinkles at the word.

"You don't like it?" Big blue eyes blink at me as her face falls dramatically. "I guess I'll have to stick with Asshat."

"Or you could call me by my name," I say, picking out the rest of the supplies I want for my soon-to-be masterpiece. Okay, masterpiece might be a stretch—well, more than a stretch. But it'll be better than whatever Clara paints. I mean, I've seen the girl's handwriting. It's not pretty. Hell, it's barely legible.

"Not an option, Asshat," she answers, dipping her brush into the teal paint.

"Wait!" I stop her just as she's about to paint her first brush stroke. "I want to change the terms if I win."

That familiar look she gives me in AM returns to her features. "To?"

"A favor to be cashed in at a later date."

"Fine, it doesn't matter," she says, bringing her brush to the canvas with a light stroke. "You won't win, anyway."

I bite back my smile and turn my focus on my blank canvas. It doesn't take me long to find something to represent my inner anger. With the blues and purples, I bring my vision to light.

I could say it didn't take long for my painting to take form, but that would be a lie. Forty-five minutes into our two-hour paint session and I had to restart three times. Each time, coating the paint down into a dark background. Every once in a while, I sneak a glance at Clara, only to discover her giving her canvas all of her attention. She furrows her brows, and her eyes harden as she studies her work. Her seriousness has me sweating.

What if she's good? Impossible. Or is it? I know nothing about her. Not even what she does for a living.

Shit. Did I just walk myself into a trap? My heart pounds at the thought of being alone with her at a bar. I'm not sure my dick and big mouth could handle that, especially after a drink.

After another thirty minutes, I'm pleased with my outcome. I wait for Clara to finish assessing her art. We both step away from the table, leaving the wet paintings to dry.

We move around the studio, looking at the creations on the walls, admiring and scrutinizing as we go. We take half an hour to make it through the whole gallery with the way we both comment on every single piece of art, coming up with theory after theory to describe what the artist's intentions could have been. Some of our guesses range from world peace to sperm and the creation of life itself. Our faces and body language mirror each other as we hide our amusement with each other.

After our interpretations, Clara convinces me to wrap up my painting to show her once we get to the bar. I follow her down the sidewalk, painting in hand. This is a bad idea, one I will probably end up regretting, but for now, I just want to enjoy spending time with this snarky woman.

CHAPTER NINE

Clara

Is this really happening? Did I actually talk Mr. Perfect into a bet and going to a bar with me? What the ever-loving fuck is up with me? Ever since seeing him so vulnerable last weekend, I've had the urge to be his friend. It seemed like he could use one. And if I am honest, I could too.

I watch him over the rim of my glass; he sips on the beer in front of him, grimacing as if it's offensive to him. But the margarita in my hand is heavenly. Its frozen strawberry goodness coats my tongue.

"Are you sure you don't want to try it?" I tip my glass in his direction.

He eyes the drink before chuckling. "You've seen what beer does to me...Do you really expect me to handle tequila?"

I shrug, tipping the glass up to my lips. The bar isn't exactly what some would call packed, but it's Sunday. There is still quite the collection of characters here. As we sit in silence, I can't help but watch them, wondering who they are. Or why they're always here.

I recognize some of the old men sitting a few stools down from us. I lift my drink in the air toward the two with scraggly gray beards and old tattoos that I assume are old prison or military tats. Either way, those two can be a lot of fun to hang out with.

In the years I've been coming to this hole in the wall, with tattered stools and a sticky floor, I have never once been in here without those two. And I have never learned their names. It's one of those things that make those old bar rats even more fun.

Tap. Tap. Tap.

Kamdyn drums his finger on the bar. The noise brings my attention back to him and the alcohol I'm hoping he'll drink. His beer is only missing a few sips. Shit, getting Asshat to go away and let loosey-goosey Kam out is going to be harder than I expected. I examine my drink and find it's on its last few gulps. I need to slow myself down.

Gone was the fun guy from art class. The relaxed, sexy man from yoga, yeah, he's nowhere to be seen either. No, in that man's place is Mr. Perfect—the stuck-up, stiff-ass jerk I know and hate.

I watch him carefully pull at the cuff of his jacket as he ensures his tattoos are perfectly covered.

His incessant tapping continues, etching away at my nerves. My hand slaps down over his. "For the love of God, stop," I say.

His hands fly up. "Sorry." He lifts his beer to his lips. "You could have just asked."

"Ugh!" I hiss. "Can you try to enjoy yourself even the smallest amount?"

This earns me a glare. "You knew very well I wouldn't have any fun when you brought me here."

I swivel in my seat to face him. "Then why would I bring you here?"

"Because you're evil. And mean." He takes a swig of his beer, holding a finger up to me. "You hate me and want me to suffer for some unknown reason."

I blink at his words. "Damn, Kam. Tell me what you really think." I want to say more, but I find myself speechless. Unable to find the words. The right words. Is he right? Did I invite him here to make him suffer? He assumes I'm a horrible person. Maybe I am a little. The revelation leaves a nasty taste in my mouth that not even my margarita will wash away.

I turn back to face the bar, not wanting to look at him while he's probably at least somewhat right about me. The expression I'm wearing must scream internal deliberation or pending breakdown because Benny, the bartender who works the day shift instead of Lex, brings me another margarita. And to my surprise, he brings a second, handing it to Kamdyn.

Kamdyn takes the drink in his hands, thanking Benny as he does. He brings the large goblet to his lips. His face softens as he takes his first drink, and I swear a moan slips from him.

"You like?" I ask.

A smile stretches across his handsome face, and he nods as he takes another sip. Only this time, it's not a sip, it's a full-on drink. Hell, it could constitute a chug if you ask me.

"Whoa there, buddy," I say, grasping his wrist and pulling it down from his face. "You're going to get a—"

Face twisting in agony with a loud groan, he presses his hands to his forehead. "Brain freeze."

I scoot my stool closer to him, placing my hand on his back. I rub up and down, all while singing, "Hush, little baby, don't say a word.

Mama's gonna buy you a mockingbird."

"God, I hate you," he utters with his head pressed against the cool bar counter.

Chuckling, I say, "I know."

Only a few seconds later, he recovers, cursing the tastiness of the frozen adult beverage. But that doesn't stop him from continuing to drink it.

"Okay," he says, placing his empty margarita glass down. "How are we going to do this?"

My head cocks to the side. "Do what?"

"Judge the paintings."

"Oh yeah, about that," I say. My shoulders lift as I straighten, ready for his reaction. "They're already being judged."

His forehead crinkles, and somehow, even when he looks like an idiot, he's still handsome.

"So, when we got here, you know how you went to the bathroom?"

"Yeah," he says, nodding at me to get to the point.

"I kind of gave Benny the paintings to display at the entrance with cards for people to vote on which was better."

His mouth falls open, a flush creeping up his face as his eyes narrow. The expression makes me want to laugh.

"Don't worry," I say, my hand patting his shoulder. "I didn't look at yours."

He looks like he's about to sweat. He shifts away from my touch. "That's not what I'm worried about. I'm worried about the whole AM part of it. What if someone I know sees?"

"Why does that matter? It's not like I said it was for our court-ordered Anger Management class or wrote your name beside it."

His hand shakes as he covers his face. He's scared. No, not scared. Terrified. Terrified of someone finding out. "I'll lose my job. It's the only thing I have left. I can't lose it."

My voice goes soft as I lean closer to his face. "Hey, you aren't going to lose your job. No one will ever find out it was for AM." He turns his head to face me, eyes clouded with worry. "I'm sorry I put the painting out for judging without talking to you first."

"Thanks." He grasps his empty mug and throws his head back, groaning. I flag Benny over, ordering two more margaritas.

One-and-a-half frozen margaritas.

That's all it took to get him to loosen up.

Tequila is Kamdyn Cook's kryptonite. The man is a lush. Give him the frozen drink, and he won't stop drinking and yammering on about his favorite teacher Linda, the old lady he works with.

I'm two margs in and nursing the third. If I finish this one, I might be on the same level as my current companion. And my tipsy brain loves the way his full upper lip skims across his teeth whenever he smiles. I'm captivated by his storytelling and his lips. I watch his mouth move in a way that shouldn't be seductive but is.

"Asshat," I say, interrupting his over-the-top, in-depth description of why Hamilton, the Broadway musical, should be shown in all US history classes and even world history classes. "First, Hamilton taught me a shit ton, but the biggest lesson I took away from it was that Alexander Hamilton was trash and a cheater. That all men are trash, no matter how smart they are, they're still trash."

His head rears back as if I slapped him, and I'm not sure if it's because I spoke ill of Hamilton or men. "Second," I say, lifting two fingers, "shall we go see who won the bet?"

The moment his feet hit the ground, Kamdyn is grasping my

shoulders, laughing to himself as he tries not to sway.

"I regret bringing your lightweight ass with me," I say before leading him to the spot where our art is on display.

Just as I'm about to round the table to see what his painting looks like, he pulls me back, knocking me into his chest. His *hard* chest. My body hums with arousal as I'm pressed deeper into the definition of his muscles that I can feel through the fabric. But my back isn't the only part flush with his body.

Yep, my ass is planted right in his crotch. This innocent touching, or at least I'm pretty sure it's innocent, has me falling over the edge. An ache builds deep in my core. I turn my head, peeking over my shoulder at him. "Did you just want to cop a feel, or was there a reason you stopped me like this?"

A blush rises up his face, turning his already drunkenly rosy cheeks to a crimson shade. It isn't fair he has a body and face meant for Greek gods. Maybe it's to make up for the fact that the man can be a grade-A dick. But apparently, I'm the only person who notices that fact.

He lets go of my shoulders as his hips move off my ass, leaving my body frustrated but my mind thankful. He clears his throat before looking away and back at me. "I want to read the results before we look."

"Why?"

"Because you got to choose the method of judging, and I want to choose the method of revealing the world's eighth wonder to you."

I throw my hands up, surrendering to his drunken show of power. "Have it your way."

He wiggles his eyebrows at me, and his finger finds my nose, giving me a "boop" as he touches it. With a slow turn, he heads back to his stool while I stand there with a stupid-ass, goofy smile lingering on my face.

I bring the box of votes back to the bar and patiently wait as Kamdyn tallies them up.

"No fucking way," he mutters before giving me a glassy-eyed glare.

"What?" I question, needing to find out what could get his panties in a bunch. I assume I won, of course.

He hands over the votes. "Count them." He crosses his arms against his chest and leans back to wait.

Fifteen votes for Kamdyn.

Fifteen votes for me.

It's a tie. A motherfucking tie.

I peer over at him and laugh. "Tiebreaker?"

Kamdyn cracks his knuckles as he hops up and down. He looks like he's preparing for a fight, not a drunken tiebreaker.

"What are you doing?" I ask as he rolls his neck in circles.

"Psyching myself up," he says, giving me a face that screams "duh."

Now outside the bar on the sidewalk, we both stand with our paintings displayed in front of us, still not knowing what the other's looks like. We wait for someone to pass by to begin.

At the sight of a couple walking toward us, I squeal. "On the count of three," I say, while peering at the couple. "One, two, three."

Both of us speed into action, basically catcalling the couple to us to see our art. We try to talk them into voting for the better painting. The first person to get a vote is the winner. But that didn't work out so well because all we got was couple after couple, each person voting for a different painting.

The tie continued for five couples before a group of girls that had to be around twenty stopped in front of us to ogle Kamdyn. They were far too young for him, but that didn't stop him from using their attraction to him to his advantage.

He got all five of them to vote for him. Hell, I don't even think the girls looked in my direction once. I'm pretty sure all of them wrote their phone numbers on the paper slips with their vote.

"Didn't expect you'd fight dirty, Mr. Cook," I say as we walk back into the bar to sober him up a little, as well as pay the tab.

He lowers his head, trying to fight the grin creeping up his face. "I don't know what you're talking about, Ms. Doyle."

"Bullshit. You so do." I shove his shoulder.

"It's not my fault they found me irresistible."

"Sure." I slide the glass of water Benny gave me across the table to him. "Are you going to call them?"

He quirks his eyebrows as the glass touches his lips, taking a long sip. "Why do you want to know?"

"Because weren't they a little young?"

Forearms on the table, he leans in, getting closer to me across the small space. "They told me the youngest was turning nineteen later this month." He winks. The dick winked at me.

"That's disgusting," I say, my mouth filling with saliva. "You're disgusting."

"I'm joking, Clara," he says, still grinning at me.

I turn my head, refusing to look at him, to talk to him.

"Clara," he says, all humor gone from his voice. "I really was joking. I'm not a pervert. Those girls are young enough to have been my students.”

I glance over at him. His face is serious, and his eyes are pleading with me to recognize the truth.

“Well, it wasn’t a good joke, now, was it?” I reach across the table, stealing the water from him. I don’t drink it, though. I hold it, letting the condensation from the glass cover my palms.

He breaks our silence. “Wanna see the winning piece?”

Black, blues, purples, pinks, and whites fill the space of Kamdyn’s canvas. I tilt my head, examining his work. It’s interesting, that’s for sure.

The colors are spun together to create darkness with patches of light poking through. It looks like the night sky, but not really. More like the sky you imagine in fantasy novels. With all the swirling colors, I can’t keep my eyes off it.

“I like it,” I say, still staring.

He takes it from my hands, setting it down on the table. “Let’s just hope Stean does too.”

My hand flies to my heart.

“What?” he asks, drawing his eyebrows together.

“You said Stean.”

“Shit,” he mumbles under his breath before picking up my canvas. I wait as he takes it all in.

“Oh my fucking God,” he says, looking down at my painting. He lifts his eyes to find mine. “This—this is what your inner angry monster looks like?”

“Yep.” I nod. “Pretty frightening, I know.”

His face falls, erasing all expression. “It’s a cat.”

“I am aware. I was the one who created that brilliant piece of art, remember?”

"It's a motherfucking cat." His voice grows gravelly before he bends at the waist. A strangled noise comes from him, and I freeze. It sounds like crying. I don't do crying.

Unsure what to do next, I ask, "Kamdyn?"

Now he's crouching, the noise becoming even louder. I have no choice but to get closer. I'm just about to ask if he's okay when he lifts his head. Tears are in his eyes, and he's gasping for breath. He lets out a loud cackle, holding his stomach.

My hand grasps my chest in relief. "Why are you laughing?"

"A cat." He pushes out between laughs. "Why a cat?"

"It's pretty obvious. They're so sneaky, and they have this diabolical look in their eyes. I swear they always look like they're plotting to overthrow the human population. I'm telling you; cats are as angry as they come."

I put Kamdyn in an Uber before calling my own. I have to admit that today was fun; he wasn't as much of the uptight ass I'm used to seeing. He seemed like an actual person. I already knew drunk Kamdyn wasn't the same as Mr. Perfect, but it was still nice to see that the sober him does indeed have a personality.

When I wake up in the morning, I've never been so glad to have cut myself off from drinking. Even two-and-a-half margaritas have me suffering like a car hit me. Well, not that bad. Maybe more like a motorcycle or horse-drawn carriage. Both sound unappealing and painful.

The mild hangover lasts the entire day, turning the simplest tasks into torture. During a facial with extractions, usually my favorite part, I nearly vomited at the sight of puss. I spent my entire day choking back my urge to vomit all over clients. When did I become this intolerant of alcohol? Is it my age? Does entering your late twenties trigger some sort of sensitivity to fun? I sure as shit hope not, but right now, it's the only explanation I can find.

I leave work early, needing to get some rest. To fight off this lingering hangover. But that didn't work.

The next morning, I wake up and rush to the bathroom. I barely make it to the toilet before the contents of my stomach force their way out of me.

I stay that way for the next two days. Sick to my stomach. Definitely not a hangover. I'm not sure if I should be overjoyed that I'm still young enough to drink a few mixed drinks without suffering or if I should cry because whatever is going on with my body is miserable.

Even with my body trying to kill me, I was somehow a little relieved to spend the week at home. It was like a staycation. An impromptu, sad staycation. But still, a staycation.

By Thursday, I manage to keep some food down. My limbs have a heaviness that is weighing me down. My couch and I have become well acquainted. Wrapped up in my fluffy robe, I lie there watching mindless Hallmark movie after movie. I figure I could at least get this part of my AM assignment for the week out of the way while I give my body time to recover.

But it turns out that the more Hallmark movies you watch, the more you want to watch Hallmark movies. It only takes two of the sappy movies to warm my icy heart. Tears filled my eyes with every single happy ending. I get sucked into the rabbit hole of a small town needing saving, along with the added benefit of hunky farmers. How could I ever resist? The goodness of the purely intentioned romances had me longing for something like that.

Simplicity. Love. But more than anything, I want the happiness I see. I want my version of that. But without the farms or big city corporations threatening to tear my hometown down. I just want to experience joy in the small things. And hot sex. I want nasty, can't-wait-to-tell-my-best-friend-about-it sex. It's not too much to ask for.

When it's time for Anger Management on Friday, I'm finally feeling like myself again. *Thank God.* I cannot afford to miss a class for anything. If I do, it's so long freedom, hello jail. So missing is not an option. Along with not being able to skip a class, there is no way in hell I would have been able to sit through the annoyingness that is AM while my insides fight death.

I take my normal seat next to Kamdyn. Oddly enough, I don't want to scratch his eyes out at this moment. It's a strange sensation, not hating his smug ass. I'm not sure what I think about it. If he isn't acting like the social-conforming jerk I've come to hate, how am I supposed to act?

"Hey," I whisper.

He gives me a small wave and a closed, tight-lipped smile.

What the hell? Is he being shy right now?

I don't have time to think about why he's acting weird because Stean steps into the circle. "People," he cheers, his hand cupped around his mouth, amplifying his words, even though everyone in the class was more than close enough to hear him regularly. "We've made it to week six of Anger Management. How exciting is that?" He claps before encouraging us all to join in. Most of the class does as he says.

I do not.

I quickly look at Kamdyn to see he's doing the bare minimum to not hurt Stean's feelings. And now I feel like an asshole. I'm not sure why I have to be such a defiant or pessimistic person. It's just who I am. I've been this way for a while now. And it didn't start with this legal mess I'm in. I wish I could pinpoint the exact moment when I stopped being the smiling girl with friends out the ass to this shell of a person.

I ponder other hollow things that could describe people other than shells. Like trees that have been injured or chocolate Easter eggs. Why not call someone empty like a chocolate egg? I mean, they could be delicious and empty, like me.

"Learning how to identify constructive criticism and disagreements is essential to controlling your inner-anger demon. With this tool, you might understand and not react negatively. You might take the time to see what the other person is trying to tell you, and vice versa," Stean says, sitting on a chair with his denim-short-clad legs crossed.

"I understand that this can be hard," he continues, "to let another's words that might hurt not affect you deeply. To not react. But I believe in you."

A smile tugs on my lips at the sincerity in his voice and on his face. Stean might dress like he can't recall what decade it is, but he is genuinely a caring guy.

As usual, we are split up into groups. Unsurprisingly, Kamdyn and I are paired together by Stean again. He must be oblivious to our clashing personalities, or he's some sort of sadist. Either way, I take back the kind thoughts I had about him earlier.

In this partner activity, Kamdyn and I are supposed to come up with scenarios where someone might overreact to another's words and figure out how to spin the situation in a constructive direction before lashing out.

He's still acting awkward, and his silence is unnerving. A week ago, I would've loved to walk into this flat, quiet version of Kamdyn. But his lack of acknowledgment toward me has my blood boiling.

I thought we had turned over a new leaf last weekend. But I guess I was wrong.

If this is how he wants to play it, fine. Two can play that game. Hell, I'll even take it up to an extra level. Bring on the bitchiness.

As we sit across from one another, I decide to go first. "I admire how brave you are," I say, watching his eyebrows squish together. "I wish I could not care about how I looked."

And just like that, his eyes light up with fire. A sneer forms on his lips as he leans back in his chair. His gaze studies me as it roams up and down my body.

I squirm in my seat. There's something in the way he looks at me that gives me a shiver.

"Thanks," he says. "I find it makes others like you more comfortable. They say imitation is the sincerest form of flattery."

My mouth drops open. Did he just say that? I glance down at my ombre pastel maxi dress before glancing back at him. "How kind of you." I recognize we aren't doing this assignment right. That we should figure out what we would do if someone said that to us, but I can't stop myself. I need to throw another punch. "I heard you're a really great teacher"—he narrows his eyes as if he knows I'm not finished—"for a man."

A choked laugh comes from him. And just like that, I can't tell if he's mad or amused. Maybe he's impressed.

Kamdyn shakes his head, leaning forward with his forearms braced against his thick, muscular thighs. God, how can he wear that long-sleeve shirt in here? I don't understand why he's hiding his tattoos. I mean, why get a full sleeve if you never show it? It makes zero sense.

"Clara, Clara, Clara," he says. "You are something else."

Flipping my hair over my shoulder, I wink at him. "Thank you."

"I didn't say it was a compliment."

I narrow my eyes and pull my brows closer. "You're such a dick."

"Is that why you invited me to the bar with you last weekend? Because you want my...?" He leans forward, curling the edge of his lips into a taunt.

"Don't worry, Asshat, it won't ever happen again. I promise." I fold my arms across my chest, adding a little extra push to my boobs. I do this knowing he stares at my breasts. I've caught him twice, but I wasn't sure enough to call him out until last weekend. My dumbass didn't go in for the kill. I could have embarrassed him, made him feel like the asshole he is, but instead, I hung out with him, laughing and telling jokes.

I whip my head to the side and pretend to ignore him. I have never been so glad that my hair is in a ponytail as right now. I need my cleavage to be hiked up on full display for him. It takes all of ten seconds for his eyes to glue themselves to my propped-up tits.

A sense of satisfaction radiates through me like a drink of hot coffee. It fills me with energy and warmth. A smirk forms on my face, and I wait for him to realize I've caught him. After almost a minute, he glances up to see the knowing smirk plastered all over my face. I raise my eyebrows as his throat bobs, his cheeks flushing from either discomfort or lust. Either way, the two looks are eerily close.

"Did you need something, Asshat?" My voice is sweet and thick with amusement. I flick my gaze down to my chest and back up to him, fluttering my lashes to make this moment everything I could ever want.

Kamdyn opens his mouth to reply when Stean arrives, examining the tension of our standoff. "What's happening, guys? You two look like you're ready to do a round in the ring." He places his hands on his hips, waiting for someone to speak.

"You would love to get your hands on me, wouldn't you, Kammy?" I taunt. I don't expect him to reply, but he does.

His large hands roll up the sleeves of his light-gray jacket as his gaze penetrates mine. "You have no idea."

My breathing stops, and I blink back a rush of dizziness that he not only replied to me but that he responded like that. From the outside, it might only look and sound like an aggressive taunt, but his eyes tell a different story.

His beautiful multicolored eyes deepen as he stares, and the dark circles in the center of his eyes widen. I've never watched someone's pupils dilate. My body overheats, betraying me as his eyes emit a want and need toward me.

I clasp the front of my dress with a pinch, pulling it out, then in, fanning myself. I train my sights back on Stean, who looks like a disappointed dad right now.

He lets out a huff. "What am I going to do with you two now?"

Not understanding what he's talking about, I see Kamdyn has the same questioning look on his face, which is a relief. I hate being the only clueless one around.

"Everyone else has partnered up for their mandatory nature activity," he says with his pointer finger and thumb pinching the bridge of his nose. The dude isn't happy. That's a first.

Kamdyn interjects, "I don't see what the problem is." I nod, still confused by this situation with Stean, as well as the one with Kamdyn.

"Ugh, do you two want to go to jail? Is that what's going on? You both would rather spend a month in a cell than a few hours each week playing nice and learning how to be a decent human being?"

He's speaking at a normal volume level, but I still feel like I'm being yelled at. I lower my head and find a nice, cracked tile to stare at while he continues.

"You come into my class with different attitudes not only toward each other but to the subject material every week. Why? To test the rest of us? Cause I am telling you right now, you are testing the H-E-Double-Hockey-Sticks out of me right now."

Kamdyn lets out a snort at Stean's aversion to cussing, and I fight the urge to do the same. I end up biting the insides of my cheeks to stop myself from joining him on Stean's now even larger shit list.

Stean's left eye twitches as he tries not to react to the laugh. He takes a deep breath before sighing. "Like I was saying before, I have paired you together for the mandatory partner nature assignment. You both—"

"Wait," I say, interrupting as I hold up a palm. "Are you saying it's a mandatory nature thing, and people are partnering up? Or are you saying it's mandatory to have a class partner for this assignment?"

Stean cocks head to the side. "The latter."

"Can we trade partners?" Kamdyn pipes in, running his hands through his mussed hair, catching beams of light with every movement.

"No," Stean says, holding up a finger. "Don't even try it, Mr. Cook. It's a done deal." He turns on his heels, walking about ten paces away before shouting over his shoulder, "I will require picture proof. Both of you must be in the picture together."

I watch as he walks away, muttering to myself, "Pictures or it didn't happen."

Just then, Kam's large palm reaches toward me. "Give me your phone."

I don't. I'm still a little shocked. Well, that and I'm confused by him.

"Come on, Clara, I don't have all day. Class is over, and I would like to enjoy some of my night."

I reach into my purse, pulling it out. With the passcode entered, I hand it to him. He dials his number before saving. "There, now I have yours, and you have mine."

"Why did we need to exchange numbers?" I ask, still speculating about his motives.

He gives me an expression that I can only assume means he thinks I am a total idiot. "So we can plan the assignment."

"Oh, yeah." I shake my head, trying not to be embarrassed because I thought he was asking 'cause he wants my body. My hands fidget with my ponytail, pulling the elastic out. My hair goes down, then back up into a messy bun before going back to being down.

Without another word, he gets up. His long, toned legs lead him out the door, leaving me boggled. How the fuck do I read this guy?

Chapter Ten

Kamdyn

One week ago

After Clara places me in an Uber, I go home and eat an entire large cheese pizza, all while staring at the "art" I created earlier that day.

My eyes lock on the painting on my coffee table while I grin to myself. I had so much fun not only painting it but also with Clara's dumb competition. She may have a poor attitude 90 percent of the time, but that other 10 percent is something else. She's fun and compassionate, even though it seems to make her uncomfortable to be recognized as such.

It's that 10 percent that makes me question what caused her to be ordered into Anger Management. She doesn't seem like the type who would be in a situation like this. Clara might be the definition of trouble, but not the legal, criminal kind.

I spend the rest of the night thinking about her, comparing every aspect of her to my time with Steph.

Waking up the next morning, I'm on the floor beside my bed, wearing nothing but a pair of socks. I lift my head off the floor, unsure of how I ended up here, and wipe the drool off my chin. I don't remember moving from the living room or falling asleep on the floor. Then there's the fact that I'm starfishing it nude against the cool hardwood floor.

The throbbing pulse in my head forces me to lift myself off the ground slowly. My knees hit the back of the bed, and I fall onto my back. My brain sloshes around, hitting my skull with an intense force—just another reminder of why I don't drink. My body has always been like this, refusing to permit me any overindulgence. It punishes me for every indiscretion. While my mind is full of self-hatred.

There is no way in hell I'm going on my daily run. Even if I could talk myself into picking myself up, my body would probably go into some sort of shock and die. My dad would roll over in his grave if he saw me, for more reasons than one.

Brent Cook was one of the most charming men, or so I'm told by everyone who met him. That wasn't my experience with him. It's funny the different faces people can wear—the one for the public, and the one for their families.

My dad's ability to put on a new persona at any time is the thing I hated and admired the most about him. The social butterfly that had it all. The perfect job, perfect family, perfect life. Beloved by all who knew him, but that was all a lie. He was beloved, just not by his wife and child. Dad was a monster in his own way, caring more about outer appearances than anything. God forbid my mom or I not look put together and perfect at all times. He was always focused on how we represented him. He would flip his shit if I gained a pound or two. I won't lie, I had some baby fat, but I was fourteen, just months away from a growth spurt. But Dad didn't want a chubby kid. So he made me run.

I ran early in the morning.

I ran when I misbehaved.

Hell, I had to run before I could eat.

I assumed that was the final straw for my mom. When she found out about the miles and miles he forced me to complete before breakfast or dinner, she packed our bags and drove us to my grandparents'.

Even then, I still tried everything I could to make him proud. I kept up the running on my own. I joined the football team, and just like that, my pudgy baby fat disappeared, and practically overnight, I was over six feet tall and built of muscle. But that wasn't enough for him. It never was.

My rocky relationship with him continued until the summer before college. After I graduated from high school, my mother came out. She had been in love with the same woman for years and was waiting until I graduated, hoping she wouldn't embarrass me. Which was insane. I love my mom no matter what. Her sexual orientation wouldn't and doesn't affect that. But years with my father made her afraid. Of my reaction, of how I would feel about her and others knowing.

Even from the grave, the man manages to make my blood boil. His twisted thought process still haunts me, the unrealistic standards ingrained in me.

I let out a small laugh knowing he would have an aneurysm if he were alive to see his only son as a high school history teacher who spends his weekends in court-ordered Anger Management after his ex-girlfriend cheated on him.

I spend the entire day like this. In and out of sleep, reflecting on my whole life and how I wish I could go back and change so much.

On Tuesday, when I finally wake from my margarita-induced hangover coma, I shower off the layers of sweat coating my skin and, unfortunately, my sheets. After showering and doing a load of laundry, I feel more alive and like myself prior to alcohol's influence. While drinking a cup of coffee, I pick up my phone for the first time since Sunday night and check for texts.

Ten texts and two missed calls.

My stomach drops when I see her name. *Steph.*

The two missed calls were from her, along with six of the texts.

My thumb hovers over her thread. Why would she contact me? It's been over a month since I ended things. And there is no coming back from what she did, anyway.

My heart speeds up as I open the thread.

Me: Stephy, my ex-y.

Steph: Hey, Kammy.

Me: What are you doing, Stephy?

Steph: I'm in bed, Kammy. What are you doing texting me? I assumed you never wanted to speak to me again.

Me: I don't. But I do. I am going to call you.

Shit. Shit. Shit.

Please, please tell me I didn't call her. *Please.* With a glance at my call log, my suspicions are confirmed.

I did.

Snippets of our conversation replay in my mind—memories of how I let my every thought of her slip through my loose lips flooding back in.

I called her. I fucking called her—and made a fool out of myself. Twenty minutes. I spoke to the woman who slept around on me for twenty minutes on Sunday night.

A groan rumbles up my throat, turning into a full laugh at the fact I never gave her a moment to speak as I rambled on and on before hanging up on her.

Steph: What did you mean by that?

Steph: Kammy, please talk to me.

Steph: You can't bring shit like that up, then hang up. We need to talk.

Steph: Please, Kamdyn.

This. *This* is why I can't drink alcohol. I always look like a fucking idiot when I do.

I wish I couldn't remember a fucking thing I said to her. I just want to forget about it. Pretend it never happened. That's healthy, right?

The other messages are from Marcus and Taylor, his lovely wife. All in a group chat. I guess I needed friendship and conversation.

Me: Marcus, I miss you.

Me: Marcus!

Taylor: K-Man, Marcus is taking a bath.

Me: Lies. He doesn't bathe, and you know it.

Taylor: He really is, I swear. Girl Scout's honor.

Me: Prove it.

Taylor: *Picture of Marcus in the bathtub* Believe me now?

Me: Oh, I believed you the whole time. I just wanted to see if you would send me a nude of Marcus. You know he used to walk around our apartment stark-ass naked all the time? I miss it.

Taylor: OMG! Lol. You are killing me.

Marcus: What the FUCK, you two!

Me: Marcus, finally!

Marcus: Naked pictures of me in the tub. REALLY?!

Taylor: What? It's not like K-Man and I haven't seen everything before.

Marcus: Not the point.

Taylor: So the point.

Me: Yeah, what she said. Also, I might have had a margarita or three-ish tonight.

Marcus: Kamdyn, I'm ashamed of you. I expect this kind of thing from Taylor, but from you...I assumed you were more mature than this. And I do mean the pictures and the booze.

Marcus: I hate both of you.

Taylor: Nah, K-Man and I are both on the same level, and you love us for it.

I can't help the gigantic smile from spreading across my lips as I read these messages. Those two are the best. I can only hope to find something like that. I want to have the type of love the two of them share. That person who makes my life better.

I'm not ashamed to admit I'm jealous of their relationship. Reason number one is because I want my best friend to always be there for me, but he can't be because Taylor and the baby are his number one priority. This brings me to reason number two. I'm jealous that they have each other. A person who they love and who loves them back. That they complement each other so well. That they're best friends and lovers. I want all of that.

The envy I hold for them can sometimes be all-consuming. Even with Steph, I would feel that twinge of my heart straining for that type of love. I guess I knew even then she wasn't right for me. Maybe I just couldn't see the truth. Didn't want to admit it to myself. But I guess Steph didn't have that problem.

She knew.

She just didn't want to give me up. She wanted it all. Steph was always selfish like that. Her selfishness ranged from eating my leftovers to fucking around on her live-in boyfriend of two years.

Thinking of her leaves a bitter taste in my mouth. I rub small circles into my temples with my fingers as I fight the dull ache that thinking of her brings on. She's to blame for all my current problems.

The need to clear my mind is undeniable, so I find my running shoes and Beats before heading out for a five-mile run.

My mind stills as I run away from my issues. The movements a meditation. The former punishment is now the only place I can escape what troubles me. My body gets in exercise while my mind gets to rest. To clear itself from everything in the world but my body moving in the rhythmic pattern.

With each pound of my feet on the pavement, I feel more and more peace flowing through my veins.

I run all around my neighborhood before moving along to the city sidewalks. My run takes me past a children's park where adult heads turn to observe me passing. If I didn't have my headphones in, I'm positive I would hear some sort of catcall from the mothers with their children because of the way their eyes strip off my clothing.

On the way back to my house, I stop by the animal rescue to visit Samson and Sunny, two dogs I've been walking each week. Both are overjoyed to see me when I step into their yard. Sunny, the yellow Great Dane, gallops to me with the grace of a toddler, knocking me on my ass in a swift motion of pure joy. Even though she's around four years old, she's a big puppy at heart. Samson, being eight years old, is as calm as a cucumber. He saunters over to where I lie on the ground, tail wagging the whole way.

If I had the space and the yard they need and deserve, they would be mine. They've already stolen my heart, and I wish more than anything that my place was what they needed. I want nothing more than to give these dogs the life they deserve, but until I can buy a home with a backyard large enough for a couple of dogs and kids to run around, I can't do that to them. To any dog. It wouldn't be fair to them.

Samson lies down beside me, his large black head resting in my lap. He is a full-blood Labrador. It's insane that such a gentle and caring dog, with a breed like his, would be at a shelter. But people don't want older animals. They want shiny, new, and cute. They want puppies. There's also the weird big *black* dog factor. It scares people, as if his fur color means anything.

I stay like that for a while, petting the rambunctious, giant star and the dark, silent teddy bear. When I can finally stand, I'm covered in fur. Long black hairs stick to my skin and clothing.

"I look like a yeti," I tell the two of them as they walk with me to the gate. Their faces are full of so much love and devotion that it breaks my heart every time I leave them here.

I snap the gate's latch into place and am turning to give the dogs one last smile when I hit a small body. I lift my head around just in time to spot Justine, the rescue owner's daughter. Her attractive, twenty-year-old daughter.

"Shit," I mutter, grabbing her shoulder to prevent her from falling backward. Her hands fly to my wrists, clenching them for support.

Her eyes widen as she stares up at me. As she's grasping my wrists, a crimson blush rises on her cheeks before she straightens, letting go of her hold on me.

"Justine, are you okay? I'm so sorry. I wasn't looking. You know how I get with Samson and Sunny. Anyway, I was in a rush leaving and looked back one last time—again, I'm sorry," I say, blurting out the rambled apology, hoping to get out of here before her mother sees us together.

Most mothers want to keep their beautiful daughters away from older men, but not hers. No, Darla has been obsessed with setting us up ever since I started coming here. The first few times Darla brought it up, I brushed it off as a joke. But it soon became clear she wasn't joking. Luckily for me, I had just started seeing Steph, so my excuse was solid.

But now I'm single, and Darla knows it. The only saving grace I have now is that I know Justine has a boyfriend, thank God. She's a beautiful girl and is very nice, but she's way, way too young for me.

Justine lets out a small laugh. "Damn, Kam, did you even take a breath between those words?"

"Nope. Runner's lungs, we can go minutes without breathing properly. It's a gift."

She laughs again, her blond hair shaking in the high ponytail atop her hair. "You're something else, you know that, right?"

"I do indeed."

"Why were you rushing out of here like a bat out of hell?" she asks.

I glance around before saying, "No reason in particular. Just wanting to get back home."

Her face lights up. "You didn't want anyone to see you."

I shake my head. "Eh, wrong."

"Nope, I'm right. Is it someone in particular you're avoiding?"

My eyes flick away instinctively.

"Ah-ha, I knew it. Who is it?"

"No one."

"Is it Trevor? Lucy? My mom?" She stops, her face growing brighter and brighter as she jumps up and down and squeals like a kid hopped up on candy and soda. "It's my mom, isn't it? Oh my God, it is. Tell me everything."

"Shh," I say, placing my hand over her mouth.

"Okay, okay." She lifts her hand to her lips, giving me the zipped lips gesture.

"I haven't wanted to see Darla ever since I broke up with Steph." Her eyes grow with recognition of what I said. "So if she caught me, it would be question city, and if she saw me with you, it would be worse."

She pulls her eyebrows together. "Why would it be worse if she saw us together?"

"I guess you don't know. For the past few years, your mother has been trying to get me to fall in love with you."

A loud laugh spills out of her mouth. "Oh my God. She has?"

"Yeah. You're great and attr—"

She puts her hand up to stop me. "You don't need to explain anything, Kam. I get it. No one wants to be pushed on anyone, especially after a breakup."

My shoulders sag a little as the tension I was holding dissipates from my body. "Thank you for understanding."

"Absolutely!"

"Look, I have to go. But again, I'm sorry for running into you," I say, stepping around her. She shoots me a gigantic wave as she shakes her head, still laughing about her mother's crazy antics.

The rest of the week passed in a blur of wagging tails and never-ending chores. Friday afternoon is busy, thanks to a to-do list from June I need to complete before Anger Management this evening. The woman loaded me up with tasks, all while refusing to come with me because she wanted to "catch up on her stories." The woman uses and abuses me. I should be annoyed, but I'm not. Instead, I find her endearing. With her always perfectly coifed hair and layers of necklaces that reach her waist, she is too hard not to love.

Between her cooking meals for me just because and telling me that my tattoos make me look like a "hooligan," she throws in some not-so-subtle flirts. Her technique ranges from saying things like, "if I were a few years younger" to "you know women only get better with age. I'm always here if you want to find out for yourself." And my favorite, "Boy, I would let you bend me over right here and take me from behind if it weren't for these bad knees."

If she were anyone else, I would have run for the hills at the first explicit comment, but June is June. And damn if I don't love her, come-ons and all.

I've already stopped at two craft stores, buying up the specific yarns and fabrics she requests—or I should say demanded in extreme detail. Now at the grocery store, my cart is filled with spices and ingredients for many things that I couldn't even figure out the use of. Like, what the hell do you use cream of tartar for? Tartar sauce?

My face must scream confusion because I am continuously being flocked by women. Old, young, it doesn't matter. They see my eyes searching the shelf and the long list in front of me, and they can't seem to help themselves. I don't know what it is about men in grocery stores, but it's like Viagra for women. They can't get enough of it.

It's not just me either. It happens to Marcus too. He says it's even worse when he has the baby with him. He described it as being "the last drop of water in the desert, and they've been walking for days."

I'm halfway through the never-ending list, having escaped the grip of yet another housewife, when I turn onto the frozen food aisle, only to stop dead in my tracks. My hands grip the cart, turning my knuckles white at the sight in front of me.

Steph is here. In the middle of the aisle with him. The same man I witnessed her giving head to. My blood boils as I see the flowing summer dress she wears. It's the type of dress she never wore with me because she always had to work. Always pencil skirts and pantsuits. Her skin is bronze like she's been soaking in the sun for days. Bright matching smiles are on their stupid cheating faces.

My lips curl, and a sour tang fills my mouth. Turning my cart around, I forget the rest of June's list. She'll have to live without her frozen peas.

I drop off the items I was able to collect, and as predicted, June isn't so pleased with the few missing items on her list. But she could tell there was something off, so she lets me off with a mild tongue-lashing.

I spend the next few hours fuming on my couch, on the ride to AM, and again in the cold steel chair in the rec center. I had hoped that after last Sunday, things were turning around, at least somewhat. But damn, was I wrong. Now my mind is a mess. Blow after blow, I can't catch a break. Every part of my life is crumbling. And all I can do is sit back and watch it fall apart. Piece by piece, part of me is chipping away.

Clara saunters into the room and takes her unofficial seat beside me, but I disregard her, unable to handle everything that is her today. I do my best to give her the brush-off, but that just ignites her petty side, making it nearly impossible for me to sit in peace and quiet. Out of the corner of my eye, I can see the wheels turning. She's going to pounce on me the moment we split up.

Sure enough, the entire experience goes exactly how I imagined. Clara isn't holding back any of her little taunts. Her eyes practically glitter with each insult wrapped in a blanket of kindness she throws at me. I fight every urge to smile back at her. She's chipping away at my foul mood, insult by insult, and I adore her for it.

My body aches as she huffs with each slight I throw at her. Chest heaving the slightest bit as she crosses her arms, displaying the most perfect pair of tits. I don't fight my basic instinct to stare. I want to take in her body. The same body that has been haunting my dreams.

A hard lump forms in my throat as I itch to put my hands all over that curvy body of hers. To have her tell me all the things that are wrong with me. My admiration of her assets doesn't go unnoticed. She bolsters a smile, claiming her win against me.

The rush of desire running through me doesn't stop when Stean comes over to reprimand the two of us for our shitty behavior. I can barely pay attention to a word he says because I'm busy imagining pulling up that dress to find out what kind of panties Clara wears.

If she is a full-coverage type of woman. The kind that wears classic briefs or boy shorts. Or if she's a little sexier than that with cheeky, barely-there panties or thongs. Or maybe she's the dirty little vixen

I think she is by wearing nothing to cover up her sweet core.

Then she says, "You would love to get your hands on me, wouldn't you, Kammy?" If she thinks this will trip me up or embarrass me, she's wrong. She just opened up something inside me that I'm not sure she's ready for.

With my eyes locked on hers, I admit, "You have no idea."

Her body flushes. I want to say more to keep this going, but Stean makes sure that isn't going to happen. Laying down what he assumes is going to be a punishment for us. Which it slightly is because I'm not sure how much longer I can hold out on either losing it on this woman or losing myself in her.

I get her number under the pretense of needing it for the project, which is true. But it's not the whole reason. I want to talk to her. To have someone to talk to about this shitty situation we're in. Someone who understands what I'm going through. Who's going through the same things.

Chapter Eleven

Clara

The need to talk to someone about the tension between Kamdyn and me during that last class is bubbling up, threatening to burst at any moment. I would talk about it with anyone. I want and need unbiased advice. Normally I would text Lex or Chloe for guy help, but one of them is a soul-crushing bitch, and the other will just tell me to ride him like the stallion he is.

Thankfully, I have a new friend in Stevie. She agrees almost instantly to an emergency drink and guy-debriefing session. The only problem is that I haven't told her about the whole anger management thing. It just hasn't come up. But to tell the truth, I don't want her finding out about it. So I do the next best thing—I lie, ignoring the rising flush of shame.

We meet up at this local bar-coffee shop, both getting Irish coffees. I waste no time drinking down my mixture of booze and caffeine. I reflect on everything about this evening and my past few encounters with Kamdyn with a few minor tweaks. Instead of the humiliation of being forced into a rage support group, I am taking a twelve-week course to work on conflict resolution and leadership. I also refuse to call Kamdyn by his name. Instead, I stick with Mr. Perfect.

"Okay, so what exactly are you asking me?" Stevie says, her hands wrapped around a large, steaming mug.

"Am I crazy, or is he into this?" I gesture down my curves, rolling my hips.

Her head rears back. I expect to see a double chin with how far she brought her neck back, but nope. Her face is still perfect. The woman is one of the blessed with her zero neck fat. The life she must live.

"Clara! Are you that dumb?" Her blond hair bounces up as her shoulders rise with a laugh on her lips.

"What? It's confusing. One minute we're at each other's throats, and then the next, my panties are all wet." My bottom lip protrudes out, my eyes widening in question. "Help me, my brain is wonky with this stuff."

Her head shakes in disbelief. "You are too hot to be this hopeless. How have you gotten this far like this?"

"It hasn't been easy. I've made an idiot of myself every single day."

"Take comfort in the fact that you are not alone in the idiot club when it comes to romance. I, too, have been a complete dumbass in the love department."

"I call bullshit."

She laughs. "It's true, and it was with my Mr. Perfect."

"What happened?" I ask.

"I kind of royally screwed things up. But being with someone who is always charming or needs people to like him is exhausting. Even with me, he was always playing the part."

"I think that's what's making me so confused. He isn't 'on' when he's with me. He's a huge asshole most of the time. It's refreshing."

She tilts her head to the side and draws her eyebrows together. "You like that he's an asshole?"

"No, I like that he isn't afraid to be a dick with me. I'm a dick right back. With other people, he's Mr. Perfect, boring, predictable. But with me"—I pause, covering my eyes with my hands—"it's like I never know what will come out of his mouth, and it makes my stomach flip in anticipation."

A smile curves one side of Stevie's lips. "What does your friend Lexa say about this whole situation?"

I groan into my mug before taking a sip. "She thinks I should fuck him and be done with it."

"I agree. Get some R&R."

"Rest and relaxation?"

"Not that." She rolls her eyes. "R&R, ride and release."

"Oh dear God, I have become friends with Lex 2.0."

After our not-so-helpful conversation, Stevie drops me off back at my place, encouraging me to "ride and release." Once inside my apartment door, I strip off my dress, changing into an old, baggy T-shirt. With the small amount of liquid courage still in me, I text Asshat. I chuckle a little because he programmed himself into my phone like that. Just proving to me that maybe he doesn't take himself all that seriously.

Me: So tomorrow or Sunday?

Asshat: You know, it is customary to greet a person with a nice "Hello" or even "Sup" before you demand answers.

Me: Sup?

Asshat: Thank you. Now, was that so hard?

Me: Yes. Yes, it was.

Me: So tomorrow or Sunday?

Asshat: Let's do Sunday so I can mentally and physically prepare myself for spending the day with you.

Me: You could never physically prepare enough for me.

Asshat: Is that so?

Me: Yep. You'd need a lot of endurance to keep up with me.

Holy shit. *Holy shit.* Am I saying these things to him? To Kamdyn?

Asshat: Oh, I can go for hours. Maybe even all day.

That was an innuendo, right? He's flirting with me?

Me: I doubt it.

Asshat: It's true. I was once told I have the stamina of a horse.

Well, there goes the last shred of uncertainty from my mind. Yep, he's flirting. And somehow, it all circles back to ride and release.

Me: Prove it.

Asshat: I'll give you the proof you desire.

Asshat: On Sunday.

Asshat: Goodnight, Clara.

Me: Goodnight, Asshat.

I clutch my phone to my thudding heart. Did I just say all that to him? A laugh slips from my lips.

Then it hits me. *Oh my God.* I really just said those things to him. I suck in air faster and faster as the room spins. What was I thinking? I have to see this man on Sunday and at least once a week for the next six weeks.

I pick a spot on the wall, focusing all my energy on it, and count to ten. Refocusing my mind to the best of my ability. My breathing slows just as the room steadies itself around me.

Maybe he wasn't flirting back. He probably didn't even realize what was happening. Yep, that is a lie I am going to tell myself for the next few years until I can scrub this cringe-worthy moment from my brain.

I set myself up in bed with a bowl of strawberry shortcake and the new season of *Queer Eye*. It's my comfort show. Whenever I'm feeling down, nervous, embarrassed, or hell, even happy, I turn it on. I don't know what it is about the fab five that makes my heart sing.

I once invited a man I met on Tinder over after a night of drinks with Chloe. Yes, I am beyond lucky to be alive. And have stopped making such idiotic and reckless decisions since then. Anyway, while I waited for him to drive over, I put on an episode of *Queer Eye*. My little boozed-up self was in heaven and still horny.

When he arrived, I brought him inside to sit on the couch with me. He took one look at my TV and spouted off a homophobic comment about my favorite men in the entire world. It shocked me. And somehow, I kept my big mouth closed. I tolerated him for another awkward twenty minutes before I told him I was beat, and he should go. It was 3:00 a.m., and I didn't give two flying fucks what he thought was going to happen.

Did I ever talk to him again? Nope.

Do I regret that decision? Nope.

I have zero places in my life and heart for homophobia and hatred.

As I watch the guys make over a sad sap of a person into the beautiful butterfly they were always meant to be, I let myself shed a few tears for them. But mostly for me.

Meeting up with Kamdyn on Sunday is nerve-racking. Did he notice the flirting on Friday night? Did he flirt back? Is he embarrassed for me? The *what-ifs* keep running through my head, giving me zero time to prepare myself for time outdoors...with Kamdyn.

When we pull into the parking lot of the national park, I'm blown away. Even the road into this place was full of twists and turns, waterfalls, and trees taller than buildings. It's spectacular. I am in awe. Lexa parks the car, giving me a little eyebrow wiggle before nodding in the most obvious way to where Kamdyn is leaning against a black car.

I swallow down my desire as I peer at him. "He looks...like a sexy Boy Scout."

Lexa cackles. "Boy Scout? Is that what you're into now?"

"Shut up!" I shove her shoulder. "You know what I meant. He looks like he knows what he's doing."

"All I'm saying is he doesn't look like he needs a map to find a cave."

I peer at her for a moment before asking, "Are you—"

She cuts me off. "Yes, yes, I am saying he could find a vagina in the blackout. All he would have to do is listen for the sound of a babbling brook."

Flames of crimson reach my cheeks as I grab my backpack and cell phone. With my hand on the door handle, I turn back to her. "I really hate you right now."

"No, you love me and all the things I say that you're thinking." Her voice booms at me as I close the door, walking over to where he stands.

"Hey," he says, lifting his sunglasses off his face to give me a small smile. "You ready?"

"I think so. I have water, snacks, sunscreen, and Band-Aids. Am I missing anything?"

"Just your sanity, but you've never had that before, have you?" he says in a flat voice, holding a blank expression on his face for a good ten seconds before the left corner of his mouth twitches, twisting up into a full-on grin.

"You're such an ass." I brush past him, moving to the steps that lead down the trail.

He jogs to me, his face still lit up with a wide smile. "You want a big, open view with vast beauty or waterfalls with stone bridges surrounded by foliage?"

Hands on my hips, I don't bother to look at him. "Waterfalls."

"Okay then." He points to his left, and we start our hike.

The trail is full of monstrously large trees and rivers that make me feel like a little kid as we hop from stone to stone across the water. My imagination runs wild with what life would have been like hundreds of years ago when this kind of scenery was the normal, everyday view. Not something that we come to see for fun and exercise.

Just like that, I'm thinking about how much the world has changed, and if I would have fared well back in the 1800s. I already know the answer is no. I would have died from something as small as a bug bite. Despite that, I like to imagine that I would have been okay with a simpler life. That I would have enjoyed the small things.

Taking a break for a snack, Kamdyn and I sit on large stones across from one another. We stare anywhere but at each other. It's awkward and peaceful at the same time. The silence between us seems right, not because I don't want to talk, but because this place, with all its beauty, doesn't need talking. It just needs admiring.

"Have you ever been hiking before?" he asks, hazel eyes locked on the dark French braid I have draped across my shoulder.

"Nope."

He nods. "I didn't think so."

"What's that supposed to mean?" My voice rises, sharpness cutting through with every word.

He sighs, standing up to move a fraction closer to me. "I didn't mean it as something negative."

"Then how did you mean it?"

"I just meant I could tell because of the way your eyes are lighting up with every unfamiliar sight. It's refreshing. You're taking in every piece of this place and treasuring its beauty."

"Oh." My eyes lock on the water bottle lid I've been fumbling with.

"Yeah...So you ready to get going again?"

"Yep." I grab my bag, shoving it over my shoulders. "Shit," I say, turning back to him. "We need to take a few pictures...Together."

"You know, it's okay to admit you want a picture of all this," he says, his hand reaching into the side pocket of his backpack. He pulls out his phone, waving me over.

I step up to his side, leaving a good two feet between us. I need to keep a suitable distance from him. The last thing I need is to snuggle up close to that infuriating man. Kamdyn frowns at the space I left between us, rolling his eyes. "Closer."

I inch in a little more, but Kamdyn continues to wave me in.

"Closer."

I get closer and closer until we're side by side. Close enough to smell his fresh scent. I inhale the smallest amount, breathing him in. My eyes flutter shut as the aroma washes through me.

"Ready?" he asks, breaking the scent overload I'm experiencing.

I straighten up just as Kamdyn wraps his arm over my shoulder, squeezing me into his side. He snaps a picture of the surprise on my face before saying, "Cheese." Automatically, I give him and the camera a big grin. I couldn't stop it even if I tried. It's ingrained in me to smile whenever I hear that word in that specific tone.

After taking a few more photos of the two of us, he slips his phone right back into his bag. "Hey, Asshat, show me the pics."

"Nope," he says, dashing ahead.

I jog to catch up to him. Well, jog might be a loose interpretation of what I actually did. I power walked. It was pure grandmother, multi-laps-around-the-mall power walking. When I reach him, I ask, "Why not?"

"Why do you want to see them so bad?"

"Because," I say, trying to reach my hand into the pocket of his bag. He notices, swatting me away like a fly.

"Not good enough, Clare Bear."

This time, when I reach for his phone, he turns, causing me to stumble. I catch myself on a tree, hands scraping down the bark. Small cuts tear through my palms. "Ow," I yelp, pushing myself up off the tree.

Turning my palms over, I assess the damage. They're a bloody mess. I know it looks a lot worse than it is. I've always been an easy bleeder. It's my curse. Well, that and my inability to say the word Pacific correctly.

"It's not that bad," Kamdyn says, standing behind me. He's peering down at my hand from over my shoulder. "Here, let me clean them up for you." He takes one of my hands in his, and I jerk it away.

"Yeah, no. I can do it myself."

He spins me around so I'm facing him. He lifts my hand again, and I peel it away from him.

"Clara, don't be like that. Just let me wash the dirt and bark bits out."

"Why? Feeling guilty over making me fall? Because you should be."

His face falters, his tone changing from soft to harsh in an instant. "You're blaming me?" Through gritted teeth, he adds, "You know what, fuck this." Sticks snap beneath his feet as he stomps away. "Good luck wrapping your own damn hands."

I stay behind, not willing to admit he might be right. I attempt to wash my minor scrapes and place a Band-Aid on them the best I can. Hello Kitty soon covers 75 percent of the surface area of my palms. Satisfied with my job, I walk down the path Kamdyn stormed away on a few minutes prior.

I half expect to find him sitting on a log just around the first curve of the trail, but he isn't. The stillness of the surrounding wilderness is mesmerizing and terrifying all at the same time. Where is he? The farther down the dirt path I go, the more a hint of panic lodges in my throat.

Did he leave me? Would he leave me here, alone, to find my way out of these woods? My breathing increases with every passing moment, every rustle of leaves, every second I'm alone. I pull out my phone, getting ready to call him to berate him for this, only to find that I have zero service.

Of fucking course.

"Asshat," I shout into the warm breeze. *Nothing*. No response.

"Kamdyn." Still nada, not a sound.

Now panic really sets in. Tears sting my eyes, readying themselves for the outpour of emotions I'm about to release. It's like a dark cloud is hanging over me, threatening a storm.

I call out his name one more time, my voice cracking as the downpour begins. I slide my back down the nearest tree until I'm sitting on the ground. Curling my arms around my legs, I rest my face on my knees.

How could he do this? Am I that big of an asshole that he wouldn't care what happens to me?

"Fuck," someone groans in the distance.

My head shoots up, and I see Kamdyn making his way in my direction. He pauses when he sees me. His eyes drift all over my face. Another groan escapes him as he moves faster to get to me.

He looks off-kilter like he's limping, but maybe the unevenness of the ground just makes it appear that way. As soon as he reaches me, he falls to his knees beside me.

"What's wrong?" he demands, his eyes searching my body. "Where are you hurt?"

Another tear spills down my cheek. I turn from him to wipe it away. "You left me here."

He wrinkles his forehead. "So you're not hurt?"

I bite the inside of my cheeks as I break even harder. I cover my face with my hands, letting the salty drops fill my palms. "You. Left. Me," I seethe through sobs.

He clasps my hands in his, pulling them away from my face. The warm touch has me slowly calming down. His thumbs circle my inner wrists, lulling me into a new sense of security that wasn't there a few minutes ago. I glance up to find his dark hazel eyes staring at me. Blurred by tears, he looks like a mixture of emotions.

Every part of his stare makes me want to push away all emotion.

"Clara." The softness in his tone sends a shiver through me. "I didn't mean to leave you alone for so long. I would never purposely leave you alone here."

"Then why?" A strangled noise sounds from my throat.

"I needed a few minutes to myself after you made me feel like shit for getting you hurt. I swear I only meant to be gone for a few minutes, but I wasn't watching my steps and tripped." He pauses, looking at the ground. "I ended up falling down a hill and twisting my ankle. That's why it took me so long to come back."

With a sniffle, I stare at him, taking him in. He has dirt streaked across his forehead and on his clothes. He fell. "You're hurt?" I ask.

"It's fine. I'll just have to ice it tonight."

"Let me see."

"Clara, I'll be fine."

I say nothing, continuing to stare at him. Giving him my best impersonation of my mom. The look does the trick because he moves off his knees to sit on his ass, pushing his legs in front of him. Thank God for moms and their scary-ass looks.

I don't even have to ask which ankle he twisted. It's beyond obvious. His right ankle has swollen to the size of a grapefruit, visible bruising already showing.

"Holy fuck, Kamdyn." I widen my eyes as I reach down, gently touching the skin. He winces, hissing through his teeth. "This is really bad."

"It's not that bad." He attempts to wave off my concern. To prove my point, I set my hand on top of his swollen skin. He jerks back, his face contorting as he gasps in pain.

"Yeah, it's not that bad." My voice deepens as I mock him under my breath.

Still trying to ignore the obvious fact that he's not okay, Kamdyn pushes off the ground with his hands and one leg. He stumbles into a semi-hunched standing position. The strain shows on his face.

Not needing to see any more of his ridiculous posturing, I wrap an arm under his shoulders. I plan to help him walk by taking some of his weight. It would be laughable if it weren't under these circumstances. To think that a five-foot-three woman could carry half the weight of a six-foot-something man. I probably look dwarfed by him.

He stiffens on contact. "What's wrong? What else is hurt?" My hands pull at his shirt, lifting to see if he's downplaying more than just his ankle.

He tugs on my hand that's clamped on to his shirt. "Stop it, Clara. There isn't anything other than the ankle."

I narrow my eyes as I try to gauge if he's telling me the truth. "I don't think I trust you."

A wicked grin flashes across his face as he leans in a little closer. "I think you're just using that as an excuse to cop a feel."

"You perv," I say, giving him a light shove, momentarily forgetting his injury. I gasp, grabbing on to his waist, but it's pointless. He ends up having to catch not only himself but me as well by placing weight on both feet.

A strangled noise rumbles from his throat, and my stomach bottoms out. I just hurt him. With a shaky breath, he wraps his arm over my shoulder, allowing me to attempt to support his weight again.

He stays quiet, which makes me feel even worse. I fight to keep my eyes free of tears.

"Sorry." I wipe my now runny nose on my arm.

"Please stop," Kamdyn says, his voice strong and full of authority. I bet this is his teacher voice. If I were one of his students, I wouldn't know whether to be terrified or turned on by it. Hell, those two conflicting ideas are taking over my body.

And I don't know which is worse.

"Clara, don't feel bad about any of this. I provoked you, so it's okay."

"Really?"

"Yeah." His eyes light up as he looks into mine. "Besides, I don't know what to do with sad Clara. I need snarky Clara. I need you to be my Clare Bear, not this caring version of yourself. It's weirding me out."

I let out a sniffled laugh. "You sure have a way of being kind and a jerk at the same time. Did you practice that, or is it just a natural talent?"

"Baby, I was born with it." He winks at me. With a sharp inhale, I try to tamp down my growing lady boner. Not even twenty minutes ago, he had me curled up on the ground like a small child, crying over being left alone.

If this is how he affects me when I hate him, I cannot even fathom what it would be like if I liked him. If we took this relationship in another direction and pursued our flirty behavior.

He would crush the last bit of my soul and the happiness I'm clinging to.

I can't let the smiles and banter make me forget that. I can't let him any closer than he is now.

Chapter Twelve

Kamdyn

She actually does it.

Well, she does her best to support my body, helping me walk without putting weight on my left side. To say this hiking trip hasn't gone according to plan is an understatement. This has been the hike from hell.

From Clara trying to take my phone and scratching up her hands to my swollen ankle, today hasn't been the best for bonding. Not that I was too hopeful in that department. Clara has seemed even more put off by me since the meeting on Friday, and I know it's probably my fault. My piss-poor attitude—brought on by Steph—leaked into every aspect of my life. Steph showed me she still has so much power over me.

My eyes drift down to Clara. I watch her struggle to support me with every step, letting out little grunts every few steps. I can't stop the warmth flooding my chest as this tiny woman doesn't give up.

She doesn't complain at all about practically carrying me.

It's hard to believe this is the same person who calls me Asshat every time she sees me. She is so much more than what she permits the world to see. This kindness proves it. I want to know what else she stashes away from the world. Who is she when people aren't paying attention?

"Stop staring at me." She breaks my trance. "It's creepy."

I chuckle, throwing my head back. Her steps blunder as she shoots me a glare, her eyes no longer full of unshed tears.

"Ugh, I should leave you here to be eaten by the wolves," she says with a straight face. The woman is a master of schooled expressions, and right now is a testament to that. She shows no sign of humor as she continues to move me along.

I sigh, placing my right palm over my heart. "Keep saying things like that, Clare Bear, and I'm going to be in love with you in no time."

Her lips pull, fighting the smile itching to grace her pink lips.

I halt us to a stop, turning toward her. "Did I just—just render you speechless?"

"That's it," she says. "I am leaving you to be eaten."

"You wouldn't. The guilt would weigh too heavy for your incredibly strong shoulders to carry." I poke at the curve of her smooth shoulders. She inhales sharply, the smooth muscles tensing underneath my touch.

She takes a few moments to respond, shaking her head in disagreement. "Nope, I wouldn't. It's the circle of life. Your body could benefit others, which would make me exceedingly happy."

"I can think of a few other ways my body could benefit others." I pause, feeling her breathing pick up against my arm that's still draped over her. "None of them include being animal food, but some involve my mouth."

Her cheeks flare with a bright-red flush, and she swallows, refusing to look my way or acknowledge me.

We spend the rest of the painful, long trek back to my car in silence. Only stopping for a few minutes for a water break. Once there, I move to climb into the driver's side, only to have my keys swiped away by Clara.

"Oh, fuck no, Kamdyn," she says with her hands on her hips, my keys dangling from her left ring finger.

"Come on!" I reach for them, but she backs up. "I can drive. Everything's done with the right foot, anyway."

"Nice try, but the answer is still no." She points for me to get in the back seat.

"Why can't I at least sit in the front?"

"You need room to prop that thing up while I drive you to the hospital."

I shake my head, protesting, but she holds up a hand. "This isn't up for discussion. Get in the car so I can take you to the fucking hospital."

I stare at her. Dumbfounded by the way she spoke.

"Now," she says, sneering at me.

The drive is silent, with only the occasional directional question. She's so serious, observing the road with extreme caution. The only sign of her anxiousness from earlier is the frequent finger tapping on the steering wheel.

She looks so odd in the driver's seat of my car. My gaze follows every movement of her arms, her hands. She looks so stoic and beautiful. A slight sunburn turned her normally pale skin into a pinkish-red mess. The tight French braids she sported this morning are now a mess with hair pulled out in random places. She looks wrecked and undone, and I love it.

Once we arrive at the hospital, Clara still refuses to leave me. Even when I offer to call her an Uber, she won't go. I try to convince her she doesn't want to sit here waiting for what could be hours with me, but she doesn't budge.

The girl is stubborn as hell, which turns out to be admirable of her.

We get called back after an hour in the waiting room. The sole source of entertainment we had was people watching. Clara tried to guess the reasons for each person's visit. Almost every theory she had was that the man, woman, or child's wife got fed up with their shit and snapped, either poisoning them or throwing something dangerously hard at them.

After her fifth time guessing that, I had a grin that wouldn't leave my face. Even with the pain in my ankle throbbing like it had just happened, my smile doesn't waver.

Back in the small ER room, I lie back, letting the nurse and doctor poke at me, examining every part of me. All the while, Clara sits in the corner, wiggling her eyebrows back and forth between the two women. "What?" I mouth.

She responds by mouthing to me, "They totes get it on. Probably in this room."

I laugh just as the doctor rotates my ankle. My laughter dies, turning into a sudden grunt of pain.

"Does that hurt?" she asks, manipulating my left ankle.

Gritting my teeth, I nod at her. I squeeze my eyes shut as she twists and turns, determining what hurts and what doesn't. Shocker, it all hurts.

As I try to control my breathing, soft, smooth skin wraps around my hand. I open my eyes to find Clara's hand wrapped around mine. My eyes dart up to her face, and she gives me a weak smile. With a small squeeze, she tells me she's here for me.

Soon after the painful and not at all necessary movement of my limb, I'm whisked away for an X-ray, leaving Clara behind in the room. She gives me a quick thumbs up as I'm rolled away in a wheelchair.

A few hours and some strong pain medication later, I'm released, my ankle wrapped up and crutches in hand. Just a sprain, thank fucking God. Even though I didn't break it, I need to treat my ankle as if I did. I have to live by RICE—rest, ice, compression, elevation—for the next few weeks. No bearing weight on it, no running.

Without running, I'm probably going to drive myself insane with my constant worrying. It's my therapy and my workout. I need it to function. Fuck, this is going to be a long few weeks.

Since I'm on pain medications, Clara is driving once again. This time she allows me to sit in the front with her. She looks so small in my driver's seat, with it pushed all the way up, while I'm in the passenger seat, pushed back and reclining.

She glances over at me, feeling my stare. "What?" she asks, her eyes darting back and forth from me to the road.

A large grin spreads over my face. I reach over the console, taking one of her black braids in my hand. Her hair is soft and out of place as I twirl it around my fingers. "You're pretty, is all."

She lifts her eyebrows and gives me the side-eye. She lowers her head, letting out a small, quiet laugh. "Man, they gave you the good stuff."

"Huh?" I ask, sitting up to get a little closer to her.

"You're high, buddy."

I nod. "Did you know I'm a member of 4H?"

She rolls her eyes. "4H? Really?"

"Yep. Happy, horny, hungry, and high."

She laughs so hard she pulls the car over, unable to control herself. Her hands grasp on to her stomach as she moans in pain. "You're going to regret saying that tomorrow."

"Why? It's all true."

"Kamdyn!"

"What?" I ask, pulling out the rubber band that was holding her strands of hair in the braid. My fingers untangle her soft locks as she just stares at me, mouth agape.

"One, you're talking about being high. And two, you just told me you're fucking *horny*."

"So?" I glance from her hair into her eyes, which are rimmed with redness from crying and the long day. "You have soft hair. I could play with it forever."

She pulls my hand off her hair, placing it on my lap. "You know it sounds like you're trying to fuck me, right?"

I lean farther across the middle that separates us. "Would that be so wrong?"

"Oh my God," she laughs. "You know I'm going to hold everything you're saying to me against you tomorrow and the rest of our time knowing each other."

"You can hold anything and everything against me. I promise I don't mind." I give her a wink before pulling lightly on a strand of her hair again.

Her head shakes from side to side as she laughs at me. "You are insane. And way too high for your own good."

"No such thing, Clare Bear," I say, my eyes feeling heavy. I struggle to keep my lids up and open. They keep tugging down, and I'm no match against their weight.

"Kamdyn," a soft voice says. "We're at your house. Do you have an alarm?"

I mumble under my breath.

A soft hand shakes my shoulder. "Hey, Asshat! What's the alarm code?"

Beep. Beep. Beep. Beep.

My eyes shoot open, still heavy with the need for more sleep. I rear my head back when I see Clara staring at me, her hands over her ears.

She widens her eyes. "Kamdyn! The alarm."

I get up, forgetting my recent injury, and place weight on my left ankle. Pain shoots up, and I buckle under its sharpness. I grasp the car door to steady myself, looking at Clara. "8675."

She glares, rushing off, muttering something I can't pick up, but I'm pretty sure it wasn't nice.

The noise stops, and she returns to the garage. Offering me her shoulder to lean on, I take it without pause. Clara leads me into my house. My heart beats a little faster, and it has nothing to do with the pain of trying to walk.

She's at my house. My house. The one place I don't have to be anyone but myself. The one place I let go of everything. Dirty clothes and towels lay on the floor in front of the laundry basket by the washer.

Clara shakes her head in disapproval. "Such a man—can't even put the laundry an inch farther into the basket."

I ignore her blatant taunt, pointing toward my bedroom. Once in my room, she sets me down on the edge of my bed. She has me promise to stay where I am before she leaves the room to get my new pain pills and steroid out of the car, along with the crutches.

As I wait, I sink into the plush pillow top. The softness of my king-size bed has me fumbling with the blankets, attempting to cover myself so I can drift back into oblivion.

"Kamdyn." There's that soft voice again. It's calming, like watching my favorite movie on a stormy night.

"Kamdyn," she says again. This time I peek out of one eye. Clara is sitting on the edge of my bed. Her eyes scan my face, waiting for something. "Do you need anything before I go?"

I stare at the bedside table. It's covered with all kinds of drinks. Clara put a cup of water, a bottle of Gatorade, a can of orange soda, and a few snacks there, along with my new pills. My phone sits by them, plugged into the charger. "I think you covered everything." My voice is sleepy, and I'm not sure I even responded or if any of this is real.

"Goodnight." Clara grins before standing, leaving me alone in bed, surrounded by all the comforts I could ever want.

Chapter Thirteen

Clara

To say yesterday didn't go as planned would be an understatement. It was a shit show.

We didn't even finish our hike; it was horrible. Between Kamdyn leaving me alone, injuring his ankle, and the hours in the hospital, I'm surprised we didn't kill each other.

Dropping him off at his house, seeing his place, makes me think of my own and the differences between the two. It wasn't what I expected at all. The house was a little messy but still pleasant. It felt like him, the version of him that only comes out when it's just the two of us.

It was a little heartwarming and slightly endearing, seeing him that happy and high. He has me feeling things I haven't felt in forever. It was like I was a thirteen-year-old girl again. I wanted nothing more than to just sit there and stare at him, listening to him talk. Listen to him mumble on about my hair while he sports a carefree, serene smile. If this is what it takes to get a nice Kamdyn, I think I'll give him pain pills every fucking day.

After setting him up in his bed, I did a little snooping. I looked through his junk drawer in his kitchen; it was weird, not junkie enough. It surprised me because he's the type of guy who throws his laundry on the floor right beside the laundry basket. Who the fuck does that? He's a psychopath. It's the only explanation.

But what I did note was the number of empty picture frames. I want to learn what could have happened that he took out the pictures. Who was in them? What does he not want to see anymore? I wonder if 4H Kamdyn would tell me. Why do I even care?

Then there were the books strung out around his house. Some were history books that I imagine he read for his job and maybe out of curiosity. But the ones that caught my attention were the ones I recognized. A stack of two, both popular books. And from what I've heard, both are supposedly super depressing. And opposites. Literary vs. romance. The man has eclectic taste.

But that's the thing about Kamdyn. Even though we hate each other and fight constantly, days like today remind me we are both just fucking people. We might be two idiots in Anger Management ordered by the courts to keep us out of jail. But we're both idiots trying to make it through life.

It makes me think there's more than meets the eye. More than I already wondered about. More than I already knew. He's a mystery wrapped up in a hot body and bad fucking attitude.

Well, I might be the one with a poor attitude. He's just the one with a complex ensuring people like him.

I mean, honestly, does he need everybody to like him?

The man is naturally likable to some people.

I guess, maybe in some minor way, I might kind of think he is a little likable too.

So why the fuck does he need to add on all that extra charm? Why does he feel like he has to make everybody like him? And why doesn't he care if I like him? I just want to know. I want to know everything.

It's freaking annoying that I want to know everything about this asshat. I just hope that he doesn't know that. Or that I'm insanely attracted to him.

When I left his house on Sunday, I had to call Lex, giving her an update on Kamdyn and the whole damn day.

Lexa answers on the first ring. "So did you forage for nuts?" she asks, her voice blasting through the phone so loud I have to pull it back from my ear.

"Holy hell, Lexa. Tone that shit down. And I don't just mean the volume level," I say a little harsher than I meant to. But seriously, I need her to tone down the Kamdyn and me shit. It's getting out of hand. The last thing I need is someone else influencing my feelings or lack thereof for him.

"So I take that as a no, 'cause if you had gotten a sip of that, you would be a sweet, blissful angel. Instead, I get a cranky, frustrated hoe with a rapid river between her legs right now."

I can't help it. She's cracked the slightly icy demeanor I was trying to have. Laughter bursts out of me as my driver stares back at me through the mirror. There is a brief moment of uncomfortable eye contact before he glances back at the road. I can tell from the stoic expression on his face he's trying to listen in on my conversation. "Oh my fucking God. Did you just say that?"

"You bet your sex-deprived ass I did. So am I right, or am I right?"

I whine into the phone, hoping she understands my current situation without me having to say it.

"Ha," she barks out. "I knew it. You wanted him to be all up in your lady cave."

"Please, please stop with all the nature innuendos." My body sways with each turn, and my underwear starts rubbing a certain spot in all the right places. My mind strays back to Kamdyn telling me he was horny in the car, and that he didn't care that it sounded like he wanted to fuck me. God, I need to stop thinking about this. And I need this goddamn car ride to be over with so my underwear can stop with the teasing.

Lex releases a small sigh. I picture her moving her head back and forth in a disapproving manner. "Never gonna happen, girl."

"I didn't think so."

"So? Are you going to tell me what all happened today? And no detail is too small."

I go through the events of the day, everything from the fights and injuries to Kamdyn being a member of 4H. She only interrupts about every other sentence with questions about why I didn't offer to take his pain away with a kiss or a handy at the least.

If I followed any or all of her advice, I would have had at least three STIs by now. Lexa owns her sexuality and libido better than anyone I have ever known. And that's saying a lot. She even gives a few of my ex-boyfriends a run for their money. And all they did was fuck and talk about fucking, all the time.

I'm almost finished filling her in when my driver pulls up to my building. Thanking him, I step out of the car and onto the edge of the curb. I reach in to grab my backpack and cringe at the site. It's covered in dirt. The seat is also now covered in dirt. The dude is going to be pissed when he sees this mess I left. Thank God his seats are leather.

Once inside the building, I finish telling Lexa about all the craziness. Her only reply before hanging up was, "Okay, Clara, now go play DJ to the image of that sexy tree you want to climb, who I imagine has huge"—she pauses—"coconuts."

When I walk through the front door, my small apartment now appears even more cramped after being inside Kamdyn's house. His vast space compared to my crowded space has that familiar pang starting in my chest.

I rub my hand over my heart, willing the ache to end. To let my dream of owning a home slink away into the background. Disappointment from the past few months floods in, and it's overwhelming. How am I ever going to get over this when everything is a reminder of the mistakes and betrayal?

I'm careful walking through the tight space to my bathroom, avoiding touching anything with my dirt-covered self. With one glance in the mirror, I see the insane appearance I must have been sporting ever since leaving the trails.

Dirt coats my clothing. What remains of my braids is sporadically sticking out in every direction. I had forgotten that Kamdyn took out half of one braid. If that wasn't enough to make me look insane, the mascara stains were. They trail down my cheeks, starting at my eyes and running past my chin.

A huff of laughter vibrates through my throat. I don't know whether I should laugh or cry. Choosing the former, I snap a photo of my face. I look like something out of a horror movie or the after picture of someone rescued after being lost in the woods for a week.

Me: This is what I've looked like for hours…I am going to kill that asshat.

I grace both Stevie and Lex with a picture of my horrible image.

Lexa: OMG! I love him more and more every moment.

Stevie: Shit. Time for a revenge plan?

To Lex, I send a quick "Fuck you." Stevie gets a GIF of Jack Nicholson in *The Shining*, nodding his head.

I carefully peel away the dirt-contaminated clothing as the shower warms up. With another glimpse at the picture of my face, I open another text, attaching the picture.

Me: I will murder you for this.

My stomach sinks when, after a minute, there's still nothing new in the thread. It's not that I expected an immediate response. Despite that, the lack of attention makes me feel foolish. He's snowed on the pills the hospital gave him. If he were awake, I would chastise him for not resting, but the fact that he hasn't texted me back has me wanting to scream.

I step into the black-tiled box, sliding back the shower door. I wash myself three times to be 100 percent sure to get the dirt, mascara, and tangled hair in all its glory. Reddish brown water covers the tile. If I had a white shower, it would piss me off that I would have to scrub the tile ASAP to prevent staining. But thank God I have a sleek black design.

The shower is the main reason I chose this place. Yeah, it's tiny, but so am I in comparison. A single person doesn't need more than a bed and a bomb-ass shower with a multi-setting showerhead.

Damn it.

The bathroom was the one place I didn't go in at Kamdyn's. I wonder how big his shower is. It has to be large to fit his tall frame. Heat pools in my core. I picture his body in my shower, his head reaching the top of the downpour of water. I imagine water sliding down his chest and toned stomach to his engorged cock.

My eyes flutter shut as I sweep my hands over my breasts, pinching and caressing my nipples as an ache throbs between my legs. The way his large hands would engulf my breast as he shows them the attention they are overdue for. The pulsing in my clit has me grabbing for the showerhead. I position the spray in just the right spot. Hot water hits my bundle of nerves, the pressure and pleasure spreading through my limbs as the threat of release rises.

I picture his mouth on me. Kamdyn on his knees before me, his tattooed arms reaching up my body to grab one of my breasts as I moan.

The mental image pushes me over the edge. My knees threaten to buckle as my legs shake from the orgasm racing through my body. My breath and heart both race as I pull the showerhead away, putting it back where it belongs.

A low laugh slips from my lips, and I slide to the floor. The water pelts my skin, still tingling from the ecstasy the spray helped induce.

What the fuck did I just do? I would be embarrassed if it wasn't for the fresh orgasm. The post-orgasmic bliss is in full effect, and right now, I don't care if I hate myself later. I want to do it again.

Fuck, I want the real thing if I'm being honest with myself. 'Cause if that's the fantasy, I can only imagine what the reality would be like.

I'm pretty sure I fell asleep imagining and analyzing the entire day. Everything from Lexa's comments in the car to the way Kamdyn glanced back at me when he thought I wasn't paying attention.

Beep. Beep. Beep.

The beeping of my alarm startles me out of sleep, tearing me away from dreams filled with what-ifs. It pulls me back into reality, back to the place where I'm alone. My other half is missing, and it's breaking my heart. You might think I would get used to it by now, but no. Time won't mend this pain.

Chloe is gone. She left me by choice. The Thelma to my Louise left me behind to clean up her mess. To pick up every piece of my picture-perfect life that she shattered.

Silencing the alarm, I sit up, pressing my back into the headboard. With my phone still in my hand, I bypass the new alerts on my phone. My fingers tremble as I type in her number, the phone line I still pay for, hoping she'll return my calls. The line rings. With each ring, my chest tightens, threatening to rupture. To have everything I hide explode from me. All the emotions I bury build stronger, and I'm not sure how much more I can take.

Ring. Ring. Ring.

Nothing. Even her voice mail is full, so I can't even tell her off on her answering machine.

"Fuck you," I breathe out.

I'm seething as I clench my fist at my side. I need to release this darkness rising in me. With a quick strike, my fist collides with my upper thigh, and searing pain infiltrates the spot. I grind my teeth together as I scream. I'm not even sure if it's from the physical pain or the pain of having the person born to be my best friend abandon me.

The cold concrete floor connects with my feet. I flinch, my legs shooting up. Some days I relish the coolness on my skin, but today I want warmth. I need something to make me feel light.

It doesn't take me more than a few seconds to find my slippers.

With them on, I get my ass up. I drag myself to the fridge, grabbing my morning drink. Liquid crack. Well, not actual crack, energy drinks.

To-may-to, to-mat-o.

They're pretty much the same thing. I get why there are addicts out there. Does that mean I would ever touch real crack? Fuck no. I have seen what drugs can do to someone, and that shit isn't for me. I don't care if it takes away the pain and stress of every day. I would rather suffer than waste away.

It takes about ten minutes for me to gulp down the energy drink and start getting ready for my day. It's my day off, and I promised my mother I would have lunch with her. I wish I didn't feel this paralyzing weight on my chest when I think of spending time with her. Chloe is all she wants to talk about, and she doesn't even know the entire story. She doesn't know that she has disappeared from our lives. Or that I am cleaning up the wreckage from the shit storm she left in her wake.

My mom chose the restaurant, Break The Fast, a small breakfast diner downtown. She has always been a huge fan of pancakes and everything syrup related. She and Chloe were alike in that way. I, on the other hand, could do without breakfast. I love bacon. And I love eggs. Just not like this. I need bacon on a burger or with fries and my eggs boiled or deviled.

But that is part of being a matching set of children. Parents will confuse your likes with your twin's. She always forgets Chloe is the one who likes breakfast, and I'm the one who prefers anything with potatoes.

"Hey, baby girl," she says, standing to give me a warm hug and a kiss on the cheek. I relish her embrace. It makes me feel like a little kid again, and I don't feel so alone.

My mom is the typical mom you would expect to see on a sitcom. Her dark hair is shoulder length and teased high as the sky. She's beautiful and kind, but that doesn't mean she can't be my worst nightmare.

"Hi, Momma," I say, sliding into the booth across from her. "Have you been here long?"

"Oh, not too long." She smiles at me with her hands clasped on the table. "I've missed you so much. You and Chloe."

"Back at you."

"So have you spoken to your sister lately?"

I let out a sigh. That was faster than I expected. She could have at least given me time to order before going in for the kill. With my eyes fixed on the menu, I simply shake my head. If I peer up, I might break. I might tell her all the dark secrets her daughters hide from her. So I don't. I flip through the menu, looking for something to take me away from this conversation.

Just then, the server stops by our table to take our order. My mother orders a plethora of breakfast foods, from bacon to pancakes. I gladly ignore the fact that it isn't exactly socially acceptable to be drunk this early in the day and order a flight of mimosas and nothing else.

The server quirks her left eyebrow as she darts her eyes between my mother and me. "Okay, hun, I'll be right back," she says with a knowing stare.

She's speedy with the breakfast alcohol, and I down the first one as she sets it on the table. The sweet alcohol mixed with the tanginess of the fruit helps me choke down the bile threatening to crawl up my throat.

"Well, you should call her," she says. "She misses you, and it's not normal for twins to be out of touch with each other."

My fingers twirl around the flute and itch to start the irritating tapping my mother hates so much. "I know."

She adjusts her top, straightening in the seat before taking a sip of the dark soda that, without a doubt, is her signature drink—Diet Coke. "Clara, do I have to spell it out for you?"

"What are you talking about?" My voice is laced with irritation.

She blinks at me, not responding. My fingers tap on the table.

Her face falls, and a frown appears. Her gaze locks on my fingers and their repeated drumming.

The corners of my lips turn up, and she breaks. "Fine. Clara, you want to act like a child, so be it. I will treat you like one. Call your sister and apologize."

My fingers still. "Apologize? For what?"

Her mouth opens as if she wants to say something, but she doesn't. Instead, she takes a bite of her food, probably planning on how to continue this conversation without a blowup.

"Clara, I don't know why," she says, peering up at me with soft eyes that match mine. "She wouldn't say, but I could tell she's hurt by it."

I gulp down another mimosa. I'm tempted to ask the waitress for a second order of them.

"Clara! Stop drinking like that." She leans in to whisper, "It's not even noon."

I set down my drink. "Look, what's going on between Chloe and me is personal, and I don't want to talk about it."

She throws her hands up. "Fine. I'll drop it. It's not like I'm your mother and love you both or anything."

I roll my eyes as I reach across the table, stealing a piece of bacon off her plate.

After a lot more nagging and just as much hugging, we say our goodbyes, and I walk the few blocks back to my apartment, taking the time to check my texts from this morning.

Asshat: Holy shit. I don't remember it being that bad.

That little fucker let me look like I rolled around in a ditch and said nothing.

Me: Bullshit, you didn't.

Asshat: Blame it on the drugs.

Me: I looked like this before you were high.

Asshat: …

I bark out a laugh that has the people walking by staring at me. I give a small wave before continuing to text and walk to my place.

Me: I'll come to your house and murder you for this.

Asshat: Now, now, Clara. Do I need to call Stean?

Me: You keep digging your own grave. It's fine. I can wait.

Asshat: What do you want me to do? It's not like I can travel back in time and find you to say, "Oh, hey, Clare Bear, you kind of have some dirt and mascara, like, all over your facial area."

Me: You could do that exactly.

Me: Or you could apologize for being an asshat.

Asshat: Clara, my Clare Bear, my five-foot-two savior, I am sorry I let you walk around looking like the creature from *The Ring*. I was a little preoccupied with the whole ankle being almost snapped in half thing.

Me: That was almost a decent apology until you started spouting that shit about yourself.

Asshat: It's all true.

Me: Is it also true that you are a member of 4H?

Asshat: 4H?

Me: You told me all about it yesterday.

Asshat: I honestly don't know what you're talking about.

Me: *Evil hands rubbing together GIF* Never mind, I'll just wait and use this against you at the most opportune moment.

Asshat: Seriously, Clara, what does it mean? What did I say?

Me: Don't worry about it, Kammy. I'll jog your memory soon enough.

Asshat: I was high on pain pills. You cannot use anything I said or did against me.

My body must have been on autopilot during the walk because when I glance up from my texts, I'm standing in my building's elevator.

Me: Keep telling yourself that. It doesn't make it true.

Asshat: I hate you.

Laughing, I send one last text as I step off the elevator.

Me: The feeling is mutual.

Ring. Ring. Ring.

What the living fuck. He's calling me. Why?

"Hello?" I say, holding my breath to hear what he plans to say to me.

"Hey," Kamdyn says, his voice sounding gravelly yet somehow smooth like liquid, all at the same time.

"Is there a reason you called?"

"Yeah." He pauses, and I hear him take a deep breath on the other line. "Thank you. For yesterday."

"Oh, it was nothing," I say, walking down the hall to my apartment door, pausing in front of it.

"No, it wasn't, Clara. Without your help, I would have fucked my ankle up even worse."

I don't say anything. Hell, even if I knew what to say back, I wouldn't be able to respond. Goose bumps pebble across my skin.

"Clara?"

"Yeah?"

"I appreciate everything you did for me. I was a huge ass yesterday, but you stayed with me the whole time. Hell, you even drove me home and tucked me in, making sure I had everything I could need. It means a lot."

"Don't go acting all nice now, Mr. Cook. You forget I know you."

"And you forget I know you," he says.

I sigh, my voice falling quiet. "How's your ankle today?"

"Feels worse than yesterday. But the pain pills should fix that."

"Pop one of those bad boys again."

He chuckles into the phone. "I will, I will. But I wanted to cash in on my win from the painting contest."

"Doesn't my carrying your ass across a national park count for anything?" I reach for my keys to unlock my door.

"Nope, you did that willingly. This is something I'll force you into."

"What?" I whine.

"I need you to help me run some errands."

"Errands?"

"Yes, just a few."

"When?" I walk through my door and throw my purse on the floor.

"This weekend."

"Ugh, Asshat. I'm forced to spend two weekends with you."

His voice lowers, and I can sense the smirk in it. "I hate to break it to you, Clare Bear, but you've spent the past few weekends in a row with me."

"That's because one of the H's in 4H has you wanting to be around me all the time."

"It's rude to keep secrets from your forced friend."

"Whatever, I'll see you on Friday." I hang up the phone before he has another chance to keep me on the phone any longer.

My face fucking hurts from the smile that's been there since I read his first text message. He's affecting me like no one else ever has. The sound of his voice alone has my skin tingling. It's as if he ignited something in me I haven't felt in years—if ever. And I'm not sure it's a good thing.

Fuck.

I'm ten minutes late when I finally walk through the double doors into the already started Anger Management class. As the doors close behind me, everyone snaps their neck to see me stumble in.

Everyone turns to stare at me. Most are frowning, including Stean. But I don't pay any attention to the looks they're giving. The only eyes in the room I notice are his.

Kamdyn fixes his gaze on me. His stare burns into me, setting my skin on fire. Our eyes lock on to each other, and I'm trapped, frozen in my place. His tongue slowly licks his bottom lip, leaving me in a puddle of desire. Heat radiates from my core, and I know if I checked my panties, I would find them drenched.

The intensity between us is palpable at this point. Does anyone else feel it, or is it just us? But the look in his eyes makes me want him to bend me over one of those foldable metal chairs and fuck me in front of everyone and anyone.

My lips part slightly, and I suck in a small breath. I try to fight back the flush creeping up my face. "Sorry, everyone," I say, hurrying to my seat beside Kamdyn. "I had Uber issues."

Stean gives me a forced smile. "It's fine, Clara, as long as you don't make it a normal occurrence."

"I won't."

He nods, leaning forward to rest his forearms on his thighs. "Okay, where were we? Oh yes, week seven's focus. Solutions—planning and implementing. I want you all to think of solutions for the problems listed on the handout I gave you at the start of class. Then I want you to revise and use these solutions in your everyday life and anger."

I raise my hand. "I didn't get the handout."

"It's a partner activity, Clara." I swear I can see him fighting the urge to roll his eyes at me. His jaw ticks ever so slightly as his face tightens. "Your other half has the worksheet." With that, he gestures my attention over to Kamdyn, then turns his attention back to the others. "Okay, separate into your groups."

Kamdyn and I are the only two left after the circle breaks. Stean eyes us suspiciously before leaving us to move about the room to help the others.

"Partners again. Yay," I say to Kamdyn with a weak attempt at fake enthusiasm.

He leans in, bridging the small gap between our chairs. His hand finds the ends of my ponytail, his fingers intertwining with it. "Oh, come on, Clare Bear, you know you love spending every minute together."

It takes everything in me to sit there, to stay still. To not show any kind of response to him all while on the verge of coming undone because of him. Normally I would be all over him by now, taking his flirty cues and running to cash them at the orgasm bank. But the problem with Kamdyn is that I can't tell if he's fucking with me or wants to fuck me.

Our relationship, or whatever we have, is built on screwing with each other. Every action is perplexing. What if I go for it, only to ruin everything? Imagine having to be paired together every Friday after being rejected. I would rather face the jail sentence than come back here after something like that. I just couldn't handle that.

"Clara? Did you zone out again?" My eyes flicker up to his face, and I'm drawn back into wanting him. Why isn't he being the major asshat and douche that I know he can be?

"Uh, yeah. Sorry, you know how my ADD can be. Some days I can focus with no issues, but then days like today, I'm drawn into my mind every few seconds."

Shivers run up my spine as his fingers brush my neck, pulling his hand back into his own space. Kamdyn's head tilts. "Do you really have attention issues?"

"Yeah." Heat rushes through my body as my blood boils. Does he not believe me? He thinks I'm a liar.

Who am I kidding? I am a liar. Not about my ADD, but about so many other things. But that's a secret he'll never find out. It's a secret I'll take to the grave.

"Do you take meds or something for it?"

"When I was a kid, yes. But not anymore."

"I'm just surprised, is all. You seem to be pretty calm, and you never seem to bounce from one thought to the next."

My eyes grow with realization. Ah, there it is. He assumes I must either be lying or take the good shit because I'm not running around the room like a crack addict. "For one, Asshat, you are showing some ignorance. I have ADD, not ADHD. Meaning, no hyperactivity here. And two, I'm an adult. I've learned to manage it without meds, using simple behavior modifications when needed."

He rubs his left eyebrow, but his gaze never leaves me. Those lush lips that say the dumbest things clamp together.

My head shakes while smiling at him in disbelief. "Kamdyn dearest, have I rendered you speechless?"

"Never." His eyes twinkle with the sheen of amusement.

"Lies." I spin in my chair to face him, throwing my feet onto his lap.

His eyes flicker back and forth from my face down to my feet resting on his strong thighs. "Whatcha doing, Clare Bear?"

I place my palm over my heart. "Why, whatever do you mean?"

His fingers dance on the skin around my ankles, and my breath hitches as the sensation throws me into a tailspin. The pad of his thumb grazes my flesh in a slow up and down motion. Kamdyn swallows, his eyes lifting from my ankles, traveling up my bare legs to my shorts, then to my chest, where my breathing increases with every second we do this. Whatever this is.

His eyes find mine. "Clara, I—"

"Ms. Doyle, Mr. Cook," Stean calls from across the room.

And just like that, Kamdyn and I snap out of whatever lust-filled spell we were under. He retracts his hands from me while I put my legs back on the ground.

Kamdyn clears his throat as Stean reaches us.

"Either of you want to tell me something?" he asks.

Kamdyn and I glance at each other, but neither of us says a word.

"Nothing? Really?"

"I'm sorry," Kamdyn says, sitting up straighter. "What is this about?"

"I want to know how the nature assignment worked out and what on earth happened to your foot."

He lets out a breath of relief. "Oh, yeah, it was memorable."

"So you two got along okay?" he asks, squinting at us.

"You could say that." Kamdyn smirks, nodding in my direction. "Clara here carried me for miles after I fell, hurting my ankle."

Stean's face beams, and he looks like he won the lottery. "Oh my goodness. You guys sure did bond then, didn't you?"

"That's not even half of it. After carrying my fat ass all the way back to the parking lot, she then drove me to the hospital and brought me home, tucking me in like the good little mommy she will be someday."

I bite down on the grin threatening to cover my face.

"Oh, Clara, that is so kind of you," Stean says, looking down at me as he hugs his clipboard into his chest. "Okay, now I hate to do this, considering the rough time you two had, but rules are rules...Did you get the pictures for proof that you completed the assignment together?"

"Yeah, we snapped a few pictures before the day went to shit," I say.

Kamdyn pulls out his phone, handing it over to Stean. I watch as he thumbs through the pictures I have yet to see. A few times, a wide grin crosses his lips, and he looks between the two of us.

"Kamdyn, email those to the class's official email, and it'll check off the list." He hands the phone back and walks away but stops, turning to face us one more time. "Oh, and I'm done with the artwork from week five's assignment. So you guys are more than welcome to grab them from behind the table when class is over."

"You can trash mine," I say to him, and he nods, walking away.

"Well, that was...interesting." Kamdyn doesn't look in my direction. He just stares ahead at Stean talking to the man with the neck tats.

We don't speak for the next ten minutes of class, choosing to forgo the assignment in exchange for silence. The two of us silently stew in the newfound awkwardness between us. Or at least I am. I don't know what Kamdyn is thinking.

Chapter Fourteen

Kamdyn

I'm not sure why I did it, but I couldn't resist, with my legs propped up on my coffee table, I stare up at the mantle above my fireplace. Beside my painting is the teal cat on the stark white canvas.

Clara's sad but somehow captivating painting was impossible to pass up. Maybe I just wanted a memento of that night together. Whatever it is, I couldn't let it get thrown away. She worked hard on this. No matter how childish or untalented she is, it's still something she created, and that should mean something.

The teal brush strokes that make up the cat are sloppy. But something about them is methodical, like even though there isn't one artistic bone in her body, she planned out her every move with this painting.

I'm being more and more ridiculous the more time I spend with her. Maybe she's rubbing off on me like a bad influence. Or maybe she's helping set me free. Free to be the person I hide from everyone else, including myself.

There's something about her that keeps her on my mind, and it's eating away at me, wondering what this means.

Am I physically attracted to her? Fuck yes. There is zero denial there. She is gorgeous. A natural beauty that I'm not used to seeing much.

Do I enjoy spending time with her? Oddly enough, I think I do. Even though she drives me batshit crazy.

I might have misjudged her. Fuck, at this point, I know I did. A bitch wouldn't have supported my sorry ass through the whole thing. She had multiple chances to get up and leave, yet she didn't take one of them.

I almost feel bad about forcing her to help me with June's shopping. She took care of me, but that won't stop me from using our bet to my advantage. I need to explore these feelings that are confusing the fuck out of me. And if it means forcing her into getting an old woman's groceries with me, so be it.

After today, after class, I realize she needs the same thing. It was in how her body reacted to my touch. Hell, I felt it. I pick up my phone off the table and find her number.

Me: Tomorrow morning, my house at 10:00 a.m.

She responds immediately, which makes my heart leap.

Clara: I hate you.

Me: I will never believe that.

Clara: You should, because it's true.

With the world's largest grin taking over my face, I throw my phone across the couch, turning on the TV to get my weekly cheesy movie out of the way.

She's late.

It's 10:15, and Clara still hasn't shown. I run my fingers through my hair as I sit on the porch swing overlooking my yard and the street.

I texted her once, asking if she was on her way, with no response. Maybe I should call her. But it might be too pushy, and I'm trying to rein that part of me back. I want her to be comfortable with me, safe to show me who she is. And with my goddamn overbearingness, that might never happen.

A blue car pulls up to the curb. The passenger door opens, revealing white Nike sneakers belonging to none other than Clara. She pulls herself the rest of the way out of the car. My gaze travels up her body, finding her wearing a pair of short—and I mean short—athletic shorts and a tank top that shows the sexy design of her sports bra.

God, she's sexy. Once I finish appreciating her body, I see the all-knowing smirk on her face as she strides closer to me. She doesn't bother with pleasantries or any of the other bullshit. She just sits on the swing beside me. Her leg brushes mine as we sit, and I have to hold back my need to place my hand on her thigh or around her shoulder.

So instead, I do nothing, drawing my mouth into a straight line as I stare ahead, not looking at her. "You're late."

"Barely," she replies, and I don't need to see her to know she rolled those eyes that captivate me every time I look into them.

I reach for my crutches, positioning them under my arms as I stand, gesturing for her to follow. "I'll drive this time."

Once inside the car, it takes less than five minutes before she starts prodding. "I've been meaning to ask. Do you still have a driver's license?" She quirks one of her eyebrows up as she turns in the passenger seat to face me.

"Would it upset you if I said no?"

She fumbles around with the airflow knobs in front of us. "No. I was just wondering."

I nod my head, glad she doesn't care that we're doing something illegal when we're both already in deep shit and would be fucked if pulled over.

"Would you be mad if I said I didn't either?" Her voice is low and soft like she's a little nervous about my answer.

"You don't have a license either?"

"Nope. Got suspended just like yours."

Neither of us says a thing. I drive us to the farmers' market June likes, prepared to get all of her produce. Pulling the key out of the ignition, I reach for my door handle before stopping. "No," I say.

"No, what?"

"No, I'm not mad about it. Why would I be?"

"Because. I drove your car...Multiple times."

"Me too, Clare Bear. Me too. Now let's get this over with." I hand Clara the bags, setting off to find everything on June's never-ending list.

Stands fill the grounds. Booths for vegetables, fruits, honey, and other handcrafted items line up, side by side, leaving only a foot or two between them. The long gravel aisle in between was construct-ed especially for the market. A fragrance of fresh lavender wafts through the air, leaving me with a sense of solace.

Clara's eyes wander all over the place, taking in every booth. She picks up every product she can, examining it with an intensity that would make me twitchy if I were under it.

I expect her to buy something, but she just examines the product, then places it back carefully before getting a business card from the seller. Some booths seem to catch her attention a little more than others, like the booths full of soaps, lotions, and artisan-made jewelry.

I study her long enough to see that when she likes or wants something, she bites down ever so slightly on her bottom lip, contemplating what she should do. But she puts it all back. I don't know why she won't buy the damn soaps or the bracelet she wants. Either my observation skills suck, or the woman has amazing willpower.

She continues like this throughout the entire trip. It doesn't take long, though, for the apples, zucchini, squash, and more to fill the bags weighing down Clara's arms. I can see the strain of it ticking away at her. But she keeps her mouth shut, never once uttering an ounce of negativity. There's no way I would have been able to do this with crutches.

"So...these are all for you?" She stares at the bags and bags full of veggies and other homemade products, placing them into the trunk of my car.

I pull my eyebrows together. "Are you crazy? None of this shit is for me."

She throws her hands up in the air with a growl. The scowl on her face would have made me want to turn around and leave her ass where she stands a few weeks ago, but now I think she's kind of cute when she gets frustrated. She crinkles her nose, and I can't help but want to touch her. "Then why are we doing this shit?"

"Don't be like that, Clare Bear. It's for my elderly neighbor, June. I do this for her every week."

Her face softens—not much, but enough to tell me that she approves of my answer. Not that she's going to tell me that, though. "Whatever. What else is on the list?"

"That's the spirit."

The trip to the beauty store went faster than it ever has for me. Not a soul bothered me. Normally, when I come here, I'm bombarded with looks and questions. All the women want to know why I'm here, or if I'm shopping for my wife. When I tell them it's for my old lady neighbor, they practically pant with desire.

I don't mind buying this stuff, but I hate coming to these stores because of how uncomfortable all the unasked-for advice or come-ons make me.

So imagine my surprise that having Clara walking beside me was like having a huge can of bug spray. She repelled the shit out of those bloodsuckers. I still got some looks, but not a soul approached us.

The grocery store was uneventful, and I have never wanted to hug someone so badly. I need her to always come with me.

Even though the errands themselves were boring, I've never had so much fun doing them. Clara and I made a game out of everything we could. We split the grocery list in two, and the first person to get all their items would win a pizza on the loser. Then there was the guess-the cost-at-the-register game we played. *Price is Right* rules, of course.

I guess seventy-five dollars. Clara guesses seventy-four.

"Total is $74.98," the woman working the checkout line says, smiling at Clara.

"Ha," Clara shouts, jumping around in a circle with a smile that lights up her entire face.

My head rolls back with laughter as I hand the cashier my card. Clara is already halfway out the door with the groceries when the cashier hands me back my card and receipt.

She grins at me. "You two are a lovely couple." Her words radiate warmth through my body, and I give her a quick smile as the statement sinks in. It feels right.

We stop through a drive-through on our way back to the house, opting for burgers, fries, and milkshakes to reward ourselves. Aside from the few fries Clara sneaks out of the bag, we decide to wait to eat until after we bring in June's groceries.

We walk up the floral-covered sidewalk to June's front door. I stop, turning back to Clara, who slams right into my chest.

"Fuck!" She drops the bags she was carrying. Her now free hands fly to her nose, her eyes watering from the impact.

"Shit, Clara. I am so sorry. Let me see." She shakes her head, jerking away from me. My hands tighten around her wrists, pulling her hands away with more force than I was hoping to use. But it helps me get a better look.

I let out a sigh of relief. "No blood or swelling."

"Still hurts." She wipes away a newly shed tear.

I lean in closer so there are only mere inches between us. "Want me to kiss it and make it better?"

Clara does the last thing I expect at the moment; she nods her head up and down, still trying to stop the tears on the verge of spilling.

I take a deep breath, leaning down as I wrap my arms around her, pulling her into my body. She looks up at me, waiting. I bend, slowly bringing my mouth closer to her face. When my lips reach her nose, I feel her shiver in my arms. I inhale her scent, still floral, still intoxicating.

I break the embrace, feeling like I want to kiss her again. Not on her nose after injuring her by accident. I want to kiss her like I'll never have another chance, and at this moment, I think she wants the same thing.

"All better?"

She looks up at me before shoving me away, knocking my crutches from under my arm. "No, that made it hurt more. Horrible thinking there, Asshat."

I run my fingers through my hair as a chuckle rumbles through me. Clara picks up my crutches with a sigh, thrusting them into my arms before gathering the bags she dropped. "Kamdyn, was there a reason you stopped walking, or do you enjoy maiming me?"

"Oh yeah, I just wanted to warn you about June. She's a lot."

"What do you mean?"

"Oh, you'll see," I say, knocking on the front door before opening it up. "June, I'm back."

A loud thud echoes from the back of the house, followed by another thud.

My heart races, and I move toward the sound; Clara's right behind me, staying silent. Afraid I'm about to find June half dead, I reach for the handle to her bedroom, a whimper coming through the door. With a push, I open the door, only to find June nude, twisted up with an elderly gentleman behind her, grunting as he wipes sweat from his brow.

"June!" I cover my eyes with my right hand and with my left, reach to cover Clara's. "Oh my God, oh my God." I pull the door shut and hold on to Clara's hand as I drag us into the living room, fumbling with my crutches to the point that I almost slip, only to have Clara steady me with her arm.

"Oh my fucking God, Clara! Tell me we didn't just see that?" The heel of my palms rub into my eyes, trying to erase the sight.

"You mean did we just walk in on your ninety-something-year-old neighbor being dicked down?" She looks at me, eyebrows almost to her hairline, but there's something about her tone that is playful. As if any of this is funny and not traumatic. "Why yes, yes, we did."

Chapter Fifteen

Clara

Kamdyn looks like he just witnessed someone get murdered. Eyes so wide you would think it hurt. His hands rub up and down his face as he limps back and forth.

A moan comes from down the hall.

His head snaps in my direction. "Oh my God, are they still going to finish?" His voice squeaks, making it impossible for me to keep my laughter at bay any longer.

My laughter spills out to the point that I need support. I hold on to his forearm, doubling over in pain. Kamdyn stills beneath my touch, unlike the way he felt a few minutes ago when he held me in his arms, placing that one heart-stopping peck on my nose. Who knew a simple nurturing gesture could cause such a frenzy of emotions.

I try to catch my breath when I look up, discovering his cheeks are flaming red. "Is Mr. Perfect embarrassed?"

"Yes, I'm fucking embarrassed, Clara. I walked in on my elderly neighbor"—his voice lowers—"being intimate."

With a gentle squeeze of his forearm, I straighten, catching my breath. "Kamdyn, it looked like it was beyond intimate the way his—"

"No, nope. Noooo." His hands fly over his ears like a child unwilling to accept what is happening.

I throw my arms up in surrender. "I'm going to grab another load from the car. Think you can survive without me?"

"No, I'll probably die from the newly burned-in memory by the time you get back."

With a slap of my hand on his back, I say, "That's the spirit." I walk out the door, leaving him to pace back and forth. This day keeps getting better and better.

First, Kamdyn takes me to the farmers' market to carry things for him like a mule. But I end up doing much more than being his personal servant. I discovered new products and small businesses that would be amazing to feature in The Spa. Maybe with the artisan products, my boss might stop hating me so much.

Then there was the grocery store, which made me feel like a little kid again. We played games to make the time go by. Never in my wildest dreams would I have pegged Kamdyn as the type for childish shenanigans, especially in public. But he keeps surprising me, reminding me how little I know him. I only see the person he is in a class we are legally obligated to take.

I think if I had met him anywhere else, I would have been instantly into him. The more time I spend with him, the more I'm attracted to him. Which I'm unsure if it's a good or bad thing.

I mean, fuck, we met in a court-ordered Anger Management class. There could be a dark side of him I haven't seen yet. There's more to the story than he's divulging. And I'm a little scared of what that might be.

With my arms lined with yellow tote bags full of groceries, I hurry back into the house. The moment I'm through the front door, I'm met by the old woman we just saw getting her freak on.

She's short. Shorter than me, so that's saying something. Her cropped white curls are tame even with the activities she just finished. Adorned in a long blue zip-up robe with matching slippers, she gives me a wide-tooth smile.

"Well, who might you be?" she asks.

"Clara," I say, still standing in the doorway, my arms shaking under the strain of the bags. "I'm Kamdyn's unwilling accomplice for the day."

"Ah yes, where is that boy at, anyway?" She looks around before walking away, motioning me to follow. She leads me into the kitchen, pointing at the counters for me to place the bags on as she stares behind me, lips pursed. I glance over my shoulder to see Kamdyn standing behind me. His eyes locked on the ground, head shaking back and forth like a child refusing to believe the truth about Santa Claus.

"Seriously, boy? You have nothing to say to me?" June asks with a thick hum of irritation and amusement.

"Nope," he says, crossing his arms against his chest as he lifts his head, still not looking at her but at the painting of fruit on the wall behind her.

"You owe Ira and me an apology. If it weren't for Ira's new hip giving him a little extra oomph, all would have been lost from your interruption."

"Please, dear God, stop," he begs her.

"That didn't sound like an apology."

With a huff, he looks at her. "Fine. I'm sorry for interrupting your lovemaking." He cracks his knuckles, and my gaze focuses on those muscular forearms. The tattoos tracing up his left arm make me salivate a little. The hidden layer underneath the straitlaced teacher is almost too much for my horny self to bear on top of the discussion of sex.

She moves in front of him, placing her palm on his face. "Kamdyn, I think we both know what Ira was doing to me wasn't lovemaking."

He slaps her hand away and gags. "I'm going to go get the rest of the groceries."

As he's halfway to the door, June chuckles. "Try to guess if I've washed my hands yet or not."

I hear his hushed tones. "You better be fucking joking, June."

June turns to me as he leaves the room. "So you're Kamdyn's new lady?"

Lifting my hands, I shake my head. "No, no, it's not like—"

"Sure you aren't. Well, I'm just glad to see he's getting over that slut, Stephani." Her full face crinkles like she has a sour taste in her mouth. "I never liked her. My Kamdyn deserves more. Someone better than her."

I don't know what to say to that, so I pick up a bag of groceries and begin unloading it onto the counter.

"Are you that someone?" she asks.

I open my mouth to reply, to deny it. But Kamdyn hobbles in, setting down the last of the groceries from the car, and my mouth slams closed.

June gives me a wink before turning to him. "Kamdyn, be a dear and go water my plants for me."

His jaw ticks as he spins on his good foot, grumbling under his breath something about how she's more than capable of doing all this shit herself.

Once he's back out the door, she sighs, returning to placing her groceries in the proper places. "You know," she says, looking at me. "I've offered to be that someone for him multiple times. Even if it's just purely physical. But that tight ass is always turning me down."

I try to hide the smile creeping up my face. She's so serious right now, and I'm unsure if she means it or not. "Well, maybe now that he's seen all you're working with, he might reconsider."

That was the right thing to say because she barks out a loud cackle, slapping the counter. "Girl, I like you. You might just be perfect for that sweet boy. I'll tell you what, if he passes on this body again, you can have him."

With my fingers grasping my chin, I pretend to ponder her offer. "You know what, June, fuck it." My hand juts out to her. "You got yourself a goddamn deal."

She places her palm in mine just in time for Kamdyn to walk back in. He scoffs as his eyes find our clasped hands shaking. "I knew this was a bad idea. I knew it, but did I still go along with it? Yes, 'cause apparently I'm a fucking masochist."

June's eyes crinkle as her face lights up. She leans closer to me, whispering out of the side of her mouth. "He's so feisty. You think he screws with that kind of hate?"

My eyes widen as I look up at Kamdyn, his face telling me everything. He heard her comment.

He makes a throat-clearing noise to get June's attention. "Clara and I need to be heading out. I'll see you next week."

The moment we leave the house, I open my mouth, and he shakes his head. "Not yet, Clara. Wait till we're in my house."

I grab our bag of food and shakes from the car, skipping the rest of the way to meet him at his front door. Once inside, he shuts the door with his back up against it. "Okay, say what you've been holding in."

"Did you hear what she said to me?" It almost comes out as a scream, but I can't help it. I have to know.

He takes the bag from my hand and moves to the couch, throwing himself down with a loud exhale. "Which part, the part where she accused you of being with me or the part where she sexually objectified me?"

"Is there any other way to objectify someone?" I pause, glancing over at him, seeing him glaring up at me from the couch. "I mean, other than sexually?"

"She's always making comments that range from mild to slightly explicit, but now that I've seen things, it's going to X-rated." He reaches behind his back, pulling the pillow out from under his head, placing it over his face. "Smother me, Clara. Just put me out of my misery."

I brush my hand along the pillow before slapping it off his face. He squeezes his eyes shut. "Stop being dramatic. Just think of it as an inspirational story."

He opens one eye, peering up at me questioningly. "How so?"

"At least you know sex is still on the table in the golden years."

He shakes his head. "This is not how I wanted to find that out."

I move to the front of the couch, pushing his legs off the cushions as he flies up into a sitting position. Plopping down, I ignore the heat spreading through me now that we're hip to hip. Our thighs lightly brushing every once in a while. "Burger me." I hold out my hand, waiting.

We lounge together with me sitting crisscross-applesauce while Kamdyn manspreads. Our talking simmers down while we stuff our faces, eating our now cold burgers and fries with melted chocolate shakes.

I take the silence as my time to look around again, examining the place in the light of day. Everything is the same, from the books strung about to the—wait a minute, is that? On his mantle sits not only his painting from AM but mine as well.

I almost choke on my shake at the realization. But if Kamdyn notices, he doesn't let on. He took it. But why? I turn my attention to him. I want to ask about it, but I also want to let it be.

I'm keenly aware of every bite, every sip Kamdyn takes. Hell, I don't even try to hide my curiosity. I examine him so openly, and he simply allows it.

I jab my finger into his bicep. "Ow." Kamdyn grasps his arm. "Why?"

"I don't know," I say, shoving another cold fry into my mouth.

His hand rubs up and down the tattooed skin of his muscle. "You know all this abuse is going to make me question your undying love for me."

"I think you're confusing me with June."

His head flies back to rest on the back of the couch. "You couldn't give me thirty minutes? Thirty minutes without mentioning the sexual harassment I endure as the kind, attractive, smart neighbor that I am."

"I'm sorry, Asshat. If you want, I'll stop talking about it."

"Yes, please—"

"Instead, I'll talk about all the things you said while they hopped you up on pain pills last weekend."

With a quick spin in his seat, he's facing me. "What are you talking about?"

"Don't you want to hear about how you're a member of 4H? Or about how you had a certain fondness for someone's long hair?"

He widens his eyes and lifts his eyebrows. "You're lying."

"Oh, if only. Let's see, the four H's are happy, hungry, high, and...Take a guess, Kammy."

"Hopeful?"

"Ehhhhh, wrong. Try again."

"Holy?"

I roll my eyes at that one.

"Okay, what about humble? Honest? Hilarious?"

I shake my head at every word he throws out. "Honestly, are you even trying?"

"Just tell me."

"Horny...Happy, hungry, high, and horny equal the 4H's. Your words, not mine." His cheeks flush, and my smile grows even larger.

"Liar."

"Nope." I pat his thigh. "You told me while you had your fingers pulling out one of my braids." I expect him to deny it or to see his cheeks turning bright red again, but he sits there silently. His eyes lock on where my hand still rests on his upper thigh.

I pull away, but he stops me, his large hand covering mine. He turns my hand over, and my breathing quickens as his fingers trace up my palm before lacing with mine.

He's holding my hand.

Kamdyn, aka Mr. Perfect, aka Asshat, is holding my hand. And a flood of emotions drowns me. His skin on mine turns me into a raging river of want, of desire.

"Clara," he says, his voice quiet, pulling my attention away from our intertwined hands to his face.

I find him studying my face like he isn't sure if he should do this. Like he's looking for a sign of what to do next. With my free hand, I pull on his shirt, bringing him almost chest to chest with me. I lick my lips in anticipation of what's coming.

He expels a steady hiss of breath, watching my lips before closing the gap between us.

My lips touch his, and it's like a floodgate has opened.

I thought I knew what lust was, but I was wrong because this, kissing Kamdyn, is something entirely new, and my body is swimming in it.

His lips brush over mine, gently teasing before deepening the kiss, capturing my bottom lip between his sinfully soft lips. Unlacing our hands, I rake my fingers through his silky blond hair. Kamdyn moans a soft groan of pleasure, and it's all the encouragement I need.

My tongue swipes lightly at his bottom lip, and his mouth opens for me, welcoming my exploring tongue.

Rising onto my knees, I climb to straddle him, needing to feel more of his body on mine. His hands trail down my back, sending electrified shivers of promise throughout me. With my hands still tangled in his hair, I bring them to the base of his neck so my thumbs are resting on the apples of his cheeks. I cradle his face, devouring his mouth with long strokes of my tongue.

It's almost too much. It's been over a year since I've been with anyone other than my trusty vibrator, which I named Jason because if someone or something brings me that much pleasure, they need a name.

The want for him continues to grow as he takes control of the kiss. Kamdyn grips my hips with his large hands, moving me up and down in his lap. It has me hitting all the right places on his body, including the ever-growing hardness in his pants. I pull back for a moment, a shaky breath escaping from my lips. Kamdyn stills underneath me, his entire body tensing.

I look down at him. His eyes are still closed, his chest rapidly rising, but there's something unreadable in his body language. Like he's out of the moment. I lean forward, arms caging his head, and press one last tender kiss to his swollen lips before climbing off his lap back onto the cushion beside him.

He reaches his hands up to cover his face, and I'm hit with a pang in my chest. He hasn't looked at me since I left his lap. Hasn't said anything since before the kiss. He regrets this. He regrets kissing me.

It takes everything I have to not react. To not show the way I feel. I bite down on the inside of my cheeks, my teeth sinking into the scarred tissue until I taste a hint of copper. I stand up, straightening myself as I grab my things before moving to the door.

"Clara," he calls from behind me. Oh, now he has something to say. I continue moving because fuck him.

I'm halfway out the door when he wraps his hand around mine, pulling me back to him with a snap. "Don't go."

"Why not?" I look up into his eyes, demanding an answer from him. "You made it pretty clear you don't want me...here."

He scrubs a hand over the back of his neck. "Fuck. It's not like that, I swear."

I raise an eyebrow, waiting for him to elaborate.

He slips his fingers between mine. "I want you here, and God, do I want you. That isn't even a question. But I just ended a two-year relationship, and I don't want you to be a rebound."

I have to blink back my shock. Two years, Kamdyn was with someone for two years until recently. He must have loved this person if they had been together that long. My stomach aches. He must still love her.

"When did the relationship end?" I ask, gnawing on my bottom lip, awaiting his response.

He sucks in a breath. "The day I was arrested."

Chapter Sixteen

Kamdyn

"*What*," Clara shouts in my ear. "Are you telling me this chick ended your two-year relationship over one arrest?"

Her face is red with built-up anger, but it's not directed toward me anymore. She's mad for me. I shake my head, grasping her by the shoulders. "Nope, Clare Bear. Not even close." I pull her back over to the couch while I sit on the coffee table across from her.

Clara sits there, her gaze never leaving mine as she listens to me recall the entire tale of the day that changed my life. The day my heart broke and I put my career in jeopardy. She's only the second person who knows the entire story. She now sits in the same category as Marcus. As one of the two people who I trust with the truth.

When I finish, her face has fallen, and she's picking at the black nail polish coating her fingernails. "So that's the reason you don't want to explore"—she gestures between us—"whatever this is?"

"Kind of, maybe. I'm not sure."

She nods in silence, still chewing on that lip that was on my mouth—in my mouth—mere minutes ago. Fuck, why did I have to ruin this already?

"I'm sorry, Clara. It's just bad timing."

"It's fine, Kamdyn. Really, it is." A small, closed-mouth smile forms on her lips, and it's like someone punched me in the gut. God, I'm an asshole.

No, this isn't my fault. This is all Steph's fault. She can play the villain in my story, but I refuse to take responsibility for the fallout from her decisions.

"Well, I'm going to leave," she says, heading to the door.

I want to follow her, offer to drive her home. Kiss her one last time. But I do none of those things. Instead, I watch her leave, knowing that kiss was better than I've ever had. The way she took charge was insanely sexy. It took every ounce of willpower I had not to take it farther. Because God, I wanted every part of her. I wanted to taste more than just her lips. I wanted to feel her. Fuck, I still want her.

Self-hatred and the urge to chase after her and finish what we started run through my head, rendering me useless for the rest of the day. The need to get out is driving me crazy. I move back to the couch, lie on my side, and turn on Hallmark.

The sappy story of a farm girl and a rich real estate mogul comfort me, putting me to sleep.

I try multiple times throughout the week to contact Clara. She ignores my calls. Texts are a little different. She replies to some of them, but with curt responses, which makes it crystal clear that I hurt her.

I don't blame her either. She put herself out there, and I ended up giving crazy mixed signals, then rejecting her. If I were her, I wouldn't bother with me either. But that hasn't stopped me from trying to get her to talk to me again. I'm not being fair, and I know it, but I like having Clara in my life. She makes me laugh and feel more like myself than I have in years.

I sit on a wooden bench across from the musty rec center, waiting for Clara to arrive, hoping to intercept her prior to class. I will only have a minute or two to talk to her before Stean starts his lecture on self-control and finding your inner Zen spirit animal. Mine is a koala, according to the mandatory quiz Stean had us all take. Clara got a dolphin but told everyone she got a sloth instead. I'm still not sure why she did it. But I think the dolphin fits her perfectly.

She steps out of a black SUV, wearing a light purple, long flowing dress that doesn't hug one curve on her body, yet is the sexiest thing she has ever worn. Her hair is braided into a crown on top of her head. Closing the door to the Uber, she turns, seeing me. A small smile graces those lips. And I would kill to taste them again.

I wave her over. She looks around, unsure what she should do next, but she moves toward me anyway. In front of me, her fingers fidget with her bag's strap, her gaze fixed on the concrete beneath our feet.

"What's up?" she asks.

"I just wanted to talk to you before class. Clear the air and all since we haven't talked much these past couple of days," I say, using my crutches to propel me along with her as she moves toward the gym.

"Hmmm."

"Yes, hmmm indeed," I say as she pulls open the large door, letting me through first. I lean in over her shoulder, whispering softly into her ear. "Cut the shit, Clare Bear. You're mad at me, aren't you?"

Her jaw tightens. I can tell she's feeling something, and it isn't happiness.

"I don't want to do this right now," she says in hushed tones as we take our seats in the circle just as Stean stands to speak.

"Okey dokey, gang. We've made it to week eight of your journey to managing your anger." He's in what I can only assume must be his favorite outfit. Unlike his first outfit being traditional '90s dadesque mixed with a free spirit, this one screams nature man in every which way. His navy cargo shorts and signature sandals are paired with an incredibly bright orange and pink Hawaiian shirt.

The man is in a league of his own, and I, for one, fucking love it. I wish I were as free as him. But it's ingrained in me that I look like an idiot when I'm myself, when people see my tattoos in a setting like this. My father pounded into my head that who I am cannot come out in settings like this. That I am to cover or hide any part of myself that someone else might not like or find attractive.

I know his logic—my logic—is fucked up, but that doesn't stop the thoughts or behaviors from occurring.

From the corner of my eye, I catch Clara staring at me. Her pale-blue eyes peer at me. Normally when I catch her studying me, I overlook it. But ever since last weekend, I feel like we're past pretending. The sight of the crinkle around her eyes as they roam makes me wish I could be inside her head.

"Stop it," she mouths at me.

I curl my lips into a smile as I shake my head, mouthing a big "No."

"Fuck off." She turns back to Stean for a moment before glancing back at me, giving me the worst of what I can only assume is a wink. She closed her left eye tightly while her entire face scrunched up. All the while, her right eye was only partially open.

A loud laugh escapes from me, and at this moment, I don't care where I am. I couldn't control this even if I wanted to. Clara is doing better at controlling her laughter than me. She slumps forward, face buried in her legs, her whole body shaking with laughter.

"Mr. Cook, Ms. Doyle, is there something funny you would like to share with the rest of us?" Stean's hands are on his hips, his face stern. He's giving us the classic annoyed teacher look. We're being teachered.

Clara's back straightens, and she chokes back another laugh. "No, sir." The smile that continues to peek through her facade threatens the serious face she's trying to maintain.

"That's what I thought." He turns to face the other half of the room. "Like I was saying, this week's lesson is identifying hot buttons. This will require you to keep an anger log this week. Every time something makes your anger boil to the surface, log it. Date, time, incident, and feelings. I want it all written."

While Stean drones on and on about the logs and learning about ourselves, I find myself becoming more and more invested in Clara. The smooth curve of her neck, with wisps of black hair curled around the nape. God, does she even know how fucking amazing she looks right now?

I trail my eyes down her body to the flowing ruffles at the end of her dress. How did I not see it before? I always considered her attractive, but everything seems amplified ever since that night at the bar together. Like I was in a dark room, and she was a light that turned on so I could see.

Before I have time to react, Clara's fist is flying toward my arm. An ache forms upon impact. I bite down my pain, not wanting Stean's wrath again. "Why?" I mouth to her, holding my arm.

"You were objectifying me," she says quietly before adding out of the side of her mouth, "Sexually."

With a slight lean to my right, I'm close enough to whisper in her ear, "So what if I was?"

A blush rises from her chest to her cheeks. The crimson color on her soft pale skin is like fireworks in the night sky on the Fourth of July. The sight is overwhelming and beautiful. Breathtaking.

She tries to mask whatever she's feeling by stilling her facial expressions, turning once again to Stean and the lecture on how to write in a log. The extreme detail he puts into this is insane.

Does he honestly think people don't understand how to fill out a paper with spots titled with what information to put in it?

Either he thinks this class is full of dumbasses—which is fair—or he has somehow had issues with this assignment in prior classes.

Or fuck, maybe it's both.

Once Stean finishes lecturing everyone on the proper way to fill in blanks, he dismisses the class. His face falls with relief as everyone piles out, not stopping with further questions.

Clara stands, smoothing down her dress as she picks up her bag. I fold up my chair, grabbing hers to put away as well.

She reaches out, grabbing my wrist. "What the hell do you think you're doing, Asshat?"

I glance around. "Trying to be a chivalrous gentleman?"

Her stare bores into me as she wretches both chairs out of my hands. "Trying to be chivalrous," she mocks me like we're children.

"You're still on crutches. Are you trying to make sure that ankle never heals?" She takes the chairs across the room, sliding them into the holder.

We walk together to the parking lot, side by side. Her hand brushes mine every few steps, and it takes everything in me to not react to her touch. How can something so innocent have my mind reeling with fantasies of her?

"Do you think he goes home and writes about his students in an anger log?" She stops in front of my car, looking up at me with genuine curiosity.

"1,000 percent yes. I bet he even has a burn book dedicated to us," I say, placing my crutches in the trunk.

Clara just stands there, phone in hand. She turns toward the bench near the sidewalk. "Okay, well, I'm just going to wait for my ride. Talk to you later, Asshat."

"Clare Bear, wait." Lucky for me, she does. Because trying to catch up with her would have been a bit of a bitch in every fucking way. She could easily get away from me if she wanted, but she didn't.

She turns back to me, a shy, unsure smile on her face. "Yes?"

"Let me take you home?"

Eyes widening, she shakes her head back and forth. "No, it's fine. I'm going to call an Uber."

"Clara." I stare down at her, narrowing my gaze so she understands this isn't up for debate.

"Asshat."

"Can I take you home, please?"

She inhales before moving to the passenger door, not bothering to say another word as she climbs in.

"Thank you," I tell her as I pull onto the road. She puts her address into my car's navigation system.

Ten minutes.

I have her for another ten minutes before she slips away again.

She's picking at her fingernails again, something I've noticed she does a lot when she's around me.

I'm not sure why, but the thought that I make Clara nervous has my chest warming. It also makes me want to pull my hair out with how annoying it is.

Half out of irritation, half out of the need to touch her, I reach over the console, placing my hand on hers to still it. Her fingers twitch beneath mine as I turn her palm over, lacing our fingers. A small smile forms on Clara's lips as she turns to face the window.

I bring our joined hands into the middle, resting them on the cool leather of the console. My thumb rubs small circles into her skin.

Neither of us acknowledges any part of it for the rest of the drive. We just let the moment happen. Live in it. Soak up every last bit of pleasure from the contact.

When I pull up to her apartment building, she turns, still not breaking our connection, but this time, staring down at it. Her breathing shallows with every passing moment. She crinkles her forehead, and her lips form a tight line. "Why are you doing this?"

"I thought we established that I like you," I say in a joking tone.

She tries to pull away, but I tighten my grip on her hand, not willing to let her go just yet.

"No, we established you wanted to fuck someone to get over your ex, and that someone isn't me." Her voice is full of malice and hurt.

Fuck. That's what she assumes. That's how I made her feel the other night. Closing my eyes, I take a deep breath before opening them. "That isn't what I meant, Clara. Not at all."

She yanks her hand away. This time I let her. She crosses her arms over her chest and looks back toward the window. "Well, that sure as shit is how it sounded."

"I didn't mean it like that. I don't want to screw around." Her head snaps in my direction. I am not explaining this well. "Not that I don't want to screw you. 'Cause, God, do I ever. I just didn't want you to feel like a rebound 'cause you aren't. You're something else."

She rolls her eyes, reaching for the door handle. "Whatever, Kamdyn." I quickly lock the doors, preventing her from leaving.

"Clara, please give me another chance. You're all I've thought about since that kiss. Fuck, if I'm honest, you're all I've thought about for weeks. Please."

She groans, rolling her head back to peer at me. "Fine."

"Fine?"

"Yeah, fine," she deadpans.

My face lifts with the biggest grin as I lean over the console, brushing a fly away behind her ear. Her eyes meet mine, and it's like she's burning with the same intense feelings I am. I press a light kiss on her lips, feeling her smile against me as I pull her closer and take her lips between mine.

It's like a rush of heat and electricity, and I fucking love it. She pulls away, breathing heavily, and I'm hit with the sweet aroma of roses from her hair mixed with the minty scent of her breath.

Her hands find my jaw, fingertips tracing every curve as her lips touch mine. The kiss is tender and yet full of force. It leaves me breathless.

"Okay, I'm going to go," she says, hands still cupping my face.

"Hmm-hmm," I say, bringing her mouth back to mine. She gasps, and my tongue flicks her lips before caressing her tongue.

She laughs into my mouth, pushing me away from her. "I'm leaving now."

I throw my hands up, surrendering. She looks back one more time before opening the door. Lips swollen and skin flushed, she makes my heart speed up again. "Hey, Clara, want to go somewhere with me tomorrow?"

She nods. "Yeah." Walking away, she glances over her shoulder, giving me a small wave before disappearing into her apartment building.

The drive back to my house from Clara's apartment is the quickest drive of my life. She captivated me with her lips. My mind went into autopilot. Somehow, even with my brain focused on seeing her again tomorrow, I make it to my house with no problems.

Once inside the house, I need to talk to Marcus. I need his input, his advice on the whole Clara thing.

Ring. Ring.

"Hey, Kam, what's up?" Marcus asks.

"I am so fucked," I say, lying back on my bed.

"What happened?" There's a rustling of sheets in the background.

"Are you in bed?"

"Maybe," he says, the cadence in his voice telling me he wasn't sleeping.

"Ugh, tell the Mrs. I say hi."

"Will do. Now, what the fuck did you call for?"

"I asked Clara out. Well, kind of."

"'Bout fucking time. Wait, what do you mean, kind of?" he asks.

"Well, we were in my car."

"Go on."

"She was about to get out of the car, and I asked her if she wanted to go somewhere with me tomorrow."

"Did she say no? Are you confused about all the mixed signals you two keep sending each other?"

"Fuck off. She said yes. And I would say the signals are very clear now."

"So you guys are fucking?" He snickers into the phone, and I hear a loud thwack. "Ow, damn, babe. I'm allowed to ask my BFF these questions."

"Awe, Marcus, we're still BFFs even though you broke our pact to be golden bros together?"

"It can still happen," he whispers. "We just have to hold out for you know who to die, and then our plans will be back on."

In the background, there's a slap, followed by Marcus's pleas for it to stop.

I laugh at the sweet sound of Marcus getting his ass handed to him by Tay. "Okay, okay. First, I will hold you to that. And no, Clara and I aren't there yet. But fuck, the kissing is—" I groan into the phone.

"I don't see what the issue is?"

"The issue is I just broke up with Steph, and I really, really like Clara."

"Fuck Steph, she doesn't deserve a second thought from you. But Clara—Clara is perfect for you. She pisses you off, and you infuriate her."

"I'm not seeing your point here."

"The point is, she helps pull that stick out of your ass that's been there since college."

That gets another laugh from me. Marcus is right. Ever since my dad died, I've been living like I still have to uphold the unrealistic standards he set for me.

I sigh, putting an arm behind my head. "You're right."

"Like always." He snorts.

"Okay, okay. I'll let you go back to doing whatever weird, gross things you and your wife do when the child is asleep."

"Sleep. We sleep, dumbass." He chuckles into the line. "God, I hope Clara eats you alive."

"Whatever, man. Love you."

"Love you too," he says, hanging up the phone.

I stay up for another few hours, thinking of Clara. Wondering what she's doing, what she might think of where I'm taking her, what we're going to be doing. But mostly imagining her lips on mine, the sweetness of her tongue in my mouth.

When I'm around the woman, it's like I never know what will happen next. She fills every moment with anticipation and excitement for the next.

I text Clara in the morning, telling her to be ready for me to pick her up around 10:00 a.m. and to wear something like she wore last weekend. She responds with, "Don't tell me what to do." Followed by a winky face GIF.

I'm officially allowed to be off the crutches tomorrow, but I figure one day early won't kill me. I stop at the mirror in my laundry room.

Examining myself, I can't fight the smirk, guessing how Clara will react. In the past, I've pretended not to notice the subtle rise of her chest when she sees my sleeve.

With Steph, I always had to hide it because her family, friends, and career were judgmental as fuck. And I did it, for her, I did it. That was the thing about Steph. She had me hide parts of myself, just like my dad did. It was a complacent form of comfort.

But Clara—Clara seems to enjoy the parts of me I hide. So today, my tattoos are on full display with my usual running gear consisting of a dry-fit short-sleeved shirt, shorts, and Nikes.

Is this what women feel like putting on high heels and short black dresses? Like they know their clothing choice is going to push someone over the edge because, damn, it feels amazing.

When I pull up to the building, Clara is already waiting outside. Her face lights up as she skips my way. She pulled her long, straight black hair into a loose ponytail, sitting on her left shoulder. She's in tight leggings and a muscle crop top, and it looks like she had the same idea I had about the outfit, 'cause fuck, she's already turning me on, and we still have a whole date to get through.

I exhale a loud breath as she sits in the seat next to me. She eyes me, pulling her seat belt on. "What?"

I curl my lips into a smile as I shake my head. "Nothing. I'm just happy to see you."

Once facing the front again, she says, "Me too."

Chapter Seventeen

Clara

"You're taking me to get a dog?" I ask as we pull into Run and Rescue. The big red building has dogs painted on the tall fence surrounding it. It looks like a walking advertisement, which I guess is what they're going for.

He chuckles, hopping out of the car and walking around to open my door. "Why, do you want one?"

"Yes," I shout, my entire body vibrating for a moment, only to stop. "But I live in a small-ass apartment, so I can't. So it's just me and Sir Swims-A-Lot."

"Sir Swims-A-Lot?" he questions.

"My smug goldfish."

He shakes his head as he pulls my hand into his, hoisting me out of the car and up against him. We're so close I can breathe in every scent of him. The minty toothpaste lingering on his breath and the thick richness of his cologne. The manly scent of woods mixed with something sweet. Kamdyn's tongue peeks out of his mouth, wetting his bottom lip, and I can't fight it any longer.

I reach my fingers around the back of his neck, pulling him closer to bridge the gap between us as I place my lips on his. It's slow and tender. The type of kiss that can make you feel everything with its simple intensity.

He breaks away too quickly.

I want more. I *need* more.

"Come on." He tugs at my hands, walking backward to the building.

With a whine, I say, "Can't we just make out or something instead?"

There's a glint of mischievousness in his eyes as he mouths, "Later."

Kamdyn drags me into the cold building with an odd combination of wet dog and fresh-cut grass wafting through the air. He stops us at the front desk covered in boutique dog treats and collars. Behind it sits a small, stout woman with a dark pixie cut. She's all smiles at seeing Kamdyn.

"Kamdyn, I wasn't sure if you were going to be here this week. How's the foot?" she asks, coming around to examine him while ignoring me standing beside him, still holding his hand.

"You know me, Darla, I need Samson and Sunny time. No sprained ankle can keep me away for that long," he says, his voice laced with that annoying charm he uses on everyone. Well, everyone but me.

I untangle my fingers from his, bringing my hand up to my hair. I run my fingers through my long strands, trying to steady myself. Maybe this wasn't a great idea. He's already back to Mr. Perfect, and we haven't even been here for five minutes.

"So, Kamdyn, does that mean we'll see you again every week? You know the dogs love you." She leans closer to him, speaking lower. "And just between us, Justine broke up with that boyfriend of hers."

He glances at me while talking to Darla, the woman who is now blatantly ignoring my presence. Still being the charmer he is, he lets out a small chuckle. "Oh, well, you know I love the dogs and want the best for them. And as for Justine, that sucks. I'm sure she'll be just fine without him, though."

"You know, I think this is the first time both of you have been single at the same time," Darla says, and I've had enough, even though it's just begun.

I slide myself to Kamdyn and wrap my arms around his waist, one hand sliding up against the hard muscles hidden away underneath the silky-smooth shirt. "Kammy, I want to see the doggies," I say, fluttering my lashes up at him.

He bites back a grin. His hand finds my lower back, running slow, meticulous circles into my exposed skin, grasping my side in a quick pinch. I yelp, swatting away his arm.

He catches my wrist in the air as I attempt to hit him again and drags me outside, all while waving bye to a sneering Darla.

We laugh while walking down the sidewalk to a gate that leads to a yard full of barking dogs.

He reaches to unlatch the gate, stopping to glance over at me. "Are you ready to meet two of my best friends?"

I practically push him out of the way with excitement bubbling over. Yes, I want to see the dogs. It's been a lifetime since I've petted one or, hell, even been around one.

The backyard is a dog playground. There's an obstacle course, beautiful green grass, and a small splash pad with paw prints painted on the concrete. Only a few dogs are currently out playing. Some have people sitting with them, which makes my heart scream with joy. Maybe that means they'll find a home.

Behind Kamdyn, I wait to see which dogs he wants to see. Out of nowhere, a giant black dog runs over to us. His run is more of a jog, but it still catches me off guard. My heart contracts because he is beyond precious, and I already love him more than my left boob.

He stops in front of Kamdyn, tail wagging like crazy as Kamdyn strokes his black fur. The excitement of the big black teddy bear shows as he pushes into Kamdyn, almost knocking him over multiple times before he sits on the ground, with the dog taking his place in Kamdyn's lap.

I follow his lead, taking a seat on the ground beside them. Finally noticing me, the dog's tail wags even faster while nuzzling my outstretched palm, giving me permission to give him the love I've been dying to dole out from the moment he appeared.

"Oh my God, Kamdyn, I love him so much," I say, my eyes, hands, and heart glued to the dog in front of me.

"Clara, this is Samson. Samson, this is Clara, the one I was telling you about."

I shift my gaze from Samson to Kamdyn. "It better have been all good things. I'm trying to make a good first impression."

He takes his chin in his hand, massaging it back and forth with his thumb and finger. "Hmm, I'm not sure. Maybe you can jog my memory."

I give him a pointed look. "And how would I do that?"

His finger taps on his lips as he leans closer. "I'm sure you can figure something out."

I shake my head at his knowing smirk. He is ridiculous, and his flirting is so cheesy, but damn if it isn't working on me.

Just as I lean in, a big blob of yellow crashes into us, knocking us both onto our backs. I glance up to see a big tail swing with such force above me that if I attempted to sit up, it would smack me down so quickly and be anything but gentle.

Beside me, Kamdyn is getting the kiss he wanted, just not from me. Instead, the big dog standing over us, holding us down, is licking his face like he rubbed bacon all over it.

"Sunny, stop!" He laughs, moving his head from side to side to dodge her kisses. "Enough, Sunny."

It takes another minute of nonstop dog kisses before Kamdyn can push her back enough for us to sit up.

"Clara, this is my favorite girl, Sunny," he says, gesturing to the yellow giant beside Samson.

"Is she a Great Dane?" I ask.

"Yep." He nods, flapping her ears back and forth as she smiles at him.

"Why is she here?" I look around. "Why are either of them here?"

"People are assholes, that's why."

"I don't think I've ever seen a Great Dane in person before. She is definitely not what I expected."

"What did you expect?"

"A stoic statue of a dog, not this not-so-gentle, loving giant." I press my hands into her fur as she turns to give me the love she was just bestowing upon Kamdyn.

He just smiles at Sunny, who moves to lay her head on my outstretched legs.

"Why don't you adopt them?" I glance at the two dogs that are clearly attached to him. "You seem to love them, and they like you for some odd reason. I just don't understand."

His smile slightly falters before he turns to face me. "I want to, more than anything. But my yard is microscopic. They deserve room to run wild." He pauses. "I planned on buying a bigger house with a huge backyard and its own little creek. It needed pretty much everything redone in it, but it would have been perfect."

"Why didn't you buy it?"

"My ex, Steph. She was used to a certain level of living, and a ratty house with holes in the floor wouldn't cut it."

I blink back the rage and confusion running across my mind. "You didn't buy your dream house 'cause she's shallow?"

"Might shock you"—he shoves my shoulder—"but I was raised to always uphold a certain appearance. A picture-perfect facade. So when she reinforced that, I couldn't do it."

I reach over, covering his large hand with mine, which is childlike in comparison. "The more you share about her, the more I think she was the worst, skeevy hoe bag who probably thinks New England is in a different country."

"New England?"

"Yep, I actually got into an argument once about New England with a guy at a party. He legit thought it was its own country, and surprisingly, so did a lot of other people too."

"How old were you guys?"

"I was eighteen, and he was around twenty-six, I think. There was alcohol involved, but that doesn't change the facts. But on the other end of that, I thought Alaska was beside Hawaii until I was in middle school."

"What?" he shouts, startling all the dogs in the yard except the two rolling around on us.

"Yep, I know. How did this genius you see before you think such a thing? Well, they're always put beside each other on maps of the United States."

We both laugh. Kamdyn falls onto his back, pulling me down next to him. He rolls us so he's hovering over me, his eyes staring down at my lips, inching toward them at a painfully slow pace. It has my need for him growing wilder by the moment as my heart pounds in my chest.

As the warmth of his breath draws closer and closer to my face, I wrap my arms around his back, curling my fingers into his shirt. His lips are just about to touch mine when we're interrupted by the same person we escaped from earlier, Darla.

"Kamdyn, honey," she says, and we both jump apart as if we're two teenagers caught going at it by their mom. "Justine is here." She glances down at me, giving me a look of disdain before looking back at him. "I know she would love to see you."

I rear back a little, waiting to hear, to see his response. Will he go? Will he leave me for Justine, whoever she is?

"You know I would love to see her"—he pauses, giving me a one-sided smirk—"but Clara and I were just about to take the dogs on a walk. Maybe another time."

Her smile doesn't fade as she looks at him. In fact, it gets bigger. "Oh, well, I'm sure Clara here wouldn't mind letting you catch up with an old friend while she walks the dogs." Apparently, her determination grows right along with her smile.

I don't hold back my annoyance this time. I bark out a quick, "The fuck I wouldn't."

Both of their heads snap toward me. Darla's jaw drops, her eyes wide with shock that I actually spoke up. Kamdyn's eyes, though, are darkening with sparks of heat and arousal at my words. He likes this side of me.

As if I was just going to sit there and take it.

I stand, brushing the grass off my clothes. I turn to ask Kamdyn if I got all the grass off my butt in front of Darla's passive-aggressive face, knowing I sure as shit didn't even bother to wipe anything off my ass.

He stands, his hands finding my ass and wiping away any last remnants of the ground off me. With a squeeze, he lets me know he's done.

"You heard the lady, Darla. I'll bring them back in an hour or so." His arm drapes over my shoulder as he whispers in my ear, "That was so bitchy, but so fucking hot," before calling for Sunny and Samson to follow us. He grabs two leashes with their names on them and attaches them. We open the gate and leave Darla standing with her mouth agape.

"So...Justine?" I glance at Kamdyn to throw a ball for Sunny and Samson into the large open field at the park. The two jump and run as fast as they can to get it, trying to beat the other. I have to do continual double takes when Samson is the victor more often than not.

He raises his eyebrows, smirking. "I was wondering when you were going to ask about her."

"Is there something you want to share?" I step a little closer to him, examining how his eyes move.

He rests a hand over his heart. "Awe, Clare Bear, you're jealous!"

"Pssh, you wish, Asshat." But I am. The idea he might see another woman has an ache forming in my chest.

I try to move away when his arm snakes around my stomach, lifting me off my feet. He spins me in a circle, laughing as I squeal. When he sets me down on my feet, I try to break out of his arms, but he tightens his grip, holding my back flush against his front. His breath tickles the hairs on my neck. "Admit it, and I'll consider letting you go."

"Never," I say, deciding to take this to the next level. He doesn't want to let me go. Okay, fine. But let's see how he does when I play dirty.

My hips press deeper into him, circling back and forth. A hiss escapes his lips. Over my shoulder, I ask, "Ready to give up?"

He opens his mouth to answer, but I dig my ass back even deeper into his crotch. I can feel how my body is affecting him, and I love it. Feeling him twitch beneath me has me breathless.

It makes me think I can do anything. Conquer anything I set my mind to. It's intoxicating. *He's* intoxicating, and I cannot get enough.

My stomach flutters as he tries to hold me still with one arm wrapped across my stomach while the other travels down to grasp my hip. His feverish fingertips dance across my bare skin. He has me aware of every breath I take.

He splays his fingers across my hips, dangerously close to touching a part that hasn't received another's touch in what feels like a lifetime. I want to beg him to continue touching me. To have his way with me right here in public.

I can feel he wants to. His dick is throbbing on my ass. I continue circling my hips, only to be met with his shallow pants. He rests his head on my shoulder. "You're killing me. Is that what you want?"

"Maybe, I—"

His teeth sink into my left shoulder. I gasp as his sharp canines press into me, and it's like nothing I've ever felt before. Every muscle in my body tenses with pain, only to have all the tension released in a wave of tingles that has my clit throbbing.

Kamdyn interprets my gasp as a sign that he hurt me. His hands fall, releasing me as he spins me to face him. Eyes drifting to my shoulder, grimacing, he takes a deep breath. "Clara, I am so, so, so fucking sorry. I got carried away."

I tilt my head. "Kamdyn."

He doesn't glance in my direction. Instead, he looks away at the dogs still playing in the field. He clenches and unclenches his fists.

"Kamdyn," I say, grabbing his hands. He still won't look at me. Instead, he stares at our hands. "You didn't hurt me. Was I surprised? Yes. Very surprised."

He looks up at me, and I can't help but smile at his stupid, handsome face. "And want to know what else?" I lean in closer to him. "I liked it too."

He shoots his eyebrows up in question as the corner of his lips tug up. And I finally steal the kiss I've been waiting for. With my lips against his, we sit down on the grass. I straddle him as he pulls back, kissing and licking down my neck. I rake my fingers through his silky hair as the sun dances off the blond strands. It's almost blinding to stare at but impossible to take my eyes off.

With a light tug at his scalp, I direct his mouth back to mine. Our tongues rake over each other in unison. With every flick, I'm brought closer and closer to ripping off his clothes.

But alas, Samson and Sunny bound up to join us. Their hot breath is so close to our faces that it's like steam from a boiling pot on my skin. We break apart, and his face is flushed, lips plush and dark pink from excessive kissing.

"I think they're trying to tell us we have to stop, or we'll be arrested," he says, burying his head in my hair.

"Just for that, I say we get them a treat." I climb off his lap to stand, pulling him up with me.

We find a picnic table not too far from where the ice cream truck was parked. The truck not only served regular cold treats but also had pupsicles. Which I had zero idea was a thing until Kamdyn bought them.

Both of us give a dog a frozen treat made of rich peanut butter. Sunny and Samson go wild, ignoring us completely while we sit watching them chow down.

I turn to face Kamdyn. He's an unfamiliar sight. With his elbows propped on the table, his face is purely content. "They look like they're in doggie heaven," I say.

His smile widens. "Oh yeah, we stop at this truck about once a month, and they go crazy for Monet's stuff."

"On a first name basis with the owner, I see," I say with a suggestive wiggle of my eyebrows.

The smile on his face turns devilish, and my insides turn to mush. And not from the sun. He's trouble, and I know it. I cannot fathom how this will work out well for either of us, but for now, I don't care.

Apparently, neither does Kamdyn.

"Yes. Are you surprised I know people?"

I shrug, taking a bite out of the red, white, and blue popsicle, dripping a sticky mixture of colors all over my right hand.

Kamdyn's eyes narrow at me and my popsicle. "What?" I ask, taking another bite of the frozen goodness.

"Did—did you just bite that popsicle?"

The corners of my lips turn up as I take another bite. "Sure did."

He looks at me in utter disbelief. "Well, we had a good run."

"Oh, did we now?"

"Yeah, we did. But I'm sorry to say that right there is a deal breaker for me."

I purse my lips. "Do tell more, sir."

"As you probably don't know, I am well versed in a plethora of things like history, hair braiding, amateur stunts, clockmaking, and psychology." He takes a long lick of his ice cream cone. "That makes me practically licensed to diagnose you as a..." He looks around, leaning forward and whispering, "Psychopath."

My hands fly to my mouth in exaggerated shock as I lean back. "Oh, no. How did you find out?"

"It was the popsicle biting instead of licking. It gave you away in an instant. I hope you can understand."

I nod my head up and down. "Well, it was nice while it lasted." I slide out of the seat, turning my back to him, only for him to pull me against him.

His body is feverish from the sun's rays beating down on us. I wait with my head cocked to the side while I stare up at him.

"Clara." He brushes my ponytail off my shoulder. "Clare Bear."

"Yes?" I bite down on my bottom lip.

"There might, maybe, sort of be a slight chance I was wrong about the psycho thing. So we can still see each other." He leans in. My mouth waters with the want of his on mine again. It hasn't been long since our last kiss, but I want more.

"Until we get you tested, that is."

I reach my right hand up, shoving into his impossibly hard left shoulder. "Asshat."

He lets out a laugh mixed with a cry of pain before circling his arms around me again. Kamdyn doesn't waste any time. His lips are on me in a second, and the kiss isn't sweet. It's hard and needy. It's a promise of what is coming.

I open my mouth, and his tongue caresses mine with such skill that I'm unable to stop myself from wondering how it will feel on other parts of my body. My body shudders with the anticipation of being with him.

Ring. Ring. Ring.

For what feels like the millionth time today, we're interrupted just as things get more intense. I groan in protest as Kamdyn steps out of my embrace to answer his phone.

"Hello?" His voice is abrupt, clipped.

He runs his hands through his hair, taking a seat on top of the picnic table while listening to whoever it is on the other line.

"Can it not wait?" he asks as he gazes into my eyes, shaking his head as whoever is on the other line continues to talk. He reaches out his hand, wrapping it around my wrists as he pulls me into the space between his legs.

"Fine. I'll be there in less than thirty," he says before hanging up the phone.

"Just so you know"—his fingers run up my arms, the action pebbling my skin under his touch—"I'm going to be writing about this in my anger log."

I burst out laughing. "Oh, I already planned on writing all about this day in mine. From you refusing to tell me where we were going to that Darla lady and all the kissing being cut short."

"What will Stean say?"

"Never fear, my kissable Asshat. I plan to change your name, so he'll never know."

"What's the name?" He peers into my eyes with a grin pulling at the corners of his lips.

"Mr. Richard Hull." I bite my cheeks as I wait to see if the recognition will hit him.

"Richard Hull...Rich Hull." He says the name back and forth. "Rich Hu—*Dick* Hull! Dick hole? Seriously?" He laughs, resting his shaking body on me.

"Pretty good, huh? He'll never guess it's you."

"You are ridiculous." He hops off the table, calling the dogs over before extending his hand for mine. With a loud sigh, he says, "That was Darla on the phone. She said the dogs had to be back within the hour so Justine could groom them."

I fight the festering urge to say something snarky—well, something excessively snarky—about the woman I know nothing about. Who could be as innocent and embarrassed in all this as Kamdyn is.

"Oh, anything for Justine." I place my palm in his, erasing any signs of jealousy that might have been trying to surface.

We walk hand in hand to the car, where he opens my door after placing the dogs in the back seat. I know we have one more stop before the date ends. Or maybe I can convince him to come inside my apartment with zero innocent intentions.

Chapter Eighteen

Kamdyn

When we pull back up to Run and Rescue, Sunny is resting her head between us on the console, switching back and forth between licking Clara's arm or mine.

The entire drive, I tried to pay attention to the road but couldn't focus with Clara giggling at Sunny's tongue and nose tickling her. Her giggle was like lying down on your bed after a long day. My whole body unwound with ease at her melodic sound.

Before we can open our doors, Darla rushes out of the building with a look of glee. The look disappears when she sees Clara on the other side of the car.

"You're back." She stops about five feet from me. "The both of you."

"Would you look at that," Clara says, looking around before staring at Darla. "I think we are. Both of us."

I close my eyes, counting to ten, because I cannot react. If I side with Clara, I might lose Samson and Sunny. If I side with Darla, it will be a shit show of massive proportions with Clara. Either way, I'm fucked. So I do the best thing I can for myself. I ignore it all.

Darla's face contorts, and I can almost feel the hatred radiating off her. "Kamdyn, will you be a dear and take the dogs back to Justine? She's in the grooming station."

"Sure thing, Darla." Both Clara and I walk toward the building, each with a leash in our hands before Darla stops us.

She holds up her palm in the universal "stop" position. "Wait!" She plasters on an over-the-top grin, her voice turning sweet. "Kamdyn, only you can go back. Your friend here will have to wait outside."

Clara raises an eyebrow. I can tell she's fighting the urge to laugh at the bullshit Darla is trying to pull on us right now.

"Why not?" I ask.

"Only official volunteers are allowed in the back." She bobs her head up and down as she gives Clara a pouty frown. "I'm sorry, sugar."

Clara's eyes tilt up at me as she hands me the leash with one hand and opens the other, demanding my car keys. I can tell she's trying her best not to show any reaction to Darla. But it's clear as day to me that she's pissed. The way those light eyes darkened when she peered up at me said it all.

I place the keys in her hand, catching her off guard when I steal a kiss at the same time. Her cheeks flush a deep red. "I won't be long," I call back at her as the dogs lead me into the building.

Once inside, Darla breaks her silence. "How long have you been seeing that one?" she asks.

"Not very long. It's still pretty new."

The tight worry lines on her forehead smooth away, and I realize that was just what she wanted to hear.

We turn the corner to the grooming stations to find Justine bending over, scrubbing shampoo into a dog's fur in nothing but microscopic shorts and a bikini top, soaking wet. I inhale sharply, which Darla misinterprets as a good sign. Nudging me with her elbow, she gestures at her barely dressed daughter. Her barely dressed and very young daughter.

Samson barks, pulling Justine's attention from the dog she's grooming to us in the doorway. She smiles, then looks down, fluttering her lashes up at me.

Dear Lord, this is a fucking setup.

I give her a polite smile. "Hey, Justine, where do you want these two?"

She points to the open stall next to her. "There will be fine."

I bring the dogs over, telling them to stay as I leave, when she says, "Oh, Kamdyn, would you mind helping?" The shampoo bottle slips from her hands. She leans forward to pick it back up, her tiny bikini on full display in front of me.

It's quite the show. A show I never wanted to watch in the first place and never will again.

"Can't," I say, using my thumb to point over my shoulder at the door. "My date is in the car waiting for me."

Her smile falls, and she looks over my shoulder at her mom with wide, panicked eyes. "Date?"

"Yeah, sorry, though." I wave, slipping past Darla to leave.

Once I get to the front door, I sprint. Clara has made herself right at home in the driver's seat, so I rush around to jump into the passenger seat.

Panting, I tell her, "Go, go, go!"

She looks at me like I've lost my goddamn mind but still puts the car into drive, pulling away so I can finally relax.

"You'll never believe what just fucking happened in there." I scrub my hand down my face.

"Oh, I bet I can," she says, her voice tight. "Justine."

"She was practically naked, dripping wet, and dropping stuff so she could bend over." My whole body shudders with the picture in my mind.

"Don't men like that sort of thing?" She's acting like it's no big deal, but the bouncing of her left leg and the fact she hasn't taken her eyes off the road tell me otherwise.

"Not when the person is twenty, and I could have been their teacher just two years ago."

Her jaw drops. "No fucking way. Twenty?"

I nod. "Mm-hmm."

"And her mother wants her barely adult daughter with someone in their thirties?"

"Yep," I say, throwing my hands up in the air.

"Ew."

"The worst part is she's been trying since she graduated from *high school*" I gag. "But this was the first time Justine ever showed any kind of interest."

"I mean, I get the girl's point of view." She waves her hand to gesture up and down my body. "Damn, do I get it. But the mom's is just gross."

"Awe, you think I'm attractive," I say, pressing a kiss on her cheek.

"Shut up. No I don't."

"Admit it. Or be prepared to face the consequences."

She quirks up, a sly smile spreading over her lips. "What kind of consequences?"

I hadn't meant for the comment to be anything but innocent and playful, but with that expression on her face, my mind goes straight into the gutter. All I can think about is her mouth, that tight, toned body, and the things I want to do to it.

"Admit that you find me attractive, or I cut off your premium access to these lips, attached to this bod."

Her head shakes with laughter, and my dick twitches in my shorts. Fuck, do I want her. Every part of her is turning me on. It's like she flipped a switch in me I didn't even know was turned off.

I want to ask her to come to my place. I want to ask her to stay with me. I want more time. Hell, I just want her. But it's too soon for that. Too soon in whatever we're doing. Too soon after my breakup with Steph. But that doesn't stop me from feeling this way.

"Okay, no kissing, no access to your bod. It's the law—and I know you cannot afford to get into any more trouble," she says, pulling the car over to a parking spot in front of her building. A dull ache forms in my stomach. I didn't realize we were getting so close.

With a deep sigh, I stare out the window. "It always seems to come down to this, the law versus my best interest, doesn't it?"

Placing the car in park, Clara turns in her seat, pulling her knee up to rest her chin on it. "I hate you for today."

My stomach drops. Did our run-in with Darla and Justine screw everything up? "What?"

"You made me fall in love with those dogs, and I can't do anything about it."

With a breath of relief, I say, "Sorry, not sorry, Clare Bear."

"I'll cry myself to sleep because of it."

"You'll be okay." I pat her on the top of her head.

"Nope," she says, shaking her head. "I think I'll probably die of a broken heart tonight."

I unbuckle my seat belt and pull her over the middle console to straddle my lap. I tangle my hands up in her long obsidian locks as I bring her mouth down to mine.

The soft touch of her lips has me begging for more. My hand travels down her back until I find her hips, moving her against me while our mouths collide in a rushed frenzy.

Her hands grasp the seat behind me as she finds her rhythm on top of me. Clara moans into my mouth as my tongue caresses hers, causing my hips to buck involuntarily. The heat radiating off the space between her legs, combined with the continual rolling of her hips onto my lap has my dick swelling.

My mouth moves from hers, trailing kisses down her neck and throat. Her wicked smile grows wider as her hand travels farther and farther down my body. Her touch on my chest, stomach, and going lower has my breathing growing heavy. She knows what she's doing to me, and she loves it.

She dips her hand into the waistband of my shorts, and I have never wanted anything more in my life than to have her touch me. But the honking of cars around us pulls me out of my lust-filled bubble.

We're in front of an apartment building, going at it in broad daylight. I grab her wrist, stopping it from going any farther.

I groan, laying my head back on the seat. "We need to stop."

"Why?" She leans back to peer at me. Her previously flirty smile is gone, replaced by a frown that is so over the top, yet so real.

I can't help but laugh a little. She reminds me of a little kid being told they can't have any more cake. "Clara, we're parked on the street. It's the middle of the day, and neither of us can afford to get into trouble."

"Ugh!" Her head falls to my shoulders as I wrap my arms around her back, needing her physical contact against me. "I should probably go before I try to invite you up."

I close my eyes and nod. I can't look at her, or I might beg her to do just that.

She reaches for the handle, opening the door as she climbs off me to stand. I take a deep breath before stepping out of the car to walk her to her door, hoping my hard-on isn't as obvious as it is to me.

The walk to her building door is quiet as we both try to dampen our raging hormones and nerves. I don't try walking her to her actual apartment because we both know where that will lead us. So I settle for a quick, chaste kiss, leaving before either of us has the chance to do something we might regret.

Ever since Saturday, I have been in constant contact with Clara. We text every moment, yet I still want to talk to her more. I've learned more about her these past few days from texting and video chatting than in eight weeks of class. Like, Clara only likes red single pieces of candy and refuses anything else. I also learned that she has a twin sister, Chloe, and once, while playing DD for her sister, she threw said sister's phone out the window of the moving vehicle. The next day, she told Chloe that in a drunken fit, she threw her phone out the window. That was eight years ago, and she still refuses to tell the truth.

I learned Clara likes energy drinks over coffee and thinks they're a gift from God. That she sees a lot of genitals on the daily from her waxing appointments, but it doesn't even faze her anymore.

Mostly, I've learned that I really like her. She's funny as shit and makes me laugh every time I talk to her. I don't remember the last time someone made me feel like this. Did Steph make me laugh and loosen up ever? Or was it always a show? Always best face out there? Either way, it makes this thing with Clara so much more than expected.

She laughed when I told her my favorite movie was *Toy Story* and about how Marcus and I wrote poetry together for our high school girlfriends. She wanted—actually begged—me to dig up an old poem and recite it to her. I told her I didn't have them anymore, but that's a damn lie. I buried them in an old shoebox in my closet with other old memories.

She flirts with me, and it's like I'm thirteen again. My brain goes to mush while my body goes into hyperdrive. She has taken over my mind, consuming me. All I want is to see her again. I imagine fucking her, learning her body and if she likes it slow and tender or hard and fast.

My money is on rough. If the way she has taken charge in our make-out sessions is any indicator, it will be nothing less than mind-blowing sex.

When Wednesday rolls around, I join Marcus and Tay for dinner at their house with my sweet goddaughter. I park my car behind Tay's giant SUV, which she and Marcus claimed they needed for more room for a child...Their one, single child. Who is an infant...

The moment I step out of my car, I'm greeted by Marcus wrapping his arms around me. I wrap my arms around his back with a quick pat, then we release. "I missed you, man," he says as we head up the porch and into the foyer. My stomach rumbles with anticipation of whatever is on the menu tonight as garlic wafts through the air.

"You know you don't have to miss me if you would just give that whole brother-husbands idea a chance," I say as we head into the kitchen, where Tay pulls a lasagna out of the oven. The knowing grin tells me she heard my comment.

"Still haven't convinced him that a throuple is the way to go, huh?" she asks, putting the steaming dish down to give me a quick hug and kiss on the cheek.

"Nope." I shake my head. "Some people are just so closed-minded."

"Hey," Marcus whines, rolling his eyes while placing the salad and bread on the table. "I'm not closed-minded."

"Bullshit." I laugh. "You won't eat turkey unless it's on Thanksgiving, because it's 'just not right.'"

"Oh, don't forget how he can't wear Adidas slides anywhere but in a public shower because that's what they were labeled as," Tay adds.

"Why can't you two hate each other, like everyone else's best friend and spouse?"

Tay and I laugh off his irritation because, deep down, he loves all the taunts and our friendship. Honestly, it would've been hard if I had lost my best friend to anyone but Taylor. If he had married someone who hated me or vice versa, I would have been miserable, and so would he.

"Where is my baby?" I ask, scanning the kitchen and dining room for signs of that sweet baby girl. She is such a doll. I just want to hold her, spoiling her rotten every moment I am around. Her parents hate it, but that sweet curly-haired baby and I love it.

"Nooo." Marcus throws his hands up, blocking me from walking out of the room. "She's asleep and staying that way."

"What!"

"She has a set bedtime now, a routine," he says, still standing in front of me.

"Since when?"

"Since a month ago," he says matter-of-factly.

"But you knew I was coming to see her."

"Don't care. It's not my fault you've been preoccupied." He shimmies at me, his broad shoulders dancing to pry information out of me.

"I haven't been that busy. This summer has been full of nothing," I say because I haven't been doing shit this summer. Besides staying out of jail.

"Bullshit," he says as he grabs a beer and water out of the fridge. Handing me the water, he pops the tab off the beer bottle. "You're going to say that going to Anger Management once a week with a weekly homework assignment, getting June her groceries, walking the dogs, fucking up your ankle, and getting it on with Clara is nothing?"

"First, how far Clara and I have gotten sexually has nothing to do with me seeing you. And second, you know me so well." I touch my hands to my heart.

He chuckles, brings his beer to his lips, and then pauses. "Wait, so you and Clara haven't...?"

With a shake of my head, he sets his beer down on the counter beside him. "Why not? Is this because of fucking Steph? 'Cause I swear—"

"No, it has nothing to do with her." I cover my face with my hands, groaning. "I like her."

"I'm not understanding."

"Don't make fun of me, okay?"

"Okay," he says, waiting for my reply.

"I don't want to take anything too fast and fuck it up. But also, I kind of worry that she only likes my physical appearance."

He bursts out laughing, calling Tay over to tell her what I said. She looks at me like I'm the dumbest person on earth.

Tay's hands find her hips as she tilts her gaze up. "You can't be serious?"

"You're an asshole, you know that?" I point over her shoulder at Marcus, who's wiping the tears from under his eyes with his shirt.

Tay sighs. "Oh my God, you think someone who only likes your physical appearance would not only carry your injured ass but bring you to the hospital, then home? Would help you get your elderly neighbor's groceries? Hell, would put up with any or all of your bullshit?"

"Maybe," I say, my cheeks flushing. I feel like my mom is shaming me right now.

"Stop being stupid," she says, sitting down at the table. We join her, and they continue to berate me for the rest of the evening about how dumb I am in romance. According to them, I should've dumped Steph after six months. There were flashing neon-red flags that I somehow missed.

The more they tell me how much they hated her and all the questionable things she did, the more I see them too.

Steph was never going to be "the one." She was high maintenance, shallow, and a low-key bitch. She was the one who compelled me to cover my tattoos in public places. I was going to buy my dream house, but she stopped me. Oh, and she was a cheating whore. But I guess I was so sucked up in my feelings for her that I ignored the signs.

I was the one who did all the changing, and she didn't do any. Fuck, I think the only thing that changed about her was her nail polish color every season. At first, she was fun, exciting, and beyond attractive. And my dick was doing all the thinking in the beginning.

What none of us saw coming was the cheating. Not one sign. She never stayed crazy late at work or anything, but I know now that she didn't have to. She could screw around on me all she wanted during work, and I was none the wiser.

Shit. She was sleeping around while we were having sex...Note to self: get tested tomorrow for an array of STIs.

Chapter Nineteen

Kamdyn

"Only three more weeks, people." Stean claps before placing his hands on his hips, circling the room to make sure we're all here and giving him our undivided attention.

Only three more weeks of this shit. Then I can be free, not living in fear of a parent or colleague seeing me. If they reported me or, hell, told anyone, it would fuck me. I would be the first one canned. At least Linda would be okay. She wouldn't be pushed out the door of the place she has been at for over thirty years. That reminds me. I need to call her and find out if she has heard anything more about the situation.

Last I heard, we were all to come in at the beginning of August to sign our contracts, and that was it. I can't help the restlessness that fills my bones every Friday, the sense of paranoia that something will go wrong. At the same time, I love this place because I get to spend time with Clara.

Today Clara is wearing a pair of high-waisted denim shorts that hug her ass. My mouth waters at the delicious sight. I've always been a boob guy, but her ass is changing that. Its perky roundness was almost too hard to tear my hand away from when it was time for class.

I picked Clara up thirty minutes before we needed to be at the rec center, which was only ten minutes from her apartment. Parked underneath a shady tree, we made out like there would never be another chance.

I'm not sure how much longer my self-control can last. She's testing new limits every day with that smart mouth and sinful little body. Oh, how her body rocks against me every time we're alone.

Once again, I'm left with my balls aching for a release. Unfortunately, it'll be my hand fixing the throbbing that's becoming more difficult to ignore.

Stean continues to tell us about all the ways we can accept our anger, avoid it, and, of course, alter it. You can tell he's feeling every word he says—that he believes everything he dishes out.

"Feel it deep inside you. It will be something more than a gut emotion. Reach deeper, you guys. Reach into your soul and find that anger. Use the triple A approach once you recognize it." He sits on his rolling chair in the middle of the circle. Slowly, he spins while putting his hands to his stomach. His face flashes with emotions. "Are you going to avoid the anger? Alter it? Or are you going to accept it?"

He looks out at us as if he wants us to answer him right now. Clara shifts a little closer to me, leaning to her left. "I suggest we use the triple A method for our sizzling sexual tension."

A smirk appears on my face as she continues. "So I'm thinking we can either continue to avoid the sexual frustration and buildup that is happening, pretend nothing is happening, or that there isn't anything aching to be touched. Or option number two, we could accept it. Acknowledge that it's there and we both understand it." She pauses, biting her lip as she looks away. "Or we could go with number three; alter. We finally swerve away from frustration straight into action."

I turn in my seat, completely oblivious to the fact that Stean is still talking. I bend down to her ear, brushing her long black hair behind her ear. "I think three is the magic number." I pull away, catching her eye with mine. "Don't you?"

She opens her mouth to answer when Stean stomps over, stopping right in front of us with a frown on his face. "Can't you two ever stop with the chattering and act like the damn adults I know you are?"

My jaw drops. Did he just say damn? I turn to Clara, who seems to be just as stunned. Only she has pushed herself to the edge of the chair with wonder.

He lets out a guttural groan. "You two need to get it together because you have three weeks to prove that you have taken this course seriously." His eyes flicker back and forth with his finger as he points to us. "Think you can do that?"

We both silently nod. Clara adds an extra little flair to her agreement by dragging her fingers across her lips to zip them, then with a twist at the edge, she locks them, tossing the imaginary key behind her.

Neither of us says another word until he walks to another group. Apparently, we missed the end of the lecture and everyone splitting up. Clara's eyes widen as she points to the ground behind her with extreme fury.

I eye her, the space between my brows crinkling as I mouth, "What?"

She points again, then to her lips. My head falls to my chest. Trying not to laugh, I stand from my chair to pick up the imaginary key from behind her.

She stretches her palm out, demanding that I give it to her. I pull back, out of her reach.

The scowl she gives me makes my entire body shake with silent laughter. "What are you willing to do for it?"

She cocks her head to the side and shoots her brows up over her forehead. I nod, wondering how far she'll take this little game. She gives me a shrug, with a sly smile replacing her frown.

I take that as she's interested in whatever form of payment I might request. I hold the invisible key out, dropping it into her waiting hands.

She wastes no time. Twisting it to her lips, she unzips them, gasping for air when they open. She's over the top with the show she's putting on for me, and I love it. The playfulness she has brought back into my life is a breath of fresh air in my stale existence.

I roll my head back as waves of laughter burst through my throat. Clara slaps her hand over my mouth to silence my laughter. I part my lips slightly, nipping at her hand, and she yelps. Stean's head snaps in our direction. He is fuming. A red tint flushes against his skin, and he narrows his gaze.

Class finishes with no further outbursts from Clara or me. We sat, reading our workbooks and filling in question after question until being dismissed, along with the rest of the class.

Chapter Twenty

Clara

Kamdyn drops me off at my apartment. After some—okay, a lot—of kissing and feeling each other up, he walks me to my door, holding my hand the whole time. Outside my apartment, he kisses me so softly that my heart melts into nothing but a puddle for him and him alone.

It was a test of will to leave him at the door and not drag him through my apartment and into my bed.

But tonight wasn't about Kamdyn or my aching lady bits. Tonight is a girls' night; Lex and Stevie are going to be meeting for the first time over booze and baked goods. My stomach is in knots with nerves about my best friend and my new friend meeting. Will they like each other? What if they don't?

Ugh, they have to like each other.

I throw on my favorite jeans and slinky top before heading to the bar to meet them.

Lexa was the first to arrive. She jumps out of her seat the moment

I walk in. Arms snaking around me, squeezing and constricting as she does. "Clara! Are you ready to get your drink on?"

"What do you think?" I deadpan.

I grab a drink from the bar, and she leads me back to a corner booth with a magnificent view of the entire bar. As we slide in, she asks for details on Kamdyn and Anger Management. Quickly, I tell her about class and kissing that hot piece of ass.

Out of the corner of my eye, I catch a leggy blonde waving at me—Stevie. She sweeps across the bar floor, looking like every inch of the grown-up, sophisticated woman she is. Her blond hair is pulled into a French twist that would look ridiculous on me if I tried to wear mine that way. The tight pencil skirt and stilettos she is rocking are a mind-blowing combination.

"Sorry I'm late, loves, work was a nightmare. I didn't even have time to run home to change." She glances down at the "work attire" with a frown.

"You look hot, and you know it," I say, sipping on my cocktail.

"Thank you," Stevie beams, striding over to the bar to get a drink.

"Damn," Lexa mouths at me, her eyes glancing back toward where Stevie ran off to.

"I know, right," I tell her, bobbing my head to the music.

Once Stevie arrives back at the table with not one but three drinks, she introduces herself to Lexa, and they hit it off instantly. The three of us drink, dance, and laugh for a good hour or two before calling it quits back to my apartment.

When we get back to my place, the three of us are good and tipsy, and I'm in the mood for cookies. I climb on the counter, gathering supplies to whip up a batch of baked treats.

While I'm slaving away in the kitchen, I see and hear both Lex and

Stevie snicker on the couch. The two became fast friends under a haze of sweat and alcohol tonight and are now deep in conversation about their wonderful mutual friend who needs to get laid.

"I can hear you," I shout, whacking my cookie dough a little too hard with the rolling pin. They don't even acknowledge me; they just continue to talk about how Mr. Perfect and I are going to either have the biggest fuck fest full of orgasms, or it'll be an enormous disappointment that I try to forget about with hypnosis. They laugh and laugh at my expense while I bake them cookies from the kitchen, only chiming in when absolutely necessary.

"Hey, Clara, do you want some help?" Stevie stands, moving toward the small kitchen island I'm currently occupying.

I try to let my irritation go. "Please," I practically cry from the relief of having her in here with me.

"Fuck it," Lex says, climbing off the couch to join us. She sets us each up with a shot of tequila, along with a lime wedge and salt, demanding we take shots.

Who are we to deny her this small happiness?

After two shots each, she grabs some dough to create her own baking masterpieces, or I should say some rather inappropriate cookies.

An hour and a half later, we have two dozen cookies baked and decorated. The ones Lex made are all dicks and boobs. She is pure class, using icing and sprinkles to decorate them with pubic hair and nipples. On the other spectrum were Stevie's cookies. She made hearts and stars, each decorated with striped or circle patterns. They were classic and cute.

I made my cookies with someone special in mind. With Pinterest's assistance, I made giant yellow dog and black dog cookies. The simple sugar cookies are a mess and nowhere near good-looking, but I know he'll love them, and honestly, that's all that matters right now.

A few more shots later, the three of us are sitting together in my tiny living room, slurring our words and busting out into laughter every other minute.

"Okay," Lex's words run together in a quick semi-garbled clump. "We should take a girls' trip."

"Girls' trip?" My body bounces up, straightening at the idea. "When? Where?" I demand.

"Like I have any fucking idea," she says. "I never leave the city."

"Ooh, what about a wine tasting?" Stevie leans in with her cheeks rising high as she gives us a triumphant grin. "Drinks and drinks. What more could you want?"

"Sold!" I jump up a little too quickly because nausea sweeps over me. I sway for a moment, putting out my hands to try to re-center or balance myself before sitting back down.

"Ruh-roh. Someone drank a little too much." Lexa hiccups.

My hands grasp the couch. "I'm fine. Completely fine."

Stevie laughs. "Sure you are." Her fingers are tapping away at her phone as she bites her lip, shimmying her shoulders.

"I-I need water." But I don't get up. My head slinks down to the arm of my couch and stays there.

Hiccup.

Lexa is now lying back on a pile of throw pillows with her hands propped behind her head, humming to the tune of "ABCs" between hiccups.

"There is no moving me. The couch and I are one. We coexist." I press my face into the cushion, mumbling the words out to whoever is listening, which no one is.

Stevie stands, staring down at her phone. How is she so steady on her feet while I'm currently glued to this couch? She stops to give me a quick hug and blows Lex an air kiss before grabbing her cookies and purse and walking out the door without a single word.

I turn my head from watching her walk out back to Lexa. We both stare at each other in awe of what just happened. What did just happen?

"What the hell." Lex sits up, crossing her legs before pointing at the door to repeat herself. "What the hell?"

My shoulders try to lift, but lying face down and being this drunk makes it impossible. "Who knows?"

"That's." *Hiccup.* "Fucking weird."

"Yeah, but right now, I don't care. I only care that the room is spinning around like that ride."

"Huh?"

"You know?" I twirl my hand in the air.

"Nope, I don't. But whatever, we'll talk about all this sometime tomorrow." She stands, picking up the pillows and placing them back in their spots. "You gonna be good if I head out?"

"Go! I want to die alone." I lift my head to say goodbye.

The next morning, I'm more than a little surprised when I wake up in my bed with my pajamas on and hair pulled back into two braids. My head only aches slightly, and my stomach is rumbling without being the slightest bit queasy. I don't want to leave the coziness of my bed, but I need Motrin, water, and toast.

My feet slap against the floor as I pad through the kitchen, loving the cool hardwood floors. I gather up everything I need before lying back down in my bed for a day of nothing.

I scroll through my phone, looking at pictures from other people's Friday nights, where they are out at bars and restaurants, laughing and smiling. In the past, I would have had a major case of FOMO. I would have been jealous of the clothing, the friends, every part. But now, not so much. My boozy girls' night was more than enough.

My mind wanders to what Kamdyn was doing last night. He didn't text me after dropping me off, and I never asked him about his Friday night plans. Curiosity stirs in me as I type his name into the search bar on Instagram. The small circular picture of him is impossible to miss among the long list of impostor Kamdyn Cooks. I click on his profile, my heart speeding up when I see the most recent images he posted were from a few weeks ago.

They're from our hike. The sky and scenery are highlighted in all their beauty. There are photos of the trail, ponds, and waterfalls, but the catch in my breath has nothing to do with nature.

He posted the pictures we took. The ones we only took for proof that we completed our assignment.

In a few of them, I'm smiling at the camera with Kamdyn, some, he's looking down at me, and those are the ones affecting me more than anything. He's looking at me like the smile on his face is because of me. Even when we were fighting, he was looking at me like that. How did I not see that?

In the same post, there are a few pictures of me. There's one with my eyes closed, my face tilted up at the sky while we rested. The shot is gorgeous, and it's like a work of art. My hands tremble as I comment on the post with an emoji of a crutch, followed by a heart.

I set my phone down while turning on an old musical, trying to ignore the happiness fluttering in my heart right now.

It doesn't even take five minutes before I have an alert on my phone about a new follower, Kamdyn, along with a never-ending string of liked pictures. I shit you not. He liked every picture on my page.

The number of notifications I get is insane. Turning them off, I sit up to call him, hoping to get him to stop.

"Hey, Clare Bear," he says, his voice innocent and bright.

"Stop it," I say.

"Stop what?" he asks, and I swear I hear a hint of amusement in his tone. I can feel his smile through the phone.

"You know what."

"Whatever, you love it."

I fall back against my pillows. "Ugh! You're the worst."

His chuckle fills my ear. "What are you doing?"

"Having a lazy day, full of trashy movies."

"Come do that at my house. I have it on good authority that I will also be there."

I bite my lip as a grin takes over my face. "Very tempting."

"So you'll come over?"

The line is silent as he waits for my answer. "What time?"

A loud exhale rustles through the phone. "Whenever you want. But at least give me an hour to get pretty for you and buy snacks."

"What snacks?"

"What do you like?"

"Sweet and salty stuff," I say.

"Sour worms it is."

"Okay, well, enjoy your worms. I'll enjoy staying at home."

His deep laugh is music to my ears at this point. "No sour candy. Got it. See you soon?"

"I'll text you when I'm on my way." The moment I hang up, I make a mad dash for the shower, needing to wash away the smell of tequila that I'm sure is still radiating off me.

I take a few extra minutes to exfoliate every inch of my skin and shave all the hair from my lower body and pits, not that I'm expecting anything to happen. But just like a Girl Scout, I like to always be prepared. I'm as smooth as a baby's bottom by the time I get out.

I make quick work of drying my hair, leaving some natural waves in it. With a coat or three of mascara and my favorite least ratty lounge clothes on, I head out the door a little over an hour after talking to Kamdyn.

When my driver drops me off, I practically skip up the sidewalk to his front door. The dark-red wood against the brick exterior is beautiful and welcoming. It's exactly the type of impression I want my future front door to have—that is, if I ever get to buy a house.

My hand lifts to the doorbell. I press the button right as Kamdyn opens the door. His hair is damp as if he just showered. He's dressed in my weakness, gray sweatpants—dear God, help me—and a green shirt that looks like it feels like butter. His face lights up as he pulls me inside for a hug.

He smells of the woods and spice, and I inhale while pressing my face into his chest, letting his scent wrap around me. I look up at him, lifting onto the tips of my toes as I meet him in the middle for a quick, soft kiss.

He drags me into the living room, where he's set up a movie-day oasis. With twinkling lights and blankets creating a fort over the couch, I'm in awe.

"You did all this?" I stare up at him, my chest about to rupture from how much I feel for this man.

He nods before sitting down on the cushions. Candy, popcorn, and soda cover the coffee table in front of him.

"I think I like how you do a movie day more than my way," I say, sitting beside him.

"How do you normally do it?"

"I normally lie in bed with a snack or two and never move. Nothing anywhere near this," I say, waving my hands around.

"Is it too much?" he asks, his face serious.

"No," I say, grabbing ahold of his face as I turn on my cushion. "This is magical." I press a kiss to his lips. "I love it," I assure him, giving him another kiss.

A shy smile grows on his lips as he intertwines his fingers with mine. He lets out a small breath of relief before asking, "Wanna watch a Hallmark movie?"

CHAPTER TWENTY-ONE

Clara

We're halfway through the movie about a shy small-town baker whose first love comes back to their hometown, begging for a second chance, when Kamdyn pauses the movie. "Do you believe in second chances?" he asks, rubbing my legs that are now draped across his lap.

"I do," I say quietly. He doesn't respond, though, he just gives me a quick nod, restarting the movie.

"No, no, no," I say, grabbing the remote from his hand and pausing the TV once more. "You don't get to ask a question like that and give nothing in return."

His eyes lift. "What would you like in return?" He glides his hands farther up my legs, over my knees, and up to my thighs.

"Kamdyn," I warn him, trying to mask how much he's affecting my body right now. How much he's affecting *me*.

"Yes?" His eyes flicker with the same heat that's pooling inside my core.

"You know what I want," I say in as stern a tone as I can muster. Between the way he's looking at me and the ever-increasing height of his hand on my thighs, I'm wavering.

With one swift movement, Kamdyn slips from under my lower legs to hold himself above me. "I think I do." He lowers his head, and the warmth of his breath sends shivers coursing through me as he kisses my neck. The sensation of his lips on the sensitive curve is doing me in.

I try to come to my senses, pushing on his hard chest until he's looking down at me. "Asshat! You need to stop that."

Kamdyn's lips go from a sultry smile to a frown. "Why?"

"Because!"

"Because why?"

"Because I can't think when you touch me. And when you kiss me, it's like everything else doesn't exist—"

He slams his lips down on mine before I can finish. Breathless as he caught me off guard, I gasp for air against him. He uses that opening as his chance to bring his tongue to mine. He caresses me with such passion and skill that I never want this moment to end.

I wrap my hands around his back as I spread my legs, pulling him flush against me. As he settles between my legs, I relish in the effect I have on him as he grows harder. Just knowing he's turned on by me and my body has the wetness between my thighs soaking my panties.

I lift my legs, wrapping them around his waist, lifting my hips to rub against him. Kamdyn skims one of his hands down to my side, brushing against my stomach as he glides his way to take hold of my thigh. His fingers grip me as he grinds his erection against my center.

He breaks the kiss, moving down my jaw to kiss my neck again. The ache to have him inside me grows stronger by the second. I thread my fingers through his now dry, silky hair, giving him a quick tug as I direct his lips back to mine. I tease his lips with my tongue, swiping the tip against them before pulling back.

Kamdyn opens his eyes, looking at me. He smiles, crinkling his nose. Leaning back down, he brushes a kiss on my lips, smiling against them. I loosen my grip on his hair. I glide my hand down his back, sliding against the soft hunter-green shirt until I reach the end, dancing along the underside of his shirt. He lets out a shaky breath. It's all the encouragement I need.

I grasp the end of his shirt, lifting it higher until he pushes off me, leaning on the back of his legs to remove it. He pulls the shirt over his head, tossing it over the side of the couch and onto the floor. He moves back to me when I stop him, placing my hand on his bare chest, forcing him to sit up again. Kamdyn tilts his head to the side, not understanding what I'm saying.

"I want to look at you," I say, my hands trembling as I roam up his bare torso, admiring every muscle, every hair, every inch of him. His breath shallows with every passing moment that I make him stay there as I touch his beautiful body.

The swirls of black ink on his arm are speckled full of details, from the beautiful scripts to the architecture surrounded by flowers—every part is mesmerizing.

His broad shoulders are straight and stiff while I trail my fingers down his sculpted chest. A small amount of hair gracing it. I've never been into chest hair, but seeing it on Kamdyn has an electric jolt shooting through me, rewiring my brain to be turned on by it. The tuft of hair trails farther down, and my hands follow to his stomach, toned and tight beneath my touch.

I feel him tense, the muscles tightening as I explore him.

"Clara," he croaks, hooded eyes gazing at me with need.

"Kiss me," I demand. In an instant, Kamdyn's mouth is on mine, devouring me with sweeps of his tongue as his hands make quick work of my shirt. He grazes over my still-covered breasts as I grind my hips against him, wanting to have his hard length against me.

I reach up to remove my sports bra, attempting to wrestle myself out of it, only to become stuck. With my arms twisted, the tight fabric covers my face. I whine, "Help me."

He chuckles, picking himself up off me and untangling my arms from the bra, pulling it the rest of the way off. I lay on my back, my breasts bare as he reaches down. A mewl of pleasure slips from his lips as his gaze fixates on my pierced nipples. Warm hands palm my breasts as he brings his face to my chest. Lips brush against me, and I run my fingers through his hair, ready to guide him if I need to.

But I don't because, in moments, his tongue flicks my left nipple, and my hips buck in response.

"So beautiful," he mumbles, continuing to kiss and suck at my breasts.

God, I need him. I move my hands from holding on to his hair to dipping into his sweatpants. I take him in my hand, rubbing my thumb over his wet tip.

His breath falters when I stroke him, my palm moving up and down against the soft length.

"I want you," he pants into my skin.

"So do something about it," I say.

He lifts his head, showing his desire and anticipation. He abruptly stands while grabbing my hand, pulling me off the couch and down the hallway toward a dark room. He pushes the door open and claims my mouth again, grasping my hips as he walks me backward until the back of my knees hit the bed.

He lowers his hands and lifts me to throw me onto the covered bed. He wastes no time pulling off my sweatpants and panties, followed by his own pants. He stares down at me for a moment as the sun peeks through the small cracks in the blinds, allowing us to take in each other's bodies.

In the past, I might have been a little more self-conscious of my body. But with Kamdyn, he makes me feel confident and sexy in my skin. He's already proved that he likes me, and his body has more than shown his attraction, so why hide myself from him?

His chest moves up and down as his eyes rake across my body. He groans, biting his lip before moving on top of me. The tip of his erection presses into my belly as he kisses me. I gasp as his fingers touch the sensitive skin of my inner thigh, only an inch from where I want them.

He moves his finger up, rubbing into the slickness of my slit before pressing into me. My pussy tightens around his finger as he pumps it in and out, murmuring into my mouth, "You're so goddamn wet and tight."

He pulls his mouth from mine to look down at his hand as it thrusts inside me before removing his finger. He brings it up to his mouth, licking it.

It's the dirtiest thing, but fuck if it isn't the most sensual action. I reach down to grab his cock when he moves away from me.

"I want to touch you," I beg, reaching for him again, but he moves farther away, climbing off the bed.

Standing, he wraps his hand around my ankles and yanks me to the edge of the bed before kneeling in front of me. "You can touch me later," he says, spreading my thighs before he brings his mouth down to my throbbing clit. "Right now, I'm going to eat this tight pussy."

"Fuck," I pant as his tongue swirls around me. He licks and sucks on my clit, eating me like no one ever has before. My nipples harden, and my hips move of their own accord. "Kamdyn." His name falls from my lips like a prayer as he continues to fuck me with his sinful mouth.

It is pure torture and pleasure mixed into one as he consumes me. Warmth flows through my body as my orgasm builds. My legs shudder as he latches on to my swollen clit, sucking until ecstasy rushes through me.

My back arches off the mattress. Kamdyn moves his hand to the middle of my chest to hold me in place as my orgasm slams into me. I grasp his head, pressing him into me while I moan his name. As I come down, my body is weightless from the aftershock of pure pleasure.

"You taste just like I imagined you would. Sweet and salty, and so fucking delicious." Kamdyn climbs up my body, leaving a trail of kisses until he reaches my mouth. His tongue collides with mine, his mouth still slick with my essence, but I don't care. I want him.

I cannot get enough of him.

"Holy fucking hell, Asshat," I say, covering my face with my hands. "That was—"

"Amazing," he says as if he just had a mind-blowing orgasm, not me.

"Yeah." I nod as I sit up, ready to return the favor, but Kamdyn pushes me back down. "Kamdyn, let me return the favor."

He shakes his head, kissing my neck. "Nothing to return. That wasn't a favor, it was a necessity."

I reach down, grasping his cock with my hand. My fingers don't quite fit around it, which is a little concerning since I haven't had sex in years. But I want this. I want him.

I move my wrist up and down in circles. With a hiss through his teeth, he reaches over, digging in his nightstand before bringing back a condom. "I just want to be inside you right now."

"Yes, please."

He tears open the wrapper, sliding the condom down himself. Positioning himself above me, he settles between my spread legs, rubbing the tip of his dick over my still sensitive clit. I shudder at the contact, watching a smile drag across his lips before he aligns himself at my opening.

He inhales sharply as he pushes in slowly, allowing my muscles to stretch for him. I snap my eyes shut at the twinge of pain, and Kamdyn stops, finding my face with his hand. "What's wrong?"

I shake my head, opening my eyes. "Nothing. It's just been a while for me."

"Do you want me to—"

"No. I want this. I want you to fuck me," I say, grabbing hold of his head. I slam my lips into his as I push my hips up, taking him deeper into me.

Kamdyn pulls out slightly before pushing back in. He shuts his eyes and mutters a curse under his breath before thrusting into me.

His hips move, pushing into me repeatedly. The pressure is relentless. My body hums with anticipation of another release of exquisite ecstasy.

He holds my hand above my head, threading our fingers together as he kisses me. His heart pounds against my chest as he moans. He's close, I can tell. Releasing my hand, Kamdyn rubs my clit as he fucks me harder.

He presses his forehead into the crook of my neck, whispering words I can't fully make out. My legs shake as his fingers speed up, pushing me over the edge. I burst around him, the walls of my pussy clenching down on him as he speeds up his assault, chasing his own orgasm.

His breath rages against me as he shudders, his dick pulsing inside me. He slowly continues to pump in and out of me as he comes down. Collapsing on me, he rolls over, bringing me with him to lie on top of him. We lie there, our sweat-slick bodies pressed against each other, letting our bodies come down from the high.

"You're still inside me," I say, my cheek pressed into his chest.

He tightens his arms wrapped around me. "I know," he says. "It's my new favorite place."

I laugh, Kamdyn joining me.

CHAPTER TWENTY-TWO

Kamdyn

I must have dozed off after cleaning up from the amazing sex with Clara. Because right now, I'm being pulled out of a blissful sleep by the soft brush of lips. Clara's mouth is gentle as it caresses my throat, then my jaw, to my mouth. Every inch of me stirs awake at her touch.

"Kamdyn," she whispers against my lips.

I groan in response, my mind still groggy from sleep.

"Wake up," she says, climbing onto me. Her hips straddle mine while the buttery, smooth skin of her palms graze my face, pinning me to her delicious lips again.

My dick grows under her. I shift my hips upward so she can feel my body's natural response to her.

"Oh." She hums. Her voice is playful and seductive. "So one part of you is awake." Her hips roll against me, and I wish more than ever I hadn't put my sweatpants back on before falling asleep.

A moan escapes my lips, and I part them, claiming her mouth

with mine. My hands shoot to her hips. I recognize the soft fabric covering her as the shirt I had discarded at some point earlier in the day. Fuck, that somehow makes me want her more. I tighten my grip on her, moving her core against me again.

"Ha," she cheers triumphantly as she rolls off me and the bed. "I knew that would wake you up."

I open my eyes for the first time, glaring at her as she tilts her head at me. Her pale skin is rosy, her hair is in tangles, and I love that it's all because of me. I glance down her body, taking in the sight of her in my shirt. The way it hangs over her curves does nothing to help with the erection she just caused.

"I'm hungry."

I lick my lips, needing to feel, taste, fuck her again. "So am I."

She rolls her eyes before turning to leave the room. "For food," she calls back to me.

"Fine." With a huff, I stomp off into the kitchen. She's sitting on my kitchen counter, waiting for me with a smile on her face.

I stalk up to her, trying not to stare at her legs. Trying not to see where my T-shirt is hitting high on her thighs, close to the place I ache to be again. I stop in front of her, reaching beside her to turn on the coffee machine.

"That was mean," I tell her, watching the innocent expression on her face turn devious.

"You like it when I'm mean to you." She quirks one side of her lips up and grabs hold of my bicep, guiding me even closer to her until I'm positioned between her thighs. She wraps her arms around my neck until our faces are a few inches apart. Then she leans in, bringing her mouth as close as she can without touching me. "What are you making me to eat?"

My head falls to her shoulder. "Ugh, are you trying to kill me?"

She shrugs, biting down on her lower lip. Backing away from her temptation, I do what she asked. I make the woman something to eat.

I end up making breakfast for dinner. And by "make" I mean putting frozen waffles in the toaster, then smothering them with syrup. After stuffing our faces, we lie on the couch together, finishing our cheesy Hallmark movie before turning on *Toy Story*. We're nearing the end of the movie when Clara rolls over to place her head on my chest.

"Kamdyn, I'm not sure what today meant for you. But it meant a lot to me," she says, her head tilted to look at me. Her eyes are swimming with emotion, and I wonder if she thinks it doesn't mean the same to me.

"Clare Bear"—I smile down at her—"it meant everything."

"Good." She snuggles herself even closer to me, wrapping a leg over me. "I want to tell you what happened."

My heartbeat speeds up at what she is referring to. Her arrest, how she ended up in Anger Management with me.

Until now, she's been tight-lipped about the whole situation, which has only fed my curiosity. But I've respected her privacy, understanding why she wasn't being so forthcoming about something I'm sure she holds a lot of negative emotions about.

I don't respond to her. I just wait for her to begin.

"So, for starters, only one other person knows this story. Well, I guess technically two people know the truth, and you're about to be the third." She pauses. The reality that she trusts me sinks in.

I grab her hand, holding it in mine as she continues. "So, as you know, I'm a first-time offender, just like you, and that's why I got offered Anger Management over jail time. My charges are like yours but a little more severe. Despite that, since I'm a first-time offender, they went easier on me." Her fingers play with mine as she clears her throat. "They charged me with public intoxication and assault and battery."

My heart drops, hearing the pain in her voice as she lists out the crimes. Did she do those things? Clara doesn't seem capable of such things, especially now, sniffling in front of me as she tells me about it.

"Back before summer started, I got a call from Chloe. She said she was in trouble and needed my help. I didn't know what had happened, and I didn't care. My twin needed me, and I would do anything for her. I figured it was just financial, so I dipped into my house fund, wiring the money into her bank. I didn't find out until a few days later when checking the mail that it wasn't just money problems."

She tilts her head back up to glance at me. "I received a document with a court date and time," she says, studying my face. "Chloe and I are identical. And she's gotten into trouble in the past, so this would have been her second or third offense."

Her words hit my chest like a ton of bricks weighing down on me. My heart speeds up with the fear of what I hope she isn't going to tell me. "Since she had gotten arrested in early May after getting into a bar fight with her boyfriend's other girlfriend while plastered, she knew she wouldn't get off without doing jail time. So she said she was me, knowing my record was squeaky clean and this would only be a blemish on it."

I tighten my fingers around hers as the tears build up in her eyes, refusing to fall. An ache forms in my chest for this beautiful girl who doesn't deserve this. Nausea floods my senses to learn that her own sister would, could, do this to her. Not only that, but her identical twin did this.

"I was furious. I called her, demanding she come over to explain herself. And she did. She cried and groveled at my feet, explaining herself to me. She told me she was terrified of going to jail and that I would be okay. It hurt having her put me in this situation, but I still accepted it. I love her so much I would do anything to protect her, including going to jail for her if need be."

She takes a deep, shaky breath. "So I did it. I took the blame and punishment for her. I used the last of the money I had been saving for a down payment to cover the legal fees and fines. And I did so willingly for her. But she wasn't done screwing me over. I let her drive me to court that day. She couldn't come in with me 'cause the whole twin thing might give us away. Chloe was supposed to circle back and pick me up when I texted her that I was done. But she didn't. She didn't respond to my texts. She didn't answer any of my calls. And she hasn't since."

I'm speechless at her confession as she cries into my chest. I snake my arms around her to hold her closer to me. Trying to comfort her, even though I don't know how the fuck to help her. All I can do is say, "I'm so sorry, Clare Bear. I'm so sorry."

I hold on to her, giving her the permission she needs to be vulnerable with me until she's cried out. After everything the day has held, she falls asleep, plastered to my chest as I stroke her long hair. With a ton of awkward maneuvering, I climb out from under her to stand. Lifting her body into my arms, I carry her down the hall to my bed. I lay her down, covering her with my sheets before scooting in next to her. With a sigh of content, I curl my arms around her, plastering her back against my bare chest as I drift into sleep with her.

Chapter Twenty-Three

Clara

Saturday with Kamdyn was everything I hoped for while also being everything I didn't expect. I never expected the sex to be that good. I knew it would be the best I'd ever had, but I didn't expect it to be the kind that has me hungry and aching for more. But more than anything, I never expected to tell him about Chloe or the truth about why I'm in AM.

He makes me feel good. And I don't just mean sexually. Kamdyn makes me warm and giddy, something that comes from liking someone as much as I like him. I'm beyond the crush or infatuation stage. I care about him, and I can tell he feels the same.

He listened while I poured my deepest secret into his hands. What's more, I can trust him to protect it. He held me while I cried over the pain Chloe has caused me in so many ways.

Never once did he make me feel stupid for trusting her or taking the blame. No questions were asked, like why I would do something like this for her. He was there for me, and it meant the world to me.

The sound of birds chirping through the window wakes me up. Slivers of sunlight peek through the blinds. Kamdyn's body is wrapped around mine, caging me against him. I bring one of his hands up to my lips, pressing a small kiss onto it as a thank you for being there for me, for letting me make a fool of myself with him. He stirs behind me before settling back into a soft rhythm of peaceful breathing.

Turning in his arms, I stare at him. His strong jaw is riddled with a few days' more facial hair than I am used to seeing on him. Somehow, his disheveled state right now makes him even more handsome. My fingers dance over the tattoos on his arm. While I can, I study them without him knowing. I want to memorize every inch of him so that if this ever ends, I can recall every detail to keep me company.

He has swirls of flowers, words, numbers, and more drawn in ink, and I want—no, *need*—to know what it all means. Is there significance, or did he just like it? Would it make a difference to me either way? Fuck no, but I still want to know.

I maneuver out of his embrace, careful not to wake him as I tiptoe through the dark to the bathroom. I smell like sex and Kamdyn. I love it, but I also feel dirty. The layers of sweat on my body aren't helping that fact.

I turn on the shower, waiting for the water to warm, catching my reflection in the mirror. My hair is going in every direction, with tangles all around my neck. The skin under my eyes is dark. I look like I'm in desperate need of more sleep and less crying, but my actual eyes are shining with happiness that hasn't been there in years.

As I pull off Kamdyn's shirt, my attention catches on the finger-print bruises speckling my thighs and hips. I gently rub my fingers over them, and I can't help but smile, remembering how I got them.

The hot water on my skin wakes any part of me that was still asleep. I wash my hair with Kamdyn's shampoo, loving the idea of smelling like him.

I don't know how much time has passed since I stepped in here, but I'm having a hard time leaving the warmth. Just as I'm working up the will to leave the shower, the curtain pushes to the side. I jump, and a small scream flies from my lips as my hand clutches my chest.

Relief rushes in as Kamdyn's familiar laugh fills my ears. He steps into the shower, forcing me back until I hit the wall. His naked body is on full display, and I don't even try to stop myself from letting my eyes drift all over his gorgeous skin.

The water falls over his body as he walks through the stream, getting closer to me, his eyes darkening with lust as they rake up and down my wet body. He brushes his hand up my arm, sending shivers down to my toes.

"Good morning," he says, leaning down to plant a kiss on my lips before backing under the water again. He reaches for his shampoo and lathers it in his golden hair.

I watch as water slides down his body, curving over every muscle from his shoulders to his toes. I bite my lip as I watch him wash soap all over himself. Kamdyn freezes when he notices me staring.

"Clara," he warns. "You can't be looking at me like that."

"Why not?" My body heats from my head to my core under his gaze.

"Because when you look at me like that, all I want is to fuck you."

I suck in a breath, pushing off the wall to move under the water with him. "What's wrong with that?"

"Absolutely nothing, but I want to take you to get breakfast, and we both know if we start this, we won't end up leaving this house."

"You're such an annoying know-it-all, Asshat." I hold out my hand, waiting for him to hand over the loofah he had cleaned his chest with moments ago. He places it in my hands, and I move behind him, rubbing it all over his back, washing every inch as meticulously as I can while peppering a few kisses along his spine.

Satisfied with his cleanliness, Kamdyn turns off the water, stepping out to wrap a towel around his waist. He holds up another, waiting for me to step out. When I do, he wraps it around my body, tucking the end into the top by the side of my breasts before grabbing another towel for my hair.

A stupid grin continues to take over my face as he pushes me into the bedroom to dry off and get dressed. I throw on my sports bra from the day before and some of Kamdyn's sweats before meeting him in the living room.

His face lights up the moment he sees me, his eyes dragging down my body over his clothes. "God, you're beautiful," he says, pulling me into a hug just before slapping my ass with a loud smack.

"Kamdyn," I scream at the stinging pain, fighting his hold on me.

"Sorry, did I hurt that delicate ass? Want me to kiss it and make it better?" He raises an eyebrow at me.

I slip out of his hold, moving closer to the door. "Just for that, I'm not going to give you what I made you."

His head perks up at that. "You made me something?"

Biting the inside of my cheeks, I say, "Yep, but too bad you were mean."

He rushes over, lifting me up and planting kisses all over my face and neck, with a "Give me" in between each one.

"Fine," I shout through my laughter from his facial hair tickling me. He sets me down with a bounce of excitement.

I grab my purse and pull out the wrapped cookies, holding them out for him to take.

Kamdyn stares down at the cookies, laughing as he sees the penis and boobs that Lexa created. When his eyes reach the ones I made special for him, his face falls. My stomach drops. He hates them. He glances up at me and back down to the cookies. "You made these?"

"Just the dogs. The genitals were Lex, and the hearts were Stevie," I say, my voice almost a whisper.

He points at them. "Is that Samson and Sunny?"

I give him a closed-mouth smile with a nod. He turns back to me with an enormous, panty-dropping smile on his face. "Clare Bear, you just made my day."

"You say that now, but they might be gross."

Laughing, he grabs my hand, pulling me toward the garage. Kamdyn takes me to a brunch spot where we order a flight of mimosas to share. We drink, eat, and enjoy being with each other.

I can't help the way my stomach flips whenever he touches me. Even if it's just a graze, I lean into him for more. The desire to have his skin on mine is overwhelming, and I refuse to take it any longer.

"Can I ask you a question?" I stare at Kamdyn from the passenger seat of the car. His gaze is glued to the road, head bopping along to the music flowing through the stereo.

"Hmm?"

"Are you seeing anyone else?" I hold my breath, waiting for the answer. If he says yes, it's going to hurt like a bitch.

He furrows his brows, turning to study me. "No." His voice is questioning as he adds, "Are you?"

I shake my head with a rush of relief. "No. You're the only one."

"Good."

He says nothing else, but I can tell by the way his jaw moves that he wants to. He just continues to drive, his jaw subtly ticking while he sends almost unnoticeable glances in my direction.

"Oh, just ask," I say, throwing my hands up.

He swallows. "Do you want to see other people?"

"You really are an asshat if you believe that." I turn my body to face him. "No, I don't want to see anyone else. I like you. Only you. I like your stupid mind. And I like that dumb, smoking hot, fuckable body. Does that clear things up for you?"

The corners of his lips turn up into the largest, happiest grin I have ever seen on him. "Yes, yes, it does."

"Anything you'd like to say to me?" I blink, fluttering my lashes at him as I wait.

"Nope."

I shove his arm, and thankfully we're sitting at a stop sign because his hand pulls on the steering wheel with his moving body, and he laughs. The fucker laughs. "I take it all back. I hate your mind, and your body is less than subpar."

"Clare Bear, do you see that smoke?"

I look around, not seeing what he's talking about.

"Your pants are on fire."

"Ha. Ha. That wasn't funny. Like at all," I deadpan. I want to laugh at how idiotic his joke was, but he needs to be taken down a few pegs, and I am the person for it.

"Fine. I kind of, maybe sort of, a little, like you. And I might possibly want to make it official," he says.

"Really?" I ask, hesitant that he might be fucking with me. "No games?"

"Clara, does anything we've been doing this weekend seem like a game to you?"

"I don't know. It's all been really fun."

"So?"

"So?" I say back, wanting him to ask. I need him to say it.

"Ugh," he growls, pulling the car into the nearest parking lot before turning to me. "Clara, will you be my girlfriend?"

"Are you asking?"

"Yeah."

"You could have put a little more emotion in it. It was like you didn't want to ask, like it was just another chore."

"Damn it, woman! Fine. You want emotion, I'll give you emotion." He unbuckles me, wraps his hands around my body, and pulls me over onto his lap. He moves his hands to cup my face, forcing me to stare into those gorgeous eyes. "Clara, you are one of the most annoying and mean women I have ever met. But you are also one of the funniest and most caring people in my life. I think you are beautiful, inside and out. Please be mine, officially."

"Okay," I say, kissing him quickly, pulling away before he can deepen it. "But I have one note."

"Oh yeah?"

I bounce my head up and down. "Yep, you could mention something about this platinum vagine that you recently got acquainted with."

He brushes my hair behind my ears, leaning in closer, his breath caressing my neck lighting a fire in said vagine. "Ah yes, my mistake." He whispers in my ear, "I would love it if you would do me the honor of allowing me to lick, suck, and continue to fuck that tight pussy of yours."

My cheeks heat. That was more than I expected, so much more.

I push on his chest, moving him away so I can stare at that dirty mouth. "Are you sure you can handle me?"

His face is serious as he stares into my eyes with a sobering intensity. "Yes." That he answered with no hesitation makes my heart sing.

I bite my lip. "My pussy and I accept."

We both sit there smiling at each other. He reaches his hand behind my neck to pull me to his mouth. The kiss is full of passion but isn't desperate or fast. It's slow and breathtaking. The type of kiss that conveys emotion. It's a kiss that sums up our current feelings for each other.

Chapter Twenty-Four

Clara

The week flies by. Between trying to get my boss to try some of the local vendors I found at the farmers' market and spending almost every free moment with Kamdyn, I'm drained.

We've settled into the new couple's life fairly well, if you ask me. We still taunt each other, but now we get to kiss and make up, which may be my biggest motivation for pushing his buttons recently. I've never had so much fun with someone, especially not a boyfriend.

God, I'm still in shock that Asshat is my boyfriend. He's so fucking gorgeous it almost hurts to think about it. I constantly touch him, kiss him, wish I was fucking him. And boy, did he let me do all of those things. Kamdyn seems to want me just as much as I want him.

It's like when I had my first boyfriend, the constant longing and stomach roller-coaster sensation are in full swing. Lucky for me, as an adult, I can do sleepovers. So far this week, Kamdyn and I have spent the night together four out of six days. All at his house; he has so much more room, and I love being able to lie together while watching TV. My couch is not built for that, but Kamdyn's couch is like lying on a down pillow designed for two.

This is all new to me, being this comfortable with another human being, truly trusting my body and soul to another.

Friday rolls around before I know it, which means another day of Anger Management. Which also means an hour of pretending that I'm not totally obsessed with or dating Kamdyn. It's harder than it should be. He's sitting beside me per usual, but this time is different. This time, we have the excitement and fun of knowing we have a secret. The smirk Kamdyn keeps giving me tells me he loves it too.

The subtle hand grazes and secret looks keep me going as I listen to Stean talk himself in circles about putting all the things we've learned in this damn class together. Honestly, I don't pay any attention to what he's saying. I'm too busy daydreaming about Kamdyn and all the dirty things I plan on doing to his body tonight.

Class is dismissed. Once in the parking lot, Kamdyn bends down in front of me. I jump on him, having him give me a piggyback ride to the car. Tonight Kamdyn is taking me to his best friend Marcus's house for dinner and "fun," whatever the fuck that means, with him and his wife.

To say I'm nervous would be an understatement. My stomach rolls, and I'm afraid I might puke. This is Kamdyn's best friend. The friend he grew up with, trusts, and values. This is a big fucking deal. Yeah, we've only been officially together for a week, but this thing between us started long before the kissing came into play.

I'm picking at my nails when Kamdyn reaches for the doorknob. "Stop worrying, Clara, they're harmless."

I give him a pointed look. "Harmless? You literally told me yesterday that if Marcus didn't like someone, you tend not to like them either." I point a finger at myself. "So if he doesn't like me, it's basically donezo between us."

He grasps my shoulders as he gives me a small shake. "You. Are. An. Idiot." His hands fall from my shoulders and back onto the door. Turning the knob, he opens it. "But I still like you."

The entryway to their house is something out of a magazine. A family magazine, but a magazine, nonetheless. It's beautiful yet lived in. They lined the walls with pictures and memories of the family of three, along with other loved ones. There are baby toys and blankets placed in baskets on the bookshelf that covers the wall.

My eyes are still wandering when Marcus and his wife Taylor appear. They both wrap Kamdyn in a warm hug before introducing themselves to me as Kamdyn's future *Golden Girls'* life partner and partner's spouse.

Marcus is just as I remember him from the night at the bar. He's tall and beautiful like Kamdyn. From everything Kamdyn has told me about Marcus, the two were inseparable, growing up and as adults. They have matching tattoos—which ones, I have zero clue because Kamdyn is so tight-lipped about it. Every time I ask about his sleeve, he just smiles and says he'll tell me one day.

After introductions are complete, Taylor whisks me away for a glass of wine. The girl is after my heart. Or she's trying to get me drunk to confess all the reasons I'm wrong for Kamdyn. Even though she's beyond sweet, so far, I'm intimidated as fuck.

"So, Clara, Kamdyn told us you're an aesthetician," she says, sitting across from me on the patio with a glass of wine in one hand and a piece of pizza in the other. In the middle of the table is a citronella candle with a white baby monitor beside it.

"It's true. It's what I do," I say, unsure of what else to say to her. "I also rip hair off people's assholes and taints."

Taylor cackles. And not just a little; it sounds like a wicked witch about to find some children to sacrifice, cackle. She leans her elbows on the table, setting down her glass. "Tell me all the gross things you see. I love that shit."

I throw my head back in laughter. She caught me off guard with that. The next twenty minutes are full of me giving Taylor a play-by-play of the nastiest, most satisfying pops and extractions I have ever done.

We're to the point of tears when Kam and Marcus join us outside, bringing more wine and Monopoly. Kamdyn, of course, is drinking nothing more than water. The man is such a lightweight. I want to prepare him for my need to win with board games, but I also want to shove a win in his face and make him owe me a favor.

While he sets the board up, I set up the bet. "Hey, Asshat?"

He turns, looking at me with expectant eyes. "Yeah?"

Taylor and Marcus burst into a fit of laughter. Kamdyn and I stare at them with blank expressions. "Did you just call him 'Asshat'?" Taylor asks in between laughing and gasping for air. While Marcus asks, "And did you answer to it?"

"Yeah," Kamdyn and I say in unison.

The two of them continue to laugh hysterically at us while I turn back to Kamdyn. "Want to make this game interesting?"

"How so?" He settles down across from me.

"Let's make a wager; the winner gets a favor of their choice from the losers."

He eyes me up and down, picking up the top-hat board piece. "Deal."

Marcus and Tay excuse themselves from the bet but not from the game itself. Which is fine by me. I really only wanted to play dirty against one person. When Chloe and I were growing up, we would try to have game night weekly, but unfortunately, our competitiveness made it impossible. Any time we did, there would be accusations of cheating—usually the claim someone was embezzling in Monopoly. Were the accusations thrown at me first? Yes. Did I accuse her right back? Of fucking course I did.

But the truth of the matter is that I was always cheating. And I still cheat at board games. To this day, I will do whatever it takes to win.

We play for hours until the two parents can't stay up any longer, forcing us to declare a winner. Kamdyn and I take our sweet time counting our money, continuing the back-and-forth trash talk that has been going strong throughout the entire game.

As I count my money, I watch Kamdyn out of the corner of my eye. I find it suspicious that he has racked up so many properties. I spot him grabbing money from under the board, pulling it up into his hands as if it was there the entire time.

"Cheater!" I jump out of my chair, fingers pointing.

He throws his money down, peering at me through narrow slits. "Takes one to know one."

"Gasp!" My hand flies to my chest, still latched on to the fake money. "How dare you!"

A wicked smile forms at the corner of his mouth as he looks down my body before raising his eyes in question. My gaze travels down to where he's staring. I have money stuck to the back of my thigh.

"Fuck," I mutter as Marcus shakes his head.

"You two are perfect for each other."

"It truly is a match made in heaven," Taylor agrees with a yawn. "Now pick up the game and get out. I need sleep."

She hugs us both, and just before she heads to bed, she tells Kamdyn to give me her phone number because we're going to form an alliance against the men.

After cleaning up our mess, Kamdyn drives us back to his place for what is, fingers crossed, a night of sex and more sex.

CHAPTER TWENTY-FIVE

Kamdyn

Clara got called into work this morning. Ever since her legal problems began, she has been on the chopping block at work. Her boss has her come in whenever she demands, talks down to her, and seems to give her an overall hard time. Every repercussion she has faced because of Chloe's actions makes me hate her sister.

The shit Chloe pulled has affected every single aspect of Clara's life. I hate how hurt she is by it all. She can't even report her car stolen because then her sister would get in trouble. I'm not sure why that matters to her at this point. If I were in her shoes, I would have flipped my fucking lid and left my sister to clean up her own messes.

And I told her such. But she continues to make excuse after excuse for Chloe, saying I wouldn't understand. Or it's different when it's your sibling and even more so when it's your twin.

She admits to being livid. To wanting to find her sister and have her fix her mess. But it's all just words. She hasn't actually done anything.

Maybe we could fix this. Maybe there's a way to clear her name and her legal record of this disaster left by Chloe. Unfortunately, the only person who might have an idea is the last person I want to speak to. It's a route I'd rather not go down. But the way Clara's face fell when she got the text this morning about work makes all of it worth it.

I take a deep breath, placing the call to the last person I ever wanted to ask for help.

"Hello." I thought the sound of her voice would bring me back to all the hurt she inflicted, but it doesn't. It's just familiar, and yeah, it still pisses me off. She cheated on me instead of ending our relationship, but it doesn't hurt anymore. And honestly, it didn't hurt as much as it should have.

"Hey, Steph."

"Kamdyn, it's so good to hear your voice. I've missed it more than you can imagine."

I pinch the bridge of my nose. She would say something like that. As if she has any right to. "Okay, I'm not sure what you expect me to say to that."

"I want—I want you to forgive me. I thought after we talked that maybe…"

"Ha!" It comes out more like a bark than a laugh. "Forgive you? You're fucking joking, right? You cheated on me. *Cheated*." Anger boils up in me at her nerve.

"Please, Kammy, please." She sniffles on the other line. "I'll do anything. Just give me a chance to earn your forgiveness."

"Anything?"

"Yes! Whatever you want, babe, I'll do it," she says, a smile in her voice.

I let out a growl. "Let's get one thing straight first. Don't call me babe. You and I, Steph, we're done. And we will always be done. The only reason I called you is for some legal advice and nothing more."

"Oh...Okay." Her voice is quiet now. Silence sits in the air for a few moments. "So what's the problem you need legal expertise on?"

"It's a bit of a weird situation. My friend ended up taking the blame for charges that were actually committed by her sister. Her identical twin sister. Now she's fucked."

"Okay, I feel like I need more details on this."

For the next thirty minutes, I go into detail about Clara's situation with Steph, answering all her questions to the best of my second-hand knowledge.

"Okay, I can work off this information for now. Give me a few days."

"Okay. Thanks, Steph." I'm about to hang up when she chimes in again.

"Kamdyn?"

"Yeah?"

Her voice sounds shaky, as if she's unsure of herself. "Is this girl your—your girlfriend?"

"Does it matter?" I ask. "You asked for a way to earn forgiveness. This is it."

"I know, I just—"

"There is no *just,* Steph. Either you want forgiveness, or you don't."

"I do."

"Then stop being a shitty human being and help. It's that simple."

"Okay."

"Okay, text me when you figure some stuff out." I hang up, not wanting to bother with stupid pleasantries with her. It's pointless. She's aware of my feelings regarding her.

I would be nervous that Steph won't help out of spite for Clara, but she's at least better than that. She'll do anything to make herself look like the good guy, including helping her ex-boyfriend's new girlfriend.

Fuck, if helping is even possible. Either way, I'm going to at least try. Clara deserves someone in her corner. Especially when it seems like all she does is give.

The next few days pass without a single word from Steph, and I'm getting antsy. If she can't do anything to help, she could at least tell me.

To top it all off, Clara has been so tired from back-to-back clients, and I've been helping June out with her lawn, so we've barely gotten to speak, let alone see each other.

When Tuesday rolls around and Clara texts me that she's off early, I ditch my plans of letting June sexually harass me while I worked on her shrubs. It doesn't take ten minutes to shower off the sweat and grime from all of June's crazy tasks. For a woman living in that big house for so many years, she just now seems to have a shit ton of projects.

On my way to Clara's apartment, I stop, picking her up a chocolate shake at the fast-food place down the street she's always talking about.

With the shake hidden behind my back, I knock on the door

twice. Clara peers out the peephole, yelping while the door swings open. She wraps her arms around my neck, hugging me with more excitement than I probably deserve.

With careful precision not to spill the shake, I hug her back, savoring every part of her pressed against me. The smell of her hair wrapped up in a huge bun on top of her head makes my heart thump with pure joy.

"Hi," I say as she leans back before I pull her back to crush my lips to hers.

She breaks the kiss, licking her lips. "Hi." I can tell she wants more, and so do I, but I can't hold on to this melting shake in my hands much longer.

"I brought you something," I say as she ushers me into the modest apartment. I thrust the shake forward, and the woman's eyes and smile grow wide as she wastes no time taking it from me to enjoy a sip.

"You are the best," she says with a mouth full of shake.

I shrug. "I just wanted to make you smile." It's the little things with Clara. It might be the thing I love the most about her.

"Mission accomplished." She sets the shake on the counter before lacing her hands with mine, walking backward as she leads me into her bedroom.

Slowly, she rises onto her toes, her hands gripping the back of my neck, hauling me to her for a kiss. She proceeds with the pressure and flirtiness that I love, pulling away only to nip at my bottom lip before using her tongue to swipe over the same spot. With her mouth back on mine, her tongue moves in a melodic rhythm with mine, an unspoken promise of more to come.

Clara breaks away, moving down my body until she's on the floor.

She looks up, kneeling in front of me. Her hands travel up my thighs while her eyes scream with lust.

My breath shakes when she tugs down my shorts, freeing my now solid cock. Clara takes me in her hands, caressing me slowly before her tongue dips to swirl on the head. I hiss through my teeth as the sensation of her tongue flows through me.

Never once does she break eye contact. The pad of her tongue licks me from root to tip, but she stops to place a kiss on my crown before swallowing me in her mouth.

It's an exquisite and primal feeling she gives me. I watch as she sucks me, letting me fuck her mouth until I'm to the point that I can't restrain myself any longer.

"Fuck," I hiss through my teeth. "I'm about to come, baby."

With a pop, she pulls my cock out of her mouth. "I've never swallowed for anyone. Do you want me to swallow for you?"

"Fuck," I pant out as she licks the underside of the tip. My head falls backward as I struggle to maintain what little control I still have. "You have no idea what you're doing to me."

Her throat vibrates with a laugh. She works me with just her hands again. "Oh, I think I know." And with her horrible wink, she draws me back into her mouth.

Her pace is relentless, bringing me to the brink in moments, and I curl my fingers into her hair as she guides me deeper into the back of her throat, where I explode.

My eyes snap shut as my release comes in waves of unmeasurable pleasure, and it's all because of her.

I open my eyes to peer down at her while I pull out of her mouth. Her eyes are watering, but she's all smiles as I kneel on the ground beside her. "You good?" I ask, wiping away some of the fallen tears.

"Yeah." She laughs. "I did it. I actually fucking swallowed."

With my finger under her chin, I tilt her head up, touching my lips to hers. "And you were amazing. Ten out of ten. Would do it again."

She chews on her bottom lip. "Really?"

Her question throws me. This woman who just took charge with me, giving me the best blow job I've ever experienced, is unsure? I am floored. Where did that confidence go that she just had? "Clare Bear, that was without a doubt the best blow job I have ever had. I would shout it from the rooftops if I could, but I don't want anyone else to find out about this amazing talent of yours and whisk you away from me."

"You're ridiculous." She shrieks as I pick her up, throwing her onto her bed, where I plan to make her feel as good as she made me, repeatedly.

Chapter Twenty-Six

Clara

I don't know when it happened, but I am in love with Kamdyn Cook. Like head-over-heels, give-him-a-blow-job-where-I-swallow in love. He makes me want things I never have before.

I daydream about what our kids will look like someday. Will they have his hair or mine? Will they be as charismatic as him or have to fight to control their distractibility like I did growing up? Either way, I can see it. I can picture Kamdyn holding a baby in his arms, rocking them back and forth. I envision us painting rooms in the big house we bought and fixed up together. Sunny and Samson playing fetch in a massive, open backyard. Mostly, I just picture us together.

Knowing you love someone is a scary-as-shit thing. Especially if you're unsure if the feelings are reciprocated. The fear is enough to drive you away from even trying in the love game. But as I lie next to this beautiful man, tracing the ink on his arm, I know that whatever our future holds is worth the risk.

"Kamdyn?" I whisper.

"Hmm?" It's a half-awake, half-asleep hum.

I scoot myself into his arms, pressing my lips lightly against his. "I love you."

His body stills, and my heart stops. He might have been asleep a minute ago, but there is no hiding that he is awake now. He wraps his arms around me, hugging me to his chest as his lips turn up, revealing his sleepy smile. He peers at me through heavy eyes. "I love you too."

We don't make out passionately or have mind-blowing sex. We just hold each other, falling asleep knowing we're with the person we love. And it's perfect.

When I wake up in the morning, everything is sort of like a dream. Kamdyn and I have moved up a level into a genuine relationship. We aren't just dating. This is real. Once you hit the love stage, the game's done.

I wish we could've lain together longer, stayed in bed all day. Just Kamdyn and me, basking in each other's bodies, celebrating our love for one another.

Nope, instead, I'm on my way to work, leaving Kamdyn wrapped up in my floral quilt, still asleep. I could have woken him, but the way his blond hair had fallen on the pillow around his face made him look peaceful and fucking irresistible. So I did what any sane woman in my shoes would do. I took a picture, or ten, and bolted from the room.

I'm still looking at the pictures of him, smiling like an idiot, when I stop for a coffee. In my rush to get out without waking Kamdyn, I forgot to grab my energy drink and am now in need of a caffeine fix.

With my attention on my phone, I bump into the person in front of me. "Oh my God, I am so sorry," I say, cringing at myself.

The woman whips around with her familiar blue eyes and blond hair. "Clara," Stevie shrieks, engulfing me in a hug. "Oh my God, I haven't spoken to you about everything that went down on Friday."

"You mean after you left my place?" I ask.

"Yes! I was pretty drunk leaving your house, but my boyfriend came to get me so we could…"—she wiggles her eyebrows—"you know. Anyway, that's all beside the point because I might get back together with my ex."

"Your ex? Why?"

"Eh, I don't know. Maybe I made a mistake with him."

"You don't need to explain to me about regrets. I get it loud and clear."

She smiles, flipping her long hair over her shoulder, the curls falling down her back in a beautiful cascade of layers. "This is why I like you—you get me."

We move to the front of the line, chatting about our weekend plans while we wait on our coffees before going our separate ways.

I arrive at work five minutes early—thank fucking God, too, because Angelica is standing right at the entrance. Her expression is worth every second of those precious minutes.

She looks me up and down, sneering at my ponytail whipping behind me. "Good morning, Angelica," I say as I walk to my room to prep my supplies for the day. Before I can close the door behind me, she calls down the hall.

"Clara, can you come here for a moment?"

I take a deep breath, focusing on avoiding triggering her or myself. I run my fingers through the tangled strands of my ponytail hanging over my shoulder as I make my way to stand in front of her.

She looks as if what she's about to say is painful to her. "I sampled some products from the local vendors you think we should carry, and I agree."

My head lifts, jaw dropping. "I'm sorry. What did you say?"

She narrows her eyes to slits, her teeth grinding as she smiles. "I said, I agree with you. Let's contact them for a trial run."

"Thank you, Angelica. You won't regret this!" I bounce over to hug her. She stiffens with my arms around her.

"Yeah, yeah." She shrugs me off. "Get to work. We'll discuss it in more detail later."

Throughout the day, Kamdyn and I text back and forth, sending pictures of our days and any and every meme we find funny. So far, I've received multiple pictures of Kamdyn shirtless, working in June's flower bed, courtesy of none other than June herself. The woman is such a sneak. She texted me on and off anytime she could grab his phone.

She told me how she's jealous that I pinned that piece of ass down, forcing her to admire from a distance. She sent me a list of dirty things she would do to him if she were me. Then she sent me a sweet message about how happy I make Kamdyn and that she loves that we've found each other.

My chest lightens, and a hum of joy radiates throughout my body. Kamdyn and I have confessed all of our feelings, but having someone on the outside tell me she can see how much I mean to him and the impact I'm having on him makes me feel amazing. Like I can do anything.

Toward the end of the day, I want nothing more than to go home and sleep. I had more clients than normal because of another call-in, and I sat down with Angelica to discuss who she wants to offer a trial run to and what products. It was a long day. A good day, but a long one.

Kamdyn and I had talked about getting together tonight once I got off, but it turns out all of June's chores have him worn out. We agree to both stay at our own homes for the night because we need the rest, and knowing us, we would still end up humping each other until our bodies gave out.

On the way back to my apartment, I take a slight detour to pick up some Chinese food. My stomach rumbles, begging me to eat soon. With my food in hand, I walk back to my apartment, but the pain in my stomach demands penance. Unable to take it any longer, I sit down on the curb, shoving the egg roll into my face without caring how I look to anyone walking or driving by. The only care in the world I have right now is this egg roll getting into my belly.

Still chowing down a few minutes later, I catch sight of a long-legged blonde I recognize stepping out of a small Italian restaurant across the street. Stevie's face is pinched as she forces a smile. Standing at the door, she appears to be talking to someone. He's facing away from me, so I don't see his face, but I know it's not her boyfriend. From the pictures she's shown me, her man has dark hair. Not these golden-honey locks.

Whoever it is, I can sense the unease in Stevie's body language. It isn't fear but something more like awkwardness as she shifts back and forth on her red heels. Stevie reaches in for a hug, and the man steps back.

The half-eaten egg roll falls out of my mouth, landing on the street. This man just swerved her hug. I bite back a laugh. It was brutal and hilarious at the same time. Whoever this man is, he is not a fan of hers.

Note to self: call Stevie to ask who he is. Maybe I'll leave out the part about seeing the hug brush-off.

Stevie pivots on her heels after giving him a wave, and I watch the man reach for his phone, turning toward the street.

Everything around me freezes as I get my first glimpse of the man.

My heart plummets into my stomach.

Kamdyn.

A vibration courses through my veins, and my breathing becomes rapid as I try to wrap my mind around what is going on.

He said he was staying in tonight to rest. It's why we aren't together now. He said he needed sleep.

With shaking hands, I push off the ground. Nausea sweeps over me. I throw my uneaten Chinese food into the nearby trash can, hurrying home.

My phone buzzes in my pocket. I pull it out to see it's him.

It's Kamdyn.

All the air in my lungs seems to disappear as I watch my phone ring and ring until it stops.

By the time I've made it to my building, Kamdyn has sent me a few new texts.

Asshat: Hey, did you get the email about class being postponed from tomorrow to next week? Great, right? Not like we wanted this experience to be over or anything.

Asshat: Did you already fall asleep? If you did, I hope you have sweet, sexy dreams of me. If you haven't yet, call me. I want to hear your voice.

Asshat: I love you.

I'm freaking out for nothing. He wouldn't call me or text me those things if he was doing something wrong. He isn't that guy. I know it. The way he acted with her tells me there's no way he's cheating. He would never. Especially after what his ex, Steph, did to him.

Steph. Oh my God. My phone slips out of my hand, landing with a thud on the many throw pillows I own.

Kamdyn's ex-girlfriend, who cheated on him, is Steph.

Stevie was meeting up with an ex-boyfriend soon, who she fucked up with.

No, nope. I refuse to believe they are the same person. I mean, they have two different names. Steph is obviously short for Stephani, but Stevie is just a name.

I pick up my phone, deciding to put this issue to bed right now.

Me: Is Stevie short for something?

Stevie: Yeah lol. Stephani. Why?

I bury my face in my hands, fighting the moisture pooling in my eyes. My body is shaking with every emotion possible. I feel like my heart is breaking, and I'm not sure why yet.

Me: Can we meet up tomorrow?

Stevie/Steph: Yeah, want to do lunch?

Me: Okay, 11:30?

Stevie/Steph: Perfect! I'm so glad you texted me because, boy, do I have a story for you. A JUICY one!

As I wait for Stevie/Steph to arrive at the café, I'm wringing my hands. I had three cups of coffee while waiting for her. Sure, I arrived a little early, but she's also running late.

Very late.

My nerves and the caffeine are working simultaneously to generate extreme anxiety. The bistro-style table set for two is looking sad and a little desperate as I wait for her.

Just as I'm about to text her that I'm done waiting, she walks in, rushing over to the table before throwing herself in the seat. She looks flawless as usual in her white blouse tucked into a floral pencil skirt with heels that could reach the heavens. As if I can't help but compare myself to her now, I look down at my attire. Cutoff shorts, Converse, and an old My Chemical Romance concert tee I've had since high school.

It's taking everything in me not to be insecure or feel like a step down from her. Not to cry. So I plaster on a cheerful face while I wait for the information I need to come out of her mouth.

"Ugh, sorry I'm so late. I had a deposition, and"—she waves her hand around—"you know how those go."

"Totally," I say. Why in the fuck would she assume a spa employee would understand the ins and outs of legal proceedings?

"Anyway, I am starved." She scans the menu until a server comes over to take our orders.

While eating her salad, Stevie/Steph continues to tell me the ins and outs of her day. How she had to pry herself off her boyfriend at work—the same boyfriend she talked about leaving for her ex the other day. She told me how her clients are being idiots and how sorry she is about being late for our lunch date.

Even though I have a million insecurities running through my head, mostly about myself, I can't find anything to hate about her.

Yes, I despise that she cheated on Kamdyn. It's insane and unforgivable, but that action indirectly brought him to me. So I can't hate her for that. She's still the same person I met in my chair weeks ago, still the same woman who has been texting me almost daily with fun ideas for a girls' trip.

I won't hate her just because Kamdyn used to love her. I won't hate her even if he still does.

Fuck. I rub my palm over my chest. Even the notion of him loving someone else is painful. The ache from not knowing what he was doing with her, why he lied to me, is getting worse with every minute I wait for the truth. Because the scenarios I am dreaming up are driving me insane.

"It's okay, you're here now," I tell her as I mindlessly push my salad around my plate with a bronze fork. My appetite is still lacking, and until I get her to spill, it'll stay that way. "So what was this juicy story you were dying to tell me?"

She drops her fork with a clink. "Oh my God, I almost forgot." Her lips curl up, and her eyebrows dance, leaning forward. "I had that date with my ex."

"Date?" My lungs feel like all the air has been sucked out as I wait for her to confirm it.

She rolls her eyes, taking a sip from her water. "Okay, not a date, but a meeting of sorts."

Just like that, my lungs fill with oxygen, and I'm no longer suffocating. "Okay, what happened?"

"It turned out he really only wanted legal advice or help. It's whatever. Only it wasn't for him."

I lean in closer to her. "For whom, then?" I ask, but my heart already knows the answer.

"For this new girlfriend of his. And shit, does she have some problems." She chuckles, taking another bite of her salad.

"He told you about them?"

"Oh, yeah. He told me all about how this girl took the blame for a ton of shit that her sister did, only to have her sister cut town on her." She pauses, crinkling her nose. "It's actually really sad, and it's even worse that there isn't anything to do for her unless she wants to have her sister thrown in jail and face the repercussions of perjury."

I bite back my want to cry, to scream. The coppery tinge of blood coats my cheeks as I continue to chew them while Stevie/Steph tells me more about her time with Kamdyn.

"Anyway, after all the legal talk, he was done. Like didn't want to be around me at all. I even tried to give him a quick goodbye hug, but he pushed me off, saying he made it clear that we were never happening again, and that he has someone else now. Like, fuck, man, I got it." She runs her finger across her scalp, pushing back her hair as she exhales. "Anyway, tell me what you wanted to meet about."

"I...I wanted to talk to you about Mr. Perfect. I think—"

Chirp. Chirp.

"Fuck." She holds up a finger while digging in her purse to find her phone. "Hold that thought."

Her fingers type viciously against the screen, her jaw tightening with every tap. "It's work. I have to go." She sighs while standing. "Do you hate me?"

"No, never." I wave her off with my hand before giving her a quick hug, telling her lunch is my treat today.

Once she's fully out the door and out of sight, emotions flood through me.

He told her.

Kamdyn told her my secrets. Things I trusted him with. The unshed tears I was holding back finally spill.

I need to talk to someone about this. To get it all out.

I can't tell Lex. She would say it's not a big deal. That he was trying to help me. I need someone to hold me, to let me cry.

So as I sit on the metal bistro chair with silent tears streaking my face, I pick up and call the one person I know won't defend him. Who will let me just talk without saying a word.

The phone rings three times before I get the voice mail.

"Hey, Chloe." My voice cracks. "You probably won't call me back or hell, maybe even listen to this, but I need you."

Chapter Twenty-Seven

Kamdyn

The meeting with Steph was more than disappointing. First, she tried to come on to me. But once she realized that wasn't happening, that I was there for Clara and Clara alone, she got down to business. The only problem is her advice was fucking useless. The options were to get Chloe to turn herself in and Clara to admit to lying to a judge while keeping our fingers crossed she won't get into any more trouble. Or we continue to do nothing.

It fucking sucks.

I was hoping Steph would have a definite option, a solution to help the person who means everything to me. But no, she had nothing. And sadly, she did try. It's not like Steph to fuck around with her professional reputation.

After she broke the bad news, she then continued to try rubbing my forearm, but my breaking point was the hug. No way in hell was I allowing that woman to press herself against me.

Not that it would tempt me.

I have zero interest or romantic feelings for her anymore.

But I would never let another woman do that to me because of Clara. My personal space, personal touch, is for her and her alone. No one else.

Steph went on and on about how I look different. Well, no shit. I'm genuinely happy. No longer granting her or my father any sway over me. Their words will no longer force me to be something I'm not.

When I rolled over this morning, I reached to draw Clara into me, only to be met with cold sheets. I really wish I wouldn't have conceded to spending the night apart. I miss her body pressed against mine, the warmth that radiates from every inch of her.

But I had to. I needed to meet with Steph to determine what she could do to help. It was a bust, and now I regret missing any time with that exasperating woman I worship.

I force myself to sit, leaning against my headboard as I look at my phone to see if Clara replied to any of my messages. Nope. Nothing.

I check the time again at 10:00 a.m. My shoulders slump. Why didn't she text me back yet? She works on Fridays and should be there now, but that has never stopped her. Fuck, not even when we weren't together. That didn't stop her.

Me: Hey, babe, I missed you last night and this morning. Dinner date tonight?

With Anger Management canceled tonight, I plan on taking Clara out on a proper date to show her how much I love her. But until then, I'm going to spend time with one of my other favorite ladies, Sunny. And, of course, Samson.

Once at Run and Rescue, I sneak into the kennels with Sunny and Samson's leashes. The moment the yellow giant sees me, her tail goes crazy, slapping from side to side as she pops up and down, waiting for me to get to her. Attempting to put the leash on her while her whole body wags is almost an impossible feat. After being almost knocked down three times and once actually knocked over, I get the leash on her, and we walk over to get our main man, Samson.

We spend the day at the dog park. The two run wild while I throw balls and give them treats. After a while, we're all worn out, lying on the ground, taking a mini break.

Still no texts from Clara.

My mouth feels like I've been sucking on cotton. Every worst-case scenario runs through my head.

Maybe her phone is dead. Maybe she broke her phone. What if she's hurt? Did she fall? Is she in the hospital? What if she was kidnapped, and I'm wasting precious time doing nothing to help her?

I Google The Spa's number. Fuck, I hate to be this boyfriend, but I haven't heard from her in almost twenty-four hours, and I'm concerned.

"Hello, thank you for calling The Spa in downtown Bloomburgh. This is Angelica speaking. How can I help you?" Her voice is as smooth as honey, but from all of Clara's stories, Angelica is anything but sweet.

"Hi, yeah, I need to speak to Clara."

"Clara?"

"Yes, ma'am," I say, laying on the charm my father taught me so well.

"Clara is busy with a client at the moment. Is there something I could assist you with, sir? Or would you like to leave a message?"

I let out a sigh of relief. At least she's alive and okay. "A message would be great. Will you just ask her to call Kamdyn back?"

"Can do."

"Thank you, Angelica. I really appreciate it," I say, hanging up the phone. Sunny and Samson's heads are both resting on my thighs as I lean back onto my hands, basking in the sunlight while trying not to let the fact that my girlfriend might be ignoring me consume me.

After one more walk around the park, I decide it's time to call it quits. Sunny could easily handle more, but poor Samson looks worn out, so much so that he might persuade me to carry him from my car to the rescue. When we get back, Sunny bolts for the door while the black blob sits in my back seat, silently demanding I do something about it.

"Okay, okay." I throw my hands up in surrender. "You win. Now come over here so I can pick you up."

Much to my chagrin, he does. He scoots to the open door, letting me struggle to lift his almost eighty-pound body from the car. Just steps away from the door, I stop, attempting to catch my breath.

Behind the counter, Justine stands there laughing at me. "Dear God, Kamdyn. How did he convince you to carry him?"

"What can I say?" I pant. "I'm a sucker for a good puppy-dog eye."

Once the dogs settle, I wave goodbye to the other volunteers and staff as I head out. I'm halfway to my car when someone pulls on my arm, turning me to face them.

"Kamdyn," Justine calls out, "wait."

I cock my head to the side, waiting for her to say whatever she needs to.

"I-I wanted to apologize."

I clasp my hand over hers, and her face softens for a moment before crumbling as I peel her hand off me. "For?"

Her hand falls, along with her face. "For the other day"—her voice gets quiet—"with the dog baths."

"You'll have to elaborate. Do you mean where you and your mother tried to seduce me with skimpy clothing and water? Or the part where you guys were assholes to the woman I love?"

She rears back as if I physically assaulted her, her mouth opening and closing, but nothing comes out.

"Listen, Justine." My voice softens, not much but enough to take some of the sting out of my bite. "You're a great person, and a beautiful woman too. But you are so young."

She opens her mouth to interject. I hold up my hand. "No. You are. I am thirty years old. I started teaching when you were in middle school. *Middle school.* Do you understand I could have easily been your teacher?"

She nods but looks like she still doesn't understand.

I rub my fingers over my brow. "It would not only make me look like a pedophile but feel like one if I ever dated you. Do you understand now?"

"Yes." She nods, looking down at her flip-flops.

"Okay, good. I love this place and the dogs, but if any of it happens again, I'm done here."

"I'm sorry. For everything," she says, turning back to the building.

"Yeah, me too."

With the press of a button, I unlock my car, put the key in the ignition, and sit there. What the fuck is going on with today?

As the night drags on, I still haven't heard anything from Clara. Saturday was no different. I went over to Marcus's to talk with him, but nothing helped.

I called, I texted. But only got silence.

Once Sunday hits and I still haven't heard from her, it's time to take matters into my own hands.

I don't bother trying to call or text her again. Instead, I drive to her apartment; I planned everything I want to say to her, repeating it in my head as I walk with a fury I've never known before.

Once the elevator doors close behind me, the nerves hit. My whole body shakes with the fear of what will happen when I do this. What do I expect from this confrontation? I rotate my wrists, the popping joints giving me the courage to do this. The elevator doors open onto Clara's floor, and I step out.

My heart pounds in my chest with fear. Fear that she doesn't want me. That she doesn't love me. That she realizes I'm a mistake. With my mind running rampant, I crack my knuckles, one by one, releasing fuel to my fire while ignoring the knots of unease in my stomach.

I knock on her door twice without an answer. When my fist goes for a third, the door opens. Clara stands in front of me in a fitted summer dress. Her hair is piled on top of her head in a big bun. She stares at me, her eyes the same shade as always but missing her normal sparkle. My eyes trace down her body. The way she's holding herself isn't right. Something about it is off.

I lean back, cocking my head to the side. "Chloe."

She stays still, surveying me for another moment before bringing her hands together in a slow clap. "Good job, pretty boy. I am very impressed."

"Is Clara here?" My tone is sharp.

"Who's asking?"

"Tell her it's her boyfriend," I snap.

A slow smile creeps up her face as she says, "That's weird because she told me she doesn't have one anymore." She gives a little shrug.

"The fuck she doesn't." I move past her into the apartment, making my way to the bedroom, where I find Clara sitting on her bed with her knees drawn up. Her arms are wrapped around them while her face is tucked into the space.

I slam the door shut, flicking the lock as I do. Her head shoots up from the noise. She lets out a small gasp as she sees me standing there.

Her eyes are red with dark circles under them. She looks miserable. I walk to the side of the bed, sitting down beside her on the wrinkled sheets. I reach to take her hand when she scoots toward the edge of the bed. Standing, she walks over to the door, her hand shaking as she moves to unlock it.

Following her, I grip her arm, spinning her around to face me. She doesn't fight the action, letting me pull her closer. She's so close, the familiar scent of her perfume, the scent on my pillows, clings to her like a second skin. How can I ever smell roses again without thinking about her? About her body intertwining with mine. The stupid dad jokes she thinks are funny. The ridiculous way she pronounces crayons like "crowns." Most of all, I think about what she means to me.

"Are you fucking kidding me?" I ask, looking her in the eyes.

She glances down, not speaking. Her breathing becomes heavy and rapid.

"So that's it? We're through? Just like that?" I can barely hear the words as they leave my mouth over the sound of my heart beating.

Just saying those words to her has my lungs constricting, making it hard to breathe. Hell, thinking about it is excruciating.

She sucks in a gasp at my questions.

"Why?" My voice cracks. The emotions I've been fighting back with anger rise to the surface. "After everything we've been through together this summer, why now?"

She lifts her head, tears rimming her eyes as her chin quivers. But she won't even glance at me. She couldn't be any clearer with her silence.

"What did I do to deserve this? Did I do something wrong? Or was it not real for you?" I pause, clamping my eyes shut, not wanting her to see how much she's hurting me, destroying me. With a shaky breath, I continue, "Because it was always real for me. Every single part. Every fight and every laugh. All the taunts and kisses. Every part was true. Was it just one-sided? Because when you said you loved me, I believed you."

This is gutting me. She won't look at me, won't talk to me. Won't acknowledge the pain she's causing me. How could someone who claims to love me not even bother to look at me as they break my heart?

I throw my hands up, backing away. "Okay, message received." My throat tightens. "I won't bother you anymore."

Chapter Twenty-Eight

Clara

Kamdyn is here. Begging me for answers, for reasons for all of this. His face is pure torture to look at. He loves me, I can tell. But it doesn't erase what he did.

As he turns to leave, his hand stops on the door. I blurt out, "You want to know why?"

He glances over his shoulder. "Yes." It's quiet, like a whisper, but the emotions are loud and clear.

I pick up my phone, scrolling through my pictures till I find the perfect one. "This. This is why." I thrust the phone in his face with a picture of me with Stephani.

He looks down, then back at me. "You know Steph?"

"That's my friend Stevie. Who I recently discovered was your Steph, whom you talked to about me."

He stalks forward, his fists balled. "First, she isn't mine in any way, shape, or form. And two, you're breaking up with me because of Steph?"

"You think I'm mad about the Stephani or whatever the fuck her name is part?" I demand through my teeth, clenching harder by the moment. "Fuck that! I'm mad because you went behind my back. You took something I told you in confidence. Something I trusted you with, and you betrayed me."

Kamdyn's jaw ticks. "I did it to help you." His voice is gravelly and laced with anger. "Because I love you, goddamn it. Because I don't want to see you suffering. I sure as shit don't want to see you hurting to save someone who doesn't even deserve your love."

The rage that had been simmering in me boils over. I don't want to acknowledge the first part of his statement. It only adds fuel to the anger that I let loose on him, yelling, "How dare you! Chloe is my sister—my twin. The friendship, the bond we share, is something you can never understand." My eyes well with tears. "She is my everything. I would do anything for her."

His face falls as he looks at me, taking in everything I said. He steps forward, grabbing my hands to engulf mine with his. "But are you hers?" He rubs circles on my palm with his thumb. The gesture sends warmth through me, and I hate him for it. I don't want to feel these things for someone who could take my trust and crush it into the ground without considering me. "All she ever does is hurt you. You deserve better. You deserve to be someone's everything."

His forehead falls to mine. Closing his eyes, he whispers, "Be my everything."

I suck in a sharp breath as my heart breaks even more. The tears that had formed in my eyes moments ago are now rolling down my cheeks as I sob. He wraps his big hand around my head, bringing me to his chest. I hug him, needing to touch him, smell him, have him hold me. I need him in this moment of chaos and ruin.

He's the person who can break me. But he's also the person I want to put me back together. He's offering me everything I've ever wanted, asking me to allow him to put me first. To be my beacon of light when things get foggy.

I want him to be that. I want to be that for him. But I can't. Not when I'll always wonder when my trust will be thrown out the window for what he believes is the right path.

I cling tightly to him as I cry, soaking his shirt. All he does is stroke my hair and rub my back, letting me get it all out.

This is it. I can't be what he wants me to be.

"Kamdyn, how would you feel if I broke your trust? If I told someone about your arrest? You would feel betrayed. But I would never do that. Because when I love someone, I do everything in my power to heal them, not hurt them. And you, Kamdyn, you hurt me so much."

I push away from him, scratching at my chest. His eyes mirror mine right now. The pain clear on his face. "It hurts so much. It feels like I can't breathe. I can't breathe." Tears pour down my face as I clutch my stomach in agony.

"Clara, please." He steps closer to me. But I bring a hand up to block him, stepping back to put more distance between us.

"You should go."

"Clara, I—"

"Please," I cry.

He tilts his head up to the ceiling and closes his eyes, nodding as he presses his lips into a tight line. His palms come up to his eyes, pressing into them before he turns, unlocking the wood door and leaving me standing in my room crying.

My heart isn't broken. It's shattered, like someone smashed it into pieces, then walked over those parts for fun.

I sit on the floor, pinned in the same spot as when Kamdyn left, using my sleeve to wipe my running nose and eyes. I'm not sure what I should do.

I've never wanted something so much in my life. Never wanted someone as much as I want him, but I can't. He told not only my secret but Chloe's, and I can't. It's too much.

"He could tell."

I glance up to see Chloe leaning in my doorway, her arms crossed as she stares down at the floor. I was stunned earlier today when I opened the door to find her standing there, with a bag slung over her shoulder and her arms held out. It only took me a few seconds to process that she was actually there before I broke into an incoherent, blubbering mess that only she could understand.

"Tell what?" I sniffle.

"That I wasn't you. He knew the moment he looked at me that something was off."

My chin trembles as I fight the never-ending tears threatening to pour out of me. "He did?"

No one could ever tell the difference between the two of us...

She nods, moving forward to sit down in front of me, opening her arms to me as I fall into her. "Shh, it's okay." She strokes my back, her hand drawing hearts. It's something we used to do when we were little to comfort each other.

Chloe holds me while I cry for the next hour.

I collect myself enough to pull back. Sniffling, I finally ask, "Where have you been?"

She rolls her eyes. "Geesh, Mom, sorry. I didn't realize I still had to call about every brief trip I take."

I grab a pillow off the couch and chuck it straight at her head. I bend over, laughing at the stunned expression on her face.

Her eyes dart to me. "How dare you?" she asks, gripping the pillow between her hands before dropping it onto the couch. "I'll let it slide this one time because it looks like you're going through it."

I look up at her from where I'm sitting on the couch. "Answer the question. Where have you been? Do you realize what you did? What you've done to me? I've texted, I've called. Why?"

She sits beside me, gnawing on her lip and peering down at her hands. "I'm sorry. I panicked. Besides, it all ended up okay, right?"

"Okay? Okay?" I laugh as tears form in my eyes again. "What about me appears to be okay?"

"I said I was sorry, sissy. What more can I do?" She shrugs her shoulders. There wasn't anything she could do at this point to fix the situation. "How about you tell me what's causing my extremely strong sister to cry like this?"

And I did. I told her about meeting Kamdyn. About hating his perfect, arrogant ass. About loving every part of him. And I told her about the pain I felt from what he has done.

"You aren't planning to do any of that, are you? I realize I haven't been the best sister lately, but you wouldn't go so far as to turn me into the police. Right?" She cuts me off.

I blink back at her. "Don't you think if that were the case, I would have already done it?"

Her head falls onto my shoulder as she intertwines her fingers with mine. "I really am sorry about all of this, sister."

"I know."

She didn't explain where she was or why she never contacted me. But she showed up when I needed her. And that meant more than anything to me.

So, the fact that she's here now, holding me during the most painful moment of my life, shows how much she cares. That Kamdyn was wrong about Chloe.

Chloe stops drawing on my back as the tears dry up. "You gonna be okay if I go out for a while?"

"Oh...Yeah, I'll be fine." My voice is hoarse from crying. I want her to sit with me, to comfort me, but I don't say it.

"Be back in a few," she says, jumping up with a genuine smile on her face. With her purse in hand, she stops at the mirror to touch up her makeup before heading out.

And just like that, she leaves me destroyed not only from my breakup but because she's leaving me when I need her.

Chapter Twenty-Nine

Kamdyn

I make it all the way back to my car before I let my emotions get the best of me. My head rests on the steering wheel, my knuckles turning white from gripping it. It takes everything in me to not break down right here in front of her apartment building. With my eyes closed, I take deep, slow breaths, trying to calm my broken heart.

Clara dumped me. Over her sister. Over trying to help her.

How can she not see how toxic Chloe is to her? The woman straight up stole her identity, getting her into legal and financial troubles without even a genuine apology. How can Clara be so fierce with everything but her own twin?

I'm not sure how long I sit, willing my eyes to keep from watering before I can make myself leave. Once at home, I go straight to bed, throwing my keys and clothes on the floor, covering up with blankets that still have a hint of rose scent on them.

God, this fucking hurts. I don't remember it hurting this much when Steph cheated on me, and we were together for years. Fuck, how did I not realize Steph knew Clara? I'm such an idiot. I should have never reached out. Look what it got me.

I'm on the verge of crying. My chest aches like I've been stabbed, while my limbs are heavy, weighing every part of me down.

Out of all the scenarios that could have ended our relationship, I never saw this one.

My hands scrub my face. I can't sleep. My mind won't stop racing with ideas to fix what I broke.

Since sleep is obviously off the table, I turn the TV on, flipping through channel after channel, only to find *Toy Story* playing. Fuck me, I can't even watch my favorite movie now without thinking of Clara and the first time we watched it together. I turn the TV off, staring at the ceiling, watching shadows from the window dance until my eyes hurt.

If I allow myself to start thinking about her, I won't be able to stop. This ache from having the person who helped me like myself again not want me is more than I can take. And if I let myself feel all that at once, it'll be too much. It's already soul crushing, and I'm not even letting half of the pain through.

Fuck, I need someone to talk through this shit with me. I need my best friend.

Me: Clara dumped me.

Marcus: WTF, why?

Me: Because I contacted Steph about her sister and the issues she caused her.

Marcus: Kam, why would you contact your ex for your new girl-friend?

Me: Because I knew how much her sister cost her, and I was trying to do everything, anything, to get her out of this situation.

Marcus: ...I understand you love her; I do. And I would do anything for Tay in that situation too. But Steph?

Me: I know, but the Steph part isn't even what she's mad about. It pissed her off. But it was that I told someone about her situation. She said I betrayed her trust.

Marcus: I'm sorry, man. I truly am. Do you want me to come over? I'll bring queso.

Me: Queso sounds good.

It takes Marcus less than an hour to get to my place. He doesn't knock or ring the doorbell, he just walks straight in. Not saying a word as he juggles to carry a huge-ass container of queso, a bag of tortilla chips, and a six-pack of beer. We take the goods outside; sitting on my back porch, we eat the melted cheese and drink beers that will have me drunk in no time, not talking.

I spent most of my week moping around the house, drunk. I'm not proud of it, but it was the only thing that numbed the pain for a while. Monday, I spent my day lying on the couch, puking into a trash can on the floor beside me. Tuesday, I went out to buy more beer, drinking four before passing out in my bed with the bottle still in my hand. By Wednesday, I had Marcus bringing me tacos during his lunch break. The look on his face would have been hilarious if it wasn't directed at my physical state. By Thursday, every part of me spiraled deeper into myself, making it hard to get out of bed.

But this morning, when I woke up, I knew I had to get my

shit together. It was the last Anger Management class and another opportunity to see Clara. To explain, to beg her for forgiveness. Another chance to apologize. I need to not be this broken shell of a man that being without her has made me into.

For the first time since Sunday morning, I shower. I don't bother with shaving. My normal stubble is now thick, looking like the start of a full beard. My hair is a mess, mussed up in every which way. Pulling on a short-sleeve shirt, I leave my sleeve of tattoos on full display for anyone to see.

I don't give a shit about what others think anymore. The only person besides me whose opinion I give two shits about is hers.

When I arrive at the rec center, I sit in my car, trying to build up the nerve to see her. I plan out what I'll say when I sit down beside her. I walk through the door with just a minute to spare before class begins, staring at the circle of chairs, neck tat sitting in Clara's seat.

My chest aches as I search around the room, eyeing every seat until I locate her face.

Clara's eyes are fixed on the floor. Her body slouches against the fold-up chair. I stop mere feet away from the circle, away from where we normally sit together.

She moved away from me...She left me.

She hates me so much that she can't even sit beside me.

Every muscle in my body tightens as I push forward, clenching and unclenching my fists, never once taking my eyes off her.

"Celebration" streams through the overhead speakers as Stean dance-walks into the circle, pumping his fists up in the air. If it weren't for the fucking stabbing agony in my chest, I would laugh at him along with the rest of the class.

Fuck, if the last week hadn't happened, Clara and I would live off this moment for days. But instead of sarcasm and taunts, I just sit there, my face a blank slate that can't be painted with emotion. Only one person has the power to create something different.

Stean pulls out a remote, pausing the music, his face still in a contorted smile. "Can you believe it's finally our last session together? I know you all were pretty bummed you didn't get to spend last Friday together." Stean's bottom lip juts out. "Sorry about that, folks, family emergency. But enough of that, it's time to celebrate."

He presses the button on the remote again, starting the song all over again. "Come on, everyone, get up and mingle."

Neck tat smiles at me before getting up to walk over to what I assume are the friends he's made here. As I glance around, I see everyone but Clara and I have gotten up and are laughing in groups, enjoying the people they have met and friendships they've made. I don't know any of them. This entire summer, I've been infatuated with one person. Her friendship was the only one I wanted, and I lost it.

"Kamdyn?" Stean says, forcing me to look away from the groups to him, where he's now seated in the chair beside me—in Clara's chair.

I force a closed smile as he rakes his eyes over me. "Are you okay?" he asks, leaning onto his elbows to prop his chin on his fists.

"Never better," I deadpan, tightening my jaw.

With a hefty sigh, he leans back into the chair, his gaze gesturing over to where Clara sits. "Sure you are, just like I'm a bikini model."

I clamp my lips together, shaking my head while trying not to laugh at his ridiculousness.

"I'm not sure what happened between you and that one over there, but you both look like you lost your favorite teddy bear."

I swallow down his words. "Your point?"

He doesn't take his eyes off her. "The point is, don't give up on the flame when you still have a spark." He stands, clasping my shoulder before sauntering off to join the cheerful group near us.

It turns out the last class was just a formality and a time requirement. There was no final test or evaluation. Over the past eleven classes, Stean has been evaluating us as we go. We all passed with flying colors. So I spend the entire hour of my time listening to bad music and watching people talk. When the time is up, Stean thanks us all, stating our "diplomas" would be in the mail.

The moment we're dismissed, Clara darts out the door. I rush to catch up to her, only to find Clara opening the door to a crossover SUV with Chloe at the wheel.

"Clara, stop," I say, my voice borderline pleading.

Her shoulders stiffen as she turns to face me, clutching the inside door handle so tight I can see her shaking.

Everything slows as I get a good view of her face.

Red splotches cover her usual pale, rosy complexion. The skin around her wet, dull eyes is puffy with darkness encompassing it. She looks as if she hasn't slept in days. She looks as if she's cried every tear I wouldn't allow myself to.

My breath catches in my throat. "Please." I try to beg her to talk to me. To give me another chance. To love me. But nothing comes out. It doesn't matter, though, because she seems to understand what I'm asking.

She looks over her shoulder at Chloe, whose narrow gaze is locked on me, before turning to give me a sad smile. "I'll call you." She climbs into the car before stopping one last time to glance back at me. "Okay?"

"Okay." I nod, clinging to the small token of hope she just gave me.

Chapter Thirty

Clara

Chloe speeds away, leaving Kamdyn standing there, watching us drive away. Her eyes dart over to me as she sings along to the stupid song on the radio. She knows I hate listening to this electronic, over-the-top, catchy music. Mostly because once I get one of those dumb songs in my head, I can't get them out for days.

"So," she says, turning the music down. "Wanna talk about it?"

"Not really."

"Okay." She shrugs, turning the music back up, swaying and singing along.

Which lasts about thirty seconds before she turns the music back down. "Okay, I have to say it; hot damn, Clara. Your man was looking fine as fuck."

I bury my face in my hands. "Ugh, don't remind me."

"He looks like sex on a motherfucking stick, sissy. Tell me he fucks like he looks."

I snap my head up. "That's none of your business."

"Come on, share the details, or we can pull a twin switcheroo so I can find out for myself."

Anger seethes through my body. "If you ever go near him, pretending to be me, I will never speak to you again."

"Oh, come on, I was kidding." She laughs.

"I wasn't." I grit my teeth together, trying to remember everything Stean has taught me. But being with Chloe makes everything fly out the window. It's as if I never went to that damn class. "Kamdyn isn't some random guy or boy toy you can screw around with. He matters. He matters more than you'll ever know."

"Geesh, since when did you become such a bore?"

"Probably around the same time you made me take the fall for your crimes."

Chloe deflates, driving us back to my place in silence.

Once in the parking garage, she shuts off the engine, turning in her seat to look at me. "You realize I would never touch him, right?"

"I don't know shit anymore. You put me in a horrible situation, then ran off with my car."

Her hands shake as she wipes away a fresh tear. "I'm sorry. I really am."

"Why did you come back?"

"You needed me."

"I needed you for weeks, and you never came...Why now?"

Her mouth opens but then closes as she realizes I won't listen to her lies anymore.

"It's nothing." She shakes her head. "I'm just a little short on cash right now."

A laugh leaves my lips as her words penetrate my ears. "Oh my God. You don't give two shits about me, do you?"

"What! No, of course I do." Chloe reaches over the console to grab my hand.

Yanking it away, I laugh. I'm borderline hysterical. "Chloe, I can't do this anymore. I'm done. I lost my savings because of you. My driver's license, my car, and my reputation are all gone because of you. Hell, I was even going to give up Kamdyn because of you. But you can't bother to just be here for me. I am never a priority, just another thing for you to use."

"No." She shakes her head, tears streaming down her face now.

"Until you can get your shit together, like actually together, I am done." I reach into my purse, pulling out the $1500 in cash I had gotten out earlier today in case of this exact moment. "Here." I press the money into her hands, her eyes widening in disbelief. "Consider this my last favor."

"Clara, I-I'm sorry."

"I know you are..." I reach over, pulling my twin into my arms for a hug. "I love you more than words, but I don't like the person you've become or how you treat me."

"I'll get better. I'll be better," she says into my ear, her hands tracing hearts on my back. "I promise."

We release each other, not saying a word as we walk up to my apartment. I take the car keys from her, hiding them along with my wallet while she's in the bathroom.

I've given her one last night. One last night before she has to leave. So we do what sisters do best, we pretend the fight didn't happen. We snuggle against each other, watching our favorite romantic comedies while eating candy.

For one last night, we pretend like we're okay.

Chapter Thirty-One

Kamdyn

It's been a day since Clara said she would call. I wish I could say I haven't been sitting around the entire time since, staring at my phone, but I can't. At the moment, I'm working out in my living room to the video instructions of some YouTuber with a body sculpted beyond what should be possible. I didn't want to chance going on a run, being in the wrong place, and missing her call.

So here I am, shirtless, in the middle of my living room doing an endless number of burpees. I had to push the coffee table and other furniture around the room to create enough room for the heart-attack-inducing workout. My mouth won't stop watering as my muscles tremble with every movement. Twenty minutes of the thirty-minute video is all I can manage before collapsing onto my face. I want to stand; I need to stand, but my body refuses to move.

I give in to the softness of my rug, comforting the burn happening in every fiber of my being. I don't know how long I lie there. It was long enough that I fell asleep, only to be woken up by my phone ringing.

Fuck. Clara is calling.

My body protests as I scramble to lift myself up with sheer determination. I grab my phone, answering without looking.

"Hello." My breathing is ragged as I try to sound laid back.

Marcus's voice booms through the phone. "So I'm guessing she called based on your post-sex breathing."

"You think if I were having sex or just finished, I would answer your call?"

"Yeah," he says in complete seriousness.

I sink into my couch, my limbs thanking me as they release some of the tension that had built up while moving. "No. No to her calling, and no to answering your call during or after sex."

"I'm sorry, Kam. I thought she would call by now."

I close my eyelids as I take a deep breath. "What if she doesn't want me anymore?"

"Kamdyn, stop it. She loves you. Give it one more day before you do something stupid."

"I won't do anything stupid. I'll wait forever if that's how long she needs." It's true. She's the one person who I won't ever give up on.

"Okay, enough sadness. Tay wants you to come over tonight for tacos."

"Very tempting. But I'm gonna pass. I just killed myself working out, and I never want to move again."

"Understood." He laughs. "Love you, Kam."

"Love you too," I say, hanging up, prepared to live the rest of my life in this spot.

And I do. Well, at least for the rest of the day. I only move to go to the bathroom or get something to eat. The rest of the time, I'm glued to the spot, watching documentaries about British castles.

By 8:00 p.m., there's still nothing from Clara. I compel myself to get up and take the slowest shower in the history of non-masturbating showers. Every part of me is sore as I lie down for the night.

After verifying that my volume is on and the phone is charged, I fall asleep. My body sprawled across the bed like a starfish.

My phone wakes me up around 11:00 p.m., mere hours after falling asleep. I reach over, eyes still closed, pulling it to my face to answer. "Hello?"

"Hey...Did I wake you?"

Clara. Her voice is soft like a whisper, but it wakes me from my sleep like an air horn.

"Maybe, but I don't mind." I roll off my stomach and onto my back to stare at my ceiling fan as it spins around.

She's quiet, but her deep breathing comes through the line, loud and clear. "I miss you."

The corners of my mouth tug into a smile. "I miss you too."

"I can't do this." Clara pauses, and my heart drops. "Do you want to meet up and talk in person?"

Does she mean she can't do "us" or the phone conversation? "Just to be clear, when you say, 'you can't do this,' what exactly do you mean?"

"The phone part, Kamdyn."

I sit up, flipping on the light. "Okay, where do you want me to meet you?"

"How about the park where we took the dogs?"

"I can be there in about ten minutes, give or take how long I take to put on clothes," I say, stumbling out of bed.

She chuckles, and I imagine her nose crinkling as her face lights up with joy. "Not right now, you idiot. Tomorrow, late afternoon or night."

"Oh," I say, sliding back under the blankets. "Are you sure you don't want to meet now? Because I'll meet you in a heartbeat, Clare Bear. Just say the word, and I'm there."

"Yes, I'm sure."

"If that's what you want, will you at least talk to me about the recent discovery of Stean's real name?"

"Oh my God!" She laughs. "When I got my 'diploma' today, I almost peed myself. I mean, Sebastian? All we had right was the *S*."

My body relaxes with the sound of her laugh filling my ears. "I didn't believe it. So much so that I Googled it."

"Wild guess, you found the confirmation you needed?"

I sigh, rolling onto my side and pulling my arm under my pillow. "Alas, Sebastian Buford is, in fact, Stean."

"I feel like my whole life has been a lie. First Stean, what's next? Am I going to find out Chloe doesn't actually look like me, but I look like her?" I can hear the smirk in her voice.

"Impossible." I yawn into my hand.

"I'll let you get some sleep."

"No, I'm good." I yawn again. Damn it, why is my body betraying me right now?

"I heard you yawn twice now. You're exhausted."

"Okay, fine. I am, but I don't want to get off the phone with you."

"Kamdyn..."

"Just stay on the phone with me until we fall asleep?" I'm almost begging her.

"Okay," she whispers. I hear the rustling of blankets in the background as she climbs into her bed. "Goodnight, Kamdyn."

"Goodnight, Clara." I want to tell her more. I want to whisper I love you into the phone, but I don't. Instead, I listen to the sound of her breathing until I drift off.

It's nine in the morning, and June already has me running errand after errand for her pervy ass. First, she had me take out all her trash, which was full of basically everything from her fridge. She said it was all spoiled; it wasn't. I bought most of it earlier this week. Then she had me water her plants, both indoor and outdoor, before asking—no, demanding—I pick up her dry cleaning.

But nothing can stop my good mood. This morning I got a bittersweet email from the school stating that Linda has retired to spend more time with her family and that my job is safe. And I'm seeing Clara today. After last night, I'm pretty confident that we aren't over.

I head all the way across town to not just one but two different dry cleaners because she likes one for her dresses and one for her undergarments. I take a little over an hour to collect the hanging bags. One is a plain black dress, and the other is a black satin-like dress, which I can only assume goes under the dress.

When I get back to her house, I knock on the door three different times before using my key. "June," I call down the hallway. "I don't want to walk in on you having sex again."

No response.

I kick the door shut with my foot before taking the clothes down the hall to hang in her closet. I crack her door open, knocking with a light rap. "June, I have your dry cleaning." Still nothing. "June?" I open the door, and my heart sinks.

June is on her back with her eyes closed. She looks like a sleeping angel, but she isn't. I place the dry cleaning on the chair beside her vanity before walking over to her. I wrap my fingers around her cool wrist, searching for the pulse I know won't be there.

Chapter Thirty-Two

Clara

Dresses pile up on the floor as I fling shorts and shirts around my room without a care. I don't know what to wear, and I'm freaking out about it. I don't know why exactly. Kamdyn has seen me looking like a nasty mess, and he's seen me naked. The man has seen me crying and still wants me. So why the fuck am I so nervous that I can't even pick out a fucking bra to wear to see him?

I send Kam a text asking if 5:00 p.m. works for him.

An hour later, I still don't have a reply, but I've chosen an outfit. A light-gray T-shirt dress with a jean jacket and Converse. I stare at my simple makeup in the mirror, nothing more than mascara and a light swipe of bronzer, before pulling my onyx-black hair up into a messy ponytail.

From the outside, I might look calm and collected, but inside, I'm a bundle of nerves. My stomach churns as if it's going to bubble over while my heart and core are heating at the thought of being able to touch him again. Kiss him again. To have him look at me without that twinge of pain in his eyes. I want to see his eyes light up with love and pure joy when he looks at me.

My phone rings with an unknown number.

"Hello?"

"Hey, babe, it's Lex."

"Lexa, are you calling me from the bar's phone?"

There's a clanking of bottles in the background. "Yeah. I need you to come here."

"Why?" She knows I'm supposed to meet Kamdyn tonight. Fuck, she talked to me for an hour this morning when I told her about falling asleep on the phone with him. "I can't. I'm meeting Kamdyn soon."

"Just get down here...Now."

My mouth goes dry like I haven't had water in weeks. "Lex, you're worrying me."

I'm already heading to the door when her voice quiets. "Kamdyn is here."

I freeze mid-stride. "What?"

She yells at someone in the background, returning her attention to our conversation. "Just get down here."

The moment I step into the bar, I see him. He's seated at the farthest stool from the door, his head laying on his hands with a beer in front of him. It's all I need to see. Something must have happened. Did someone find out about AM? Did he not pass? Or what if it's his job? It would devastate him.

I catch Lexa's eye as I walk over to him; she gives me a flat smile. He's wearing one of my favorite shirts of his, the soft green fabric clinging to his biceps. "Kamdyn." I reach my hand out, brushing his forearm.

He lifts his head, his eyes glistening with unshed tears. He doesn't say a word as he draws my body into his, hugging me against him. With his arms wound around me, he buries his face in my neck. His scruff is now a full-on beard. It tickles along my skin as he breathes. "Babe?"

He takes a deep breath against me. "June's dead."

My breath catches. "Oh, Kamdyn." I wrap myself around him, stroking the back of his head. "I'm so sorry."

"She knew."

"She knew what?"

His voice is low and trembles slightly. "That she was going to die. She had everything for the funeral home laid out, ready for me to call."

"For you? What do you mean for you?"

He takes a few moments to gather himself and the words, but he tells me about his day and the unexpected turn it took.

"I'm sorry you had to go through that alone." My voice is gentle as I try to stay strong for him. But seeing him like this is crippling. Just knowing if I had called him sooner, or fuck, hadn't freaked out over the whole Stevie/Steph thing and broken both our hearts, maybe he wouldn't have been alone.

He pulls back to stare at me, his eyes searching my face. "You look beautiful."

My stomach flutters, and a flush rises to my cheeks. My hands leave his back, only to cup his cheeks. "Back atcha," I say, pressing a small kiss to his lips.

As I pull away, a small twinge hits the back of my throat, souring the moment. "I'm sorry, I shouldn't have done that," I say.

"Clara, never apologize for kissing me. The only thing making me feel better right now is you." His voice cracks, along with my heart for his loss.

I stare into his warm, glassy eyes. "Then I'm here for you." I fight the pressure beginning to well in my eyes as tears threaten to fall. "In every and any way you need me."

I untangle myself from him and slide a stool as close to him as I can get. I hold his hand as we sit in silence.

It turns out Kamdyn had been sitting at the bar since around noon. After finding June, he called all the appropriate parties before driving over here with every intention of having a beer to ease the pain of her loss, of having to be the one responsible for taking care of her affairs.

He ordered a beer, took one sip, then just sat there, replaying every moment. Wondering if he could have done something different.

He couldn't have. It was her time, and she took care of everything in advance. Maybe she didn't know she was going to pass at that exact moment, but she recognized it was soon.

I drive Kamdyn back to his house, fully prepared to leave if he wants to be alone. I park my car in his driveway, waiting for him to tell me what he wants. What to do. But he doesn't say a word, his eyes vacant. He opens his door, leaving me there.

I deflate. He's hurting, and I caused some of that pain, but I had hoped he would want me to be there for him. To help him, as he said at the bar.

My door opens, and Kamdyn looks at me with a sly smile on his lips. "Clare Bear, will you stay with me tonight?"

I raise my eyebrows at the question, garnering me a laugh before he adds, "No funny business...tonight. Just sleep."

I nod, taking his outstretched hand as he walks me into his house and to his bedroom. I change into one of his shirts, wearing only it and panties as I climb in next to a shirtless Kamdyn. He's only in his boxer briefs, and I suppress a moan. God, this man is so fucking sexy that it hurts not being able to touch him in all the naughty ways I dream of.

He pulls me into his chest, covering us with the blankets. We don't say a word about what this means. Neither of us asks the big question: are we together or are we not? Instead, we hold each other until we both fall into a deep, peaceful sleep.

The two days following June's death were hectic, to say the least. They were packed with funeral arrangements. Even though June had planned everything out, there was still a lot to oversee.

Kamdyn tried his best not to get overwhelmed by it all, but it was hard. I stepped up, taking over the arrangements to help him. The man was trying to grieve, and handling every stupid little detail made that arduous task impossible.

When it came time for the funeral, the mass of people present was astounding. It turns out Ms. June Green was something of a social butterfly. She had people of all ages and backgrounds there to see her off into the next life. It was beautiful.

From the grand flower arrangements she chose to the snarky,

laugh-inducing farewell speech she had written to be read aloud during the funeral, it was every bit like her. Bold and honest.

There wasn't a crazy number of sad tears shed while people shared their favorite June stories. Instead, there was laughter and tears of joy as people gathered to tell the most outrageous things June did or told them. Kamdyn and I shared the time we walked in on her having sex and all the inappropriate comments she made about his body.

Everyone celebrated June and the life they were glad to have known.

June's passing and funeral made me want to live my life like her. Being open and honest in every way possible. I don't want to hide behind fear, especially with love. Especially with Kamdyn.

Chapter Thirty-Three

Kamdyn

The past week has been a maelstrom of emotions and tasks. Between finishing Anger Management, finding out my job is safe, and June's passing, I haven't had time to talk with Clara about our relationship or lack thereof.

She's stayed with me every night since June died, comforting me with her gentle touch and presence. But I want more. More than comfort. I need that sassy mouth in every way. I need her making me laugh, making me angry, and on me in every single possible way.

Tonight I end this dance we have going. Tonight I ensure Clara understands the level of my love for her.

I ask her to meet me in front of the rec center. The place that changed my life. Now sitting under the large oak tree, my fingers pick at the viridescent blades of grass beneath me. I watch as the woman of my dreams walks up to me, crinkling her nose as she glances around.

"Hey, Asshat," she says, looking around. Throwing her hands in the air, she asks, "Why did you want to meet at this hellhole?"

I don't respond. I just take in the beautiful sight of her body in a tight sports bra and leggings as she draws closer.

"Sit down." I point to the spot in front of me. "Please."

Her lips flatten into a line, but she follows my command. With her legs planted underneath her, she glares at me. "Okay, now will you tell me why we're here?"

I lean forward, catching her off guard as I capture her lips with mine. She sighs against me as I part her soft lips at the seam, stealing the breath from her lungs and inhaling every ounce of her delicious essence.

Clara's tongue swipes at my bottom lip, and I pull away, leaving her frowning.

"I wanted to meet here because this is where I first met you." Clara bites her bottom lip as she grins. "This is the place that brought me to you."

She moves closer to me, crawling on her hands and knees until she's straddling me.

I reach my fingers into her silky locks, tangling at the base of her neck. "This is the place where I fell in love."

Her eyes grow brighter with every word. She tugs on my short beard, bringing my face a breath away from hers. "Kiss me."

She doesn't have to tell me twice. My lips crash into hers with a punishing pressure built up from weeks of desire and heartache. Her tongue wastes no time finding mine this time, caressing me with every flick and touch.

There is no telling how long we sit there beneath the tree, losing ourselves in each other's kiss.

"Clara?" I rasp against her skin. "I need us to be together. Please, tell me this means you're mine again?"

Clara tries calming her heavy breathing as she clutches my shoulders. "I love you more than words can or will ever describe. I am yours, and you are mine, into infinity and beyond."

"God, I love you," I growl into her lips, stealing another kiss from her.

It takes everything in me not to fuck her right here under this tree. But we just got out of legal trouble. We definitely don't need to be caught having sex in public.

With her hand in mine, we hurry back to my place, stripping each other of every inch of clothing in a frenzy of pent-up desire and lust. I reach out, skimming her soft, fair skin that burns beneath my touch. I pull her naked body against mine.

My breathing becomes frantic as Clara shivers against me. She glides her hands over my skin, finding her way down to the base of my cock. I almost combust right there as she palms my thickening length.

I pick her up, squeezing her ass, and she wraps her legs around my waist as I trail kisses along her neck. Her drenched pussy glides against my stomach, up and down in a breathtaking rhythm all the way to the head of my cock. It takes every ounce of control not to slip inside her. Not to take her up against the wall in the hall.

"Fuck, I've missed this," I say, laying her down on my bed. My mouth sucks on the base of her throat before coasting down to bring a nipple into my mouth. She lets out a raspy moan of pleasure as my tongue flicks the metal barbell.

"Kamdyn, please." She bucks her hips as her hand grips on to my wrist, pushing me lower till I'm teasing her entrance. I part her wet center with my fingers, coating them in her slickness.

I insert two fingers, and her wet pussy contracts around me. Fuck, I could do this all day, every day. I finger fuck her as she writhes beside me, panting as her orgasm builds. Pulling away, I smirk as she glares at me.

"What the fuck, Asshat? I was so close," she rasps.

I lick her sweet flavor off my fingers, closing my eyes as the taste of her breaks my control. I wanted this to last forever, but I can't wait any longer.

Moving onto my hands and knees, I crawl between her legs, pressing the tip of my erection into her wet center before sinking into her. Her entire body tenses as she stretches around me. I still, waiting for her body to relax before I thrust again.

Her body melts into mine. "Start moving, Kamdyn, or I'm gonna murder you."

I laugh, pressing my mouth to hers as I slam back in, giving her everything she and I have been waiting for. Clara lets out an explosive moan that almost has me coming right there. I relish in every pant, every moan, every little noise she mutters as I fuck her, watching as my cock disappears into her wet heat with every stroke.

I roll onto my back, taking her with me. "Ride me," I demand as Clara sits astride me, her palms pressing into my shoulders. She lifts her hips before sliding back down my cock, bringing me deeper than before. The circular motion has me feeling like I'm going to explode at any moment. I grasp her hips, lifting to meet her every thrust.

Clara arches her back, giving me a delicious view of her riding me. Her eyes slam shut, and the pace speeds up. Her walls clench around me, squeezing my cock as her orgasm builds. I roll us again, lifting so I can watch her as I pound into her, bringing my thumb to her clit. I press down as she breaks apart.

Her pleasure has my orgasm racing toward the surface. Clara is still writhing under me when my cock pulses, spilling into her as her body shakes in ecstasy.

I catch her mouth with mine. The kiss isn't frantic like before. It's slow and loving, conveying every unsaid word and emotion. We stay with our sweaty bodies pressed against each other, making up for all the time we spent apart. We whisper promises and declarations of love again and again with our mouths and bodies.

"She did what?" My mouth is slung open from the shock of what I must've heard wrong. I glance at Clara, whose hand is squeezing mine, her face practically mimicking mine.

The man sitting across from us behind a deep mahogany desk clears his throat. "Ms. June Green left you her house, as well as everything in it." He leans forward, resting his arms on his desk. "Now, you're aware that Ms. Green had no living relatives?"

I nod, even though I wasn't aware. I suspected as much because I was her errand boy, not some grandson or nephew. When I got the call from her lawyer, requesting I come in for a reading of her will, I never expected this. Maybe the old perv left me some old nude picture of herself from her twenties. But this...this is nothing I could have imagined.

"Now, she left some stipulations."

I furrow my brows. "What do you mean?"

"Here," he says, pushing an envelope across the table to me. "She wrote you a letter explaining it all. I will give you two a few minutes alone to read it. Just tell my secretary when you're ready for me again."

Clara lets go of my hand so I can open the envelope. With a deep breath, I tear the seal, pulling out the folded pieces of paper. My eyes scan the letter that is pure June madness.

Dear Hot Stuff,

I realize you are probably beside yourself with grief at this current moment, but snap out of it. I just left you the opportunity of a lifetime. My house and my belongings are yours now, but I have some require-ments for them. I had that legal man make them binding.

You must sell my house within six months of my death.

Now, boy, don't go getting your tight ass in a tizzy about this. It is nonnegotiable. Besides, you shouldn't have any issues selling it, especially with all the work I had you put into it for these exact reasons.

You must sell or give away whatever junk inside you don't want.

I'm telling you now, go through it all. I have some cool shit that can be worth a pretty penny. As well as some beautiful rings that would make a lovely engagement ring, should the need ever arise once you get over me.

You must sell your own house within the same six-month period.

Don't worry; I have a method to my madness.

Use all the money from this to buy a home you love.

One with land so you can get those dogs you love so much and chase after babies someday.

Now, with all of that out of the way, time for some heartfelt crap…You've been a highlight for my last couple of years. I've never met a young man so kind and patient. You put up with my bad moods and all the sexual advances, never letting it scare you away. Hell, sometimes I made myself blush with the dirty things I said to you, but you were still there. For that, kid, I love you.

I'm sorry if my passing came as a shock to you. We both know it was inevitable. I was just a little more prepared for it than you probably were.

Please use all that I have left you to start the life you want. The life you deserve.

I promise to watch over you from above...Or below, especially when you're changing or in the shower.

With all my love,

-June

P.S. The top drawer of my nightstand is all XXX, including some old photos of this smokin' hot body. Do with that what you must.

A breath of laughter leaves my lips as I shake my head, folding up the piece of paper.

"What did she say?" Clara asks, her voice soft.

"Just that I have to sell everything, including my house, within six months."

"What?" she balks.

"Oh, and her ghost plans to watch me when I'm naked."

Epilogue

Clara

It took a few weeks for the shock of not only June's death but her will to wear off. Kamdyn started back at work doing his history teacher thing during the day. And at night, we both worked through June's things. The woman was an organized hoarder. We found quite a few sentimental items, or ones we loved for ourselves.

Nervous about what we might find in her room, Kamdyn allocated the cleaning out of June's nightstands and dresser drawers to me. And it was for the best. The woman had a plethora of sex toys that would make a pornstar blush, along with a slew of dirty pictures of herself and former lovers. June was a little sex bot, and I hope to be just like her, still getting drilled by a certain hottie in the golden years.

Once we cleared the place of anything we wanted to save or trash, we had an estate sale. Almost everything sold in the three-day period, leaving Kamdyn with a huge chunk of change.

After spending a month going through all of June's belongings and selling them, her house sold in record time. In less than a week of being on the market, we sold it.

With Kamdyn's house, it took longer. It was on the market for a month with no serious offers. We ended up putting all of his furniture and belongings into storage, and he moved into my tiny apartment with me. We claimed his moving in was about selling the houses, but really, we couldn't stand not being with each other every night.

His place sold just under two months from June's six-month deadline. With the house-selling stipulation complete, we went on the hunt for the perfect place. It didn't take us long to make an offer on a two-story home that needed quite a bit of TLC. With three acres full of trees, and its own little pond, it was exactly what we both wanted.

The day we got the keys to our new home, we didn't waste any time heading to Run and Rescue to bring Samson and Sunny home. I had never seen two dogs happier than when those two went home with us. We watched them run, jump, and play all day in the yard.

We work together room by room to restore and transform this house into our home for our future. A someday, in the very far future, that will include a few mini Kamdyns running around. But as much as I want that with him, I kind of love having him all to myself. I love the fact that we can fuck whenever and wherever we want in our home. So, for now, the four of us and Sir Swims-A-Lot are one big family. And I couldn't ask for anything more.

Acknowledgments

This book was a labor of love and one of my pandemic outlets. The idea for Clara and Kamdyn's love story all started with a patient who had to watch Hallmark movies as part of his anger management course. From there, the idea sparked a flurry of what if's until it became Clara and Kamdyn's story.

To my hot mess of a son, thank you for giving me the time and space to live in my imagination and be creative. You gave me the time and space to write. But please, for the love of all things holy, never read this book.

Jeanine. You made the editing process not as scary for me. Which is a feat in itself. Your kind words and supportive input helped me better not only my story but my outlook on the entire process.

Brooklyn, you have an eagle eye that I am eternally grateful for. You definitely went above and beyond, and I am so thankful. You da best!

Ashley, you were the first person I ever trusted to know I was writing. You were my first reader. My biggest cheerleader, even in the messy first, second, and third drafts. Without your help, I might never have pursued this dream of mine.

Last but not least, thank you Loren. You stepped out of your comfort zone to read this and it meant the world to me.

And a huge thank you to anyone who gave this book a chance. Thank you, thank you for reading and helping to make my dreams come true.

About Author

Registered Nurse by day romance writer by night. Bretta dreamed of becoming a writer since she was a little girl but finally wrote her first novel during the pandemic-imposed social isolation.

A self-proclaimed triple threat, Bretta loves to read smutty books and has an unabashed addiction to Coca-Cola. When she's not writing or caring for patients, you can find her daydreaming about her next book, making sarcastic comments, or being a mediocre crafter. She lives in Oklahoma with her hot mess son and a few furry babies.